Sandra Kess-Fields, MBM, is a transplant to Arizona from the east coast where she worked as a federal government defense contractor. Her favorite authors are Robert Galbraith, Anne Perry, Elizabeth George, J.A. Jance, and Patricia Cornwell. She can be reached on Instagram and Facebook, @sandramysterywriter.

To my son, Lorin, for whom I try harder.

Sandra Kess-Fields

BLESS ME FATHER

AUSTIN MACAULEY PUBLISHERS™

LONDON * CAMBRIDGE * NEW YORK * SHARJAH

Ordering Information
Quantity sales: Special discounts are available on quantity purchases by corporations, associations, and others. For details, contact the publisher at the address below.

Publisher's Cataloging-in-Publication data
Kess-Fields, Sandra
Bless Me Father

ISBN 9798886930931 (Paperback)
ISBN 9798886930955 (ePub e-book)
ISBN 9798886930948 (Audiobook)

Library of Congress Control Number: 2023910767

www.austinmacauley.com/us

First Published 2023
Austin Macauley Publishers LLC
40 Wall Street, 33rd Floor, Suite 3302
New York, NY 10005
USA

mail-usa@austinmacauley.com
+1 (646) 5125767

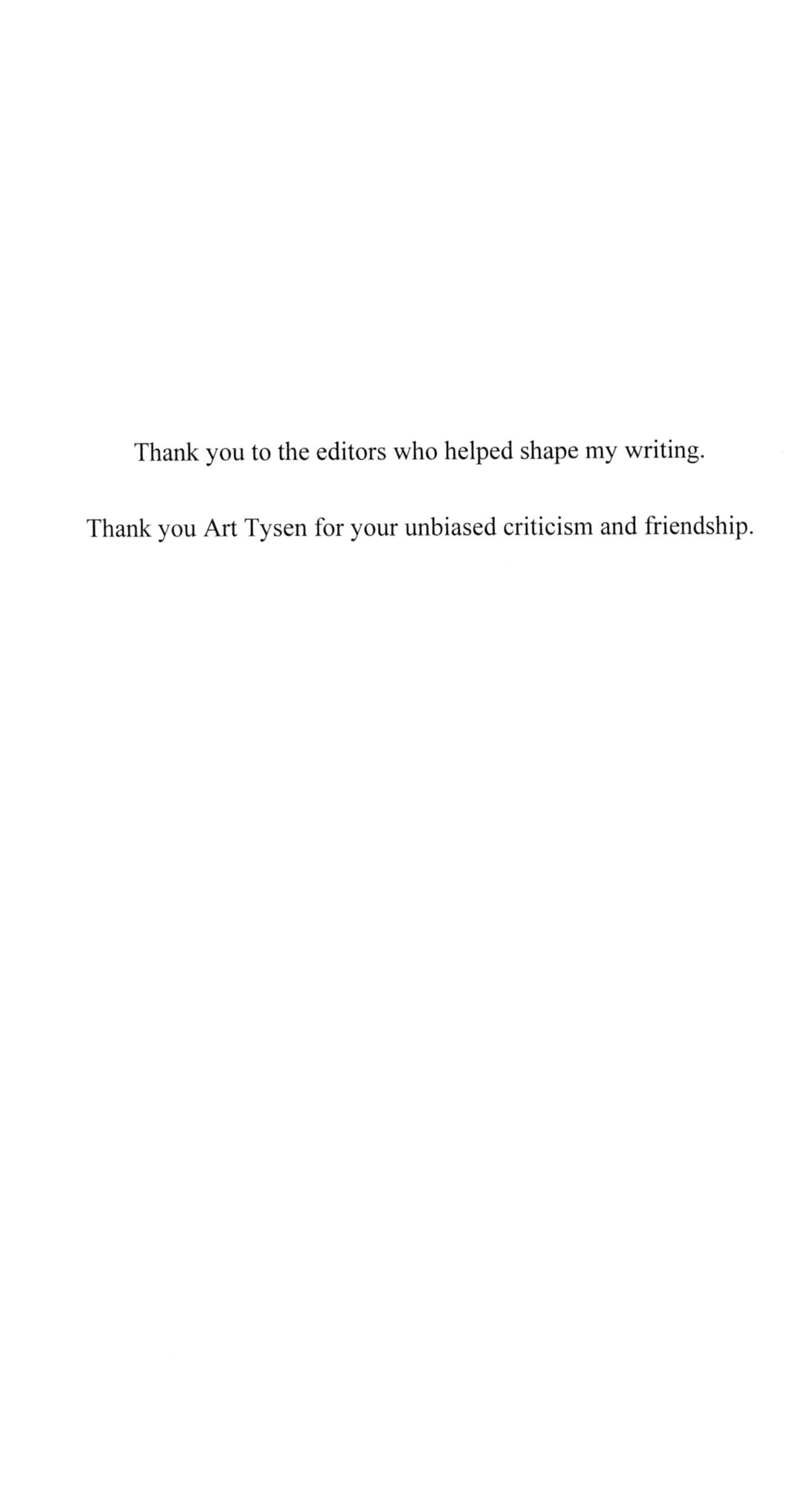

Thank you to the editors who helped shape my writing.

Thank you Art Tysen for your unbiased criticism and friendship.

Murder is born of love, and love attains the greatest intensity in murder.
– Octave Mirbeau

1

Accused of murder no way out belts out the singer on the radio as an elaborate drum riff begins and the superstitious driver switches stations. Her delicate fist bangs on the car dashboard near the air vents as she maneuvers expertly through traffic with her left hand. Maria-Teresa Rivera twists the knob on her car's air conditioner up to the max barely noticing the blurred landscape as she drives hurriedly toward a sand-colored stone building with arc-shaped doors and stained-glass windows.

Remembering the whack, she'd get from the nuns for tardiness her body is gripped by anxiety and fear knowing she is late. She weaves in and out of traffic while frantically searching the horizon practically willing the sight of the familiar square bell tower sitting on a gold dome capped by a cross to come into view. This bell tower announces the majesty of the St. Francis de Sales Catholic Church, her destination.

She exhales feeling relieved as the sprawling two-level church finally looms into view like a mirage nestled in an urban desert standing out in a quiet residential neighborhood that grew up around the church. Despite the fondest memories Maria-Teresa has of the St. Francis de Sales Catholic church, the reminders of discipline, stern rules, unacceptance, and guilt also invade her thoughts hovering just behind this morning's overwhelming sense of dread.

This weekday morning, Maria-Teresa easily finds a parking space in front of her beloved church. After parking her car slightly askew, she snatches her briefcase from the passenger seat, spills out of the car, and heads for the twelve church steps.

You are no longer a child she repeats pulling open the heavy hand-carved wooden door leading to the church vestibule. Absentmindedly, she dips her fingers in the benitier finding the holy water surprisingly refreshing as she makes the sign of the cross, tapping her forehead, chest, then once on each shoulder before hastening toward the nave. She does a half genuflect and power walks down the center aisle of the ornate nave.

The smell of frankincense, sandalwood and myrrh lingering in the air from the 6 o'clock mass ignite memories of holding her mother's hand the first time she walked down the aisle of this regal church her small mouth open in wonderment gazing at the gold crucifix on the altar, the sunlight streaming multi-colors through the stain glass windows. She knew then she would have a lifelong devotion to Catholicism.

The smells, the sounds of the bells, the sights of ornate robes, and Latin words lured her in bringing her through her first holy communion, and her wedding vows. It all falls apart when she divorces her husband of twenty years for another woman. Memories of her divorce unfailingly reignites the ache in her heart at being told by old Father Gabe that she is indeed an abomination in God's eye for divorcing Alberto for the love of another woman.

The past is the past, she tells herself while simultaneously shaking her head side to side vigorously to force her thoughts back to the present. Only the echo of her high heels clicking loudly on the marble floor anchor her to this morning as she fights to keep her steps just short of a jog for fear of disrespecting her surroundings. She checks her watch confirming she is a full thirty minutes late for her meeting with the new priest.

This Wednesday morning, she is unable to soak in the beauty of the nave with the alabaster reliefs of the twelve stations of the cross evenly placed on the side walls. She has been accepted once again into the church thanks to the new progressive priest Father Joao Santos. The last thing she wants to do is have him think she is not interested enough in the church nursery school renovation project to show up on time.

The high-pitched ceiling is marked with dark wooden beams; the colored light casting shadows placed strategically across the altar all go unnoticed as she races past them. Heading behind the altar she zips down the backstairs to the sacristy. Her chest heaving rapidly, her cheeks are the color of ripe Macintosh apples when she arrives out of breath at the sacristy door. Before knocking on the partially open door, she uses a minute to straighten her clothing and calm her breathing.

Knocking delicately and receiving no response, she pushes the door fully open, steps inside while calling out, "Father Santos? It's Maria-Teresa forgive me for being late."

Maria-Teresa scans the sacristy room. The lights are on in the large well-ordered room used for both storage and office space.

Her eyes sweep the area where the church vestments are stored and she neither sees nor hears any movement in the room. She breathes a sigh of relief that the room appears empty hoping perhaps Fr. Santos has been gone long enough that she can say, *we just missed each other*, or *I've been waiting for a while*. Feeling guilty for thinking of telling a lie to a priest compels her to repeat the rosary to herself as she walks further into the room and notices papers in disarray on Father's desk.

Half through the prayer, the hairs on the back of her neck bristle a little as the eerie silence of the office space becomes apparent to her. *Unusual for things to be this messy, perhaps Father was interrupted,* she thinks. The light blue folder marked Nursery Renovation Project stands out among the white or cream color items on the desk.

The nursery renovation project folder laying on the desk and not in the file cabinet indicates Father is indeed expecting her. She twists around and stares at the open office door which is usually kept locked when he is not here. He must be nearby, and no doubt he will be walking in soon.

The sacristy is situated so that it gets the same eastern sunlight through its stained-glass windows that streams through the nave. Usually sitting in this room makes her feel warm and nurtured but not this morning. Trying desperately to ignore her uneasy feeling she takes a seat on the wooden chair in front of Father's large hand-carved oak desk.

The ornate desk was gifted to the church about twenty-five years ago by a young priest who brought it with him from Central America. She sits her briefcase on the floor beside her chair and runs her hand along the desk admiring its craftsmanship. While moving her gaze from the front of the carved desk to its top, something grabs her attention. *What is that? Too thin for jam, maybe it's ink?*

She half rises from her chair, leans over the desktop to inspect the substance spattered on the desk's items. Holding the nursery renovation project folder out of the way she uses her index finger of her other hand to touch the unknown substance then rubs her thumb and finger together. By its feel, color, and smell, she knows that it's *blood!!*

Her body snaps to an upright position with such force that she throws the folder to the floor as if holding it will somehow sear her skin. The room spins around her and her stomach lurches and flops so violently that she tastes her breakfast in her throat. To steady herself she places both hands flat on the desktop and closes her eyes.

Her dizziness shortly subsides allowing her to open her eyes slowly focusing on the trail of blood-splattered papers rather than attend to the wet red substance now coating both her palms. Blood splashes from the top down the side of the carved desk pooling in a few deep crevices of the ornate curly ques. The uninterrupted trail of blood continues from the desk onto the old dingy white highly polished linoleum floor.

Now, the scene resembles a Jackson Pollack painting with what looks like haphazard splatters, smaller spots and dense puddles all made with red blood. The pattern of the Pollack splatters abruptly halts at a body that Maria-Teresa can now see lying on the floor face down behind the desk.

2

Frozen in place her eyes have no other choice but to peruse the body laying prone at her feet. His hair is neatly cut to a length just above the pink color tinging on what used to be his white full-neck-band clerical collar. The fabric of his dove grey short-sleeve shirt looks darker and shinier where the blood soaks heaviest and sticks tight to his skin. A larger pool of blood expands outward in a jagged pattern on his back just below his left shoulder blade then spreads out onto the linoleum floor.

Maria-Teresa shaking clutches at her chest before gripping the gold cross dangling from a chain around her neck, a childhood gift. Inhaling deeply through both her nose and open mouth simultaneously her breasts quickly move up and down. Her bloody hands clamp over her mouth to stifle a scream. Fear seizes her body rendering it rigid, momentarily restricting any movement or sound while in sharp contrast to the voice in her head that screams OH MY GOD RUN!

She feels a tightness in her chest and her heart pounds so hard and loud it reverberates in her ears as her disconnected thoughts of small children and a dead priest take turns circling in her head. *No, it can't be. Not another murder.* Now trembling uncontrollably, she wills herself to move while her eyes are still focused on the gruesome scene behind the desk. Slowly, Maria-Teresa backs up silently mouthing, *The Lord is my shepherd I shall not want. He maketh me to lie down* when her head cracks hard against the office door jamb stopping her with a jolt.

She reaches up rubbing the back of her head, to soothe the throbbing. Her own blood from the bang to her head leaves faint blood streaks through her dark curly hair resembling salon highlights. Maria-Teresa's original plans to escape are now replaced with her desire to slide down the door jamb and rest in a fetal position on the floor. Suddenly, a sound in the hallway outside the sacristy fuels panic in her at the thought that someone walking into the office might think she has something to do with this grisly scene.

Remembering how her best friend became an unwitting murder suspect just a year ago and not wanting to be put through the same kind of interrogation, she turns toward the open door and runs. The dimly lit hallway proves to be empty as Maria-Teresa silently curses her powder blue linen and silk pencil slim skirt that hampers her achieving a full gallop. Quickly, she raises her skirt to enable her to widen her stride just as she hits the nave and passes two middle-aged neighborhood women tending to the dusting of the altar.

Without stopping or asking them for help she continues her escape wild-eyed to the front door. The volunteers turn from their chores in time to see a streak of blue and a bloody face run pass them. Dust clothes in hand they call out after her, "Are you hurt? What's the matter? Why are you running?"

Ignoring them, Maria-Teresa reaches the outside where the hot dry air smacks her in the face. Running down the steps trying to think of anything except the horror left behind she repeats to herself the keyless entry code to her car. The repetition of the key code is a way of refocusing her thoughts from the dreadful sight of the dead priest. The numbers are pressed unlocking the car, she snatches open the door and climbs in.

Her quivering finger presses the button to start the engine then suddenly she stops. Her finger is poised over the letter D for drive and the blood on her hand glistens in the sunlight. Her eyes move from her hands to the red stains on her skirt then she checks her face in the rear-view mirror. She wipes at her face and rubs at her skirt, followed quickly by rubbing her face and wiping her skirt, in that order she repeats the process three times like she just developed an uncontrollable tick. She thinks, "Oh God my fingerprints are on the folder. Blood all over me. I can't stay here?"

Her shaking hands frantically search the car's passenger seat, the glove compartment, and the console between the seats for her cell phone throwing unrelated items to her search on the floor. Finding nothing she realizes it's in her briefcase in the sacristy office with the dead body. Reluctantly, she eases the car door open, swings her legs around planting both feet on the ground but remaining seated as the sensation of butterflies increases in her stomach.

Grudgingly she stands up her body; still standing between the open car door and its interior, she turns around and fixates on the church door. Moving around to the outside of the car door she leans against it quietly, pressing it close afraid that slamming it will bring unwanted attention. With each deliberate act of putting one foot in front of the other advancing up the church steps, fear once again locks its grip on her. Freezing at the top of the church steps, her mind in a fog, her body unable to move further she sits down and sinks her head into her hands.

Did I see what I thought? Father Santos is dead, who killed him? Her thoughts are moving in slow motion as she tries over and over to reconcile in her mind the last unreal moments. Images of the bloody scene play in her head while the searing heat from the sun beams down on her further confusing her ability to reason.

Maria-Teresa is sitting on the upper-most step, a little off to the side of the church door when suddenly one of the large wooden doors farthest from her swings open wide partially blocking the morning sun that now hits her directly in the face as she lifts her head. One hand automatically shades her eyes, allowing her to see a tall male figure, a figure she recognizes.

In a mental haze, she thinks everything about this morning is comprised of unforeseen events occurring in an alarming contrast to her schedule. The landscape around her begins to swirl like a vortex threatening to swallow her whole. She locks eyes with the male figure just before giving in to the overpowering sensation of falling as everything in her world goes black. Her limp body starts its unladylike descent down the front steps of the church.

The flashing red and blue lights of the Arizona police cars stop in front of the church just in time for one of the officers to assist the male figure who is running down the steps to stop the woman from rolling over and over just out of his grasp. The police officer brings her to a stop before she hits the last step. Together the office and the male from the church carry her limp body inside.

This morning, the holy water in the vestibule serves as truly a blessing and a source to help revive Maria-Teresa to consciousness. Her eyes open wide searching the face of each man kneeling around her. Her confused gaze settles not on anyone of the policeman but on the face of the male figure she saw just before she fainted. She mutters in a high-pitched quivering voice, "Why aren't you dead? I thought you were dead."

3

Walking to his car Joe P. Hobbs detective unbuttons the top button on his somewhat ironed white shirt and slides the knot in his tie down a little from his neck hoping to still appear professional while exacting relief from the morning heat. Driving out of his apartment complex Hobbs can't help noticing the play of light and shadow dancing in and out of the blue haze on the surrounding mountains. This idyllic valley scene is a far cry from east coast snow and a hell of a lot prettier.

His thoughts are interrupted by the dispatcher's voice squawking loudly over his mobile radio announcing a homicide at the St. Francis de Sales Church. Almost simultaneously the screen of the on-board computer in his police car flashes the same announcement. Joe P. Hobbs, a hulking man transplanted to the East Mesa homicide division of the Arizona police department from the Baltimore police department is on his way to his office in the opposite direction of the St. Francis de Sales Church.

Upon hearing the location of the homicide, he groans and hopes the murder has nothing to do with his friend and surrogate aunt Maria-Teresa, the smallest of his surrogate family members, volunteers, who worships at that church. Clearly out of his jurisdiction pursuing calls in the west valley, he feels compelled to investigate the particulars of the homicide call for a couple of reasons and neither has anything to do with his attendance at a church service.

He remembers recently spending a grueling two hours at a fundraiser for the nursery renovation project at that same church. Memories flood his brain of drinking diluted fruit punch, smiling at a bunch of sanctimonious strangers, all the while wishing he was someplace else smoking, cursing, and getting very drunk. Maria-Teresa's past involvement with murder is how he first met her along with her three friends a year ago. Maria-Teresa is by far the tiniest of the four women measuring half the width and the height of the six-foot-four-inch-tall detective.

The other three friends of Maria-Teresa also count as the detective's surrogate family of aunts. All the women are members of a mystery book club and fancy themselves self-appointed sleuths representing a coalition of races, one being African American, one Caucasian, one Asian, and of course Maria-Teresa Rivera, Hispanic.

Unfortunately based on prior experience, these women have a pension for insinuating themselves in police situations causing a gnawing feeling to rise in his gut while his brain urges him to make sure that she and or her friends are not somehow involved in this morning's tragedy. Instead of proceeding to his office in the east valley, he points his vehicle toward the west valley and races to the church.

The fingers of one hand absentmindedly comb through his large unkempt mustache, a thing he does when deep in thought his other large hand grips the steering wheel turning it from right to left whizzing past other cars also traveling over the sixty-five-mile an-hour speed limit. His height and the fact that his hands can palm a basketball with ease should make him a natural athlete but like so many of god's little jokes, he is the most unathletic person on the planet.

However, in his chosen profession as a police officer, his physical attributes make him quite suited for the job. His car rounds the corner to the church at a speed that would garner anyone else a ticket for reckless driving. The white stucco façade of the church looks serene and unmarred by the crime within its walls.

A few yards from the front door an excessive number of police cars line the street in front of the church. Uniform officers stand quietly in front of the church surveying the sidewalk across the street that is littered with stunned onlookers whispering and watching expectantly at the church door. Hobbs double-parks his unmarked, hops out showing his credentials to an officer approaching him, no doubt to prevent him parking.

The officer grabs Hobbs' credentials, gives them a look then hands them back. "What brings you over here?" asks the officer frowning no doubt questioning Hobbs' lack of jurisdiction.

"Personal. Who's in charge?" asks Hobbs insinuating his bulk into the officer's personal space in a calm but mildly threatening manner.

"Keating. He's inside with the suspect," snorts the officer clearly offended by this interloper. "He's touchy about his crime scenes. I'd tread lightly being you're out of your jurisdiction and all," warns the officer with a malice grin.

"Yeah thanks," snarls Hobbs over his shoulder wondering if the entire Mesa police department hates him. He bounds the steep church steps two at a time the gnawing feeling increasing in his gut as he swings open the carved wooden door and stepping inside the dim light halts his near manic movement.

Standing in the vestibule, which he remembers well from his night at the fundraiser as the last impediment between him, the outside, and a well-deserved smoke, he blinks several times before his eyes adjust to the dim lighting and bringing into focus all the people huddled in the small vestibule.

The momentary stream of light as he steps inside illuminates a slight wispy-haired man with the elongated drooping face of a blue tick hound dog dressed in poor quality plain clothes kneeling on the floor beside the seated Maria-Teresa. The man leans back sitting on his heels and looks up to see Hobbs standing just inside the doorway. Immediately his eyes narrow, his face contorts in anger as he peruses Hobbs from his head back to his feet.

The fact that Hobbs got away unpunished for a past flagrant disregard of departmental rules fuels the resentment rising in the detective in charge until the air becomes electrified with animosity between the two men. Hobbs is tired of everyone hating him for caring about the safety of a human life. A human life belonging to Grace Liu, who repaid him by using her federal connections to prevent him and his partner, Turner, from getting fired for overstepping their jurisdictional bounds by working a case in another state without permission from either state.

The priest, who came through the door just as Maria-Teresa tumbled down the front stairs stands with other officers nearby feeling the undeniable contention in the room, and instinctively turn to stare at the two men. Keating's eyes are now alert and tense like a cat ready to pounce to protect his turf.

"Detective Keating, I'm Detective Hobbs, East Valley," says Hobbs flashing his identification to the man on the floor. Keating stands up wishing to show no deference to Hobbs through his body language. Pulling himself up to his full height Keating is clearly a foot shorter than Hobbs, a hundred pounds lighter, and ten years older.

"Yeah, I know who you are, the big shot ex-Baltimore cop with the Federal connections." Keating's permanently weary eyes a result of age, too many years on the force, and god's handy work meet and hold Hobbs' stern gaze. Keating's posture is that of a man who has something to prove. "Everybody knows who you are," sneers Keating with anything but admiration in his voice.

As appreciative as Hobbs is for the federal intervention on his last case saving his ass from disciplinary action, he and his partner now suffer the draw backs, animosity from their fellow officers. The sarcasm dripping from the man's words are not lost on Hobbs as he steps closer to Keating clearly to challenge him. A couple of small scars on Keating's face draw Hobbs' attention to his weak jawline now flexing back and forth in time with the veins popping rhythmically on his forehead.

Keating looks up at Hobbs' flaring nostrils and his eyes take in the grey hairs sprinkled throughout Hobbs' unkempt mustache as he sizes up the hulking detective for what Keating knows will be a battle. The animosity between the two detectives sucks the oxygen from the vestibule causing anyone standing in their vicinity to cease conversation and focus on them.

Repressing a desire to pommel Keating, Hobbs softens his approach, "Look, I'm not here for your opinion of me. She's like family, I just want to know what happened."

Keating like most of his fellow officers is both impressed and angered by Hobbs' three-letter federal connections, even though no one knows exactly which three-letter organization is at his beck and call. Neither does Hobbs. Looking up at the big man all Keating's bravado quickly fades leaving him clear-headed and changing his tone from combative to forced compliance.

"Dead Priest, stabbed in the back. She's our prime suspect," pointing at Maria-Teresa whose body resembles a ragdoll placed with care on the floor much the way a child would put away her favorite doll on a shelf. She is seated, her back propped against the vestibule wall just at the opening of the nave, her legs splayed out lifeless in front of her.

"Two witnesses see her fleeing the scene," says Keating in a flat voice. "That bit of info is given as a professional courtesy," feeling confident that with witnesses he has a slam dunk case, Keating continues, "I'm not sharing any further developments about MY case. Even you know you're clearly out of your jurisdiction again," says Keating with a smirk.

Ignoring the warning from the officer in charge Hobbs drops down to a crouch in front of Maria-Teresa and clasps her cold tiny hand between his. Leaning in close to Maria-Teresa. "I need to ask you some questions," he says.

Her normal inquisitive dark brown eyes are unfocused unable to distinguish him or her surroundings. She is clearly in shock and is in no condition to answer questions from him or anyone else. Hobbs gently pats her hand and just says, "Things will be all right. Just hold on," in a tone he would use to soothe his mother if she were alive.

Hobbs stands up just as Keating, determined not to have his authority usurped or undermined, says to Maria-Teresa, "I'm detective George Keating. Can you tell me your name and your connection to the dead priest?" Keating repeats his questions. Maria-Teresa looks up, frowns, and swallows hard to dislodge an invisible lump in her throat.

She opens her mouth to speak but no sound comes out as she continues to stare into the horizon in a catatonic-like state. Giving up any efforts to find her voice she drops her gaze to her blood-smeared hands in her lap. Her eyes widen and she wipes her hands on her skirt and swipes at her face three times. Samples of the blood on her hands and clothes have already been bagged so no one interferes with her frantic attempt to cleanse herself.

"Her name is Maria-Teresa Rivera. She volunteers here," offers Hobbs impatiently, his protectiveness fully on display. He exhales, his hand curls in a fist as he moves in closer to Keating nearly elbowing him out of the way. Keating does not appreciate another person speaking for a suspect in an interview situation and turns to Hobbs saying sternly, "Look! I need her to answer. You interfere once more, and I'll make trouble for you, Feds or no Feds."

Keating turns his back on Hobbs and starts grilling Maria-Teresa, "When you saw Fr. Santos why did you ask, why aren't you dead? Did you intend to kill him?" Keating waits a short time for a response. Still, receiving no answers, he gets in her face and asks loudly, "Did you come here this morning to kill the priest? How long have you planned this attack?"

Tears roll down her face, and she shakes her head no. Finally receiving an acknowledgment from her he continues with "was anyone else in the office or did you pass anyone in the hallway?"

"No, I didn't see anyone else in the office. No, I didn't pass anyone leaving the sacristy."

"Are you sure?"

"Yes, I'm sure," she says in a soft childlike voice.

"I'll ask you again, why kill the priest?"

"No, no. I didn't do it," says a now tearful Maria-Teresa. "I have no reason to kill a priest. Surely that would be a sin I could never live with."

"If you are innocent as you claim, why did you run?"

"I don't know why." This answer is not entirely true. Who wants to stick around and be implicated in a murder she silently asks herself? Her close friend Samantha Jones found herself in jail because she was not able to escape from a crime scene. She did not want to repeat the same mistake.

"How long have you attended this parish?" asks Keating calmer now. She did not hear his question her mind remembers how not so long ago she, Sam, Grace Liu, and Margot Towers, her fellow amateur sleuths stood in Sam's family room gazing through her windows at an unknown corpse in her backyard.

"What?" asks Maria-Teresa in response to something Keating must have asked while she reminisced. She fidgets a little then straightens her torso focusing her thoughts on her present situation and answers.

"How long have you attended this parish?" repeats Keating. He notices the glazed look in her eyes and wonders what is taking her attention away from his inquiry. Are her thoughts germane to the murder?

"Oh, I was christened and married here," answers Maria-Teresa in a soft voice, "then I left my husband and when I came out as a lesbian I was no longer welcomed here." Looking down at her hands she says, "I just came back to church a few months ago when Fr. Santos became the new parish priest. Unlike Father Gabe before him, Santos is very accepting of all lifestyles. He preaches love and inclusion, I like that."

"So, are you pretty angry about being abandoned by the church? Did you want to get even with the priests?"

A deep inhalation, large-eyed, mouth gaped showing her surprise and indignation at the thought that she would commit the sin of murder she says, "No that's absurd, besides Fr. Gabe retired, and Fr. Santos is a member of my own book group. I don't even know the dead priest, why would I want to kill him? I couldn't do that!"

She turns her back to Keating wraps both arms around her torso hugging herself tightly and looks pleadingly at Hobbs. Suddenly, she realizes she is in as much trouble as her friend Sam was just a year ago. The helplessness in Maria-Teresa's milk chocolate eyes tug at Hobbs reminding him of the woman who haunts the nightmares that followed him to Arizona. That woman also looked at him with confusion and questions before dying in his arms.

Feeling helpless, Hobbs paces the floor just a couple of feet from Maria-Teresa mumbling under his breath *talk to her later, she's in shock and she needs help*. Finally unable to contain his concern, "Stop badgering her, damn it!" yells Hobbs letting his emotion get the best of his professionalism. Keating shoots a look of surprise in his collogues direction just as a member of the forensics' team ambles up to Keating, whispers something and Keating turns his attention elsewhere.

With Keating out of earshot, Hobbs reaches in his pocket, retrieves his phone, and calls Grace Liu. Who else but Grace, international businesswoman with a secret spy life known only to him and his detective partner Dwayne Turner, can put an end to Keating's questions and ensure Maria-Teresa's rights?

Hobbs grew up resenting the rich, their lifestyles, and the avoidance of everyday discomforts that their money afforded them. Grace Liu, however, is the only rich person he has ever liked, cared about, and appreciated. The fact that he has never known another rich person on a personal level might skew his opinion just a little.

Grace answers on the second ring with a cheery, "Hi there, detective. To what do I owe this honor?"

"Maria-Teresa needs your help. She is suspected of murder," he blurts out breathlessly.

"What are you talking about? Our Maria-Teresa? That's absurd. Where is she? Where are you?"

"We are at the St. Francis de Sales church, you know the one where she volunteers."

"Yes, so who the hell is she accused of killing?"

"A priest. He was stabbed and she is covered in blood. She's in a bad way, Grace you have to do something to help," pleads Hobbs, his voice an octave higher than normal.

"I'll send someone over. Tell her not to say a word are you involved in the investigation?"

"She's been crying, she's in shock. I can't help her, this church is out of my jurisdiction."

"Thanks for the call." She rings off and dispatches one of her attorneys to the church. Hobbs stands guard over his friend at the church until a well-dressed high-powered female lawyer appears at the church, "Hello, I'm Patricia Tom. You must be detective Hobbs?" extending her hand as she looks him up and down. "Grace described you to a tee," she says with a wry smile.

Then noticing Maria-Teresa in an almost fetal position on the floor she crouches next to her and places a hand on her shoulder, "I have been asked by Grace Liu to represent you this morning. I can help you through the basics but depending on how things proceed with the police, I will be replaced with a more experienced criminal lawyer. Do you understand?"

Standing up Ms. Tom approaches one of the uniform officers, "I am representing Ms. Rivera. Where is the detective in charge?"

Breathing a sigh of relief Hobbs looks down at the racked body of Maria-Teresa and feels confident the lawyer will take good care of his friend and reluctantly leaves the church to make his way back to his own east valley police station. Maria-Teresa is taken to the west valley police station followed closely by her attorney.

Maria-Teresa submits to regular police procedures. Crime scene techs photograph her six ways to Sunday taking scraping from under her nails, mouth swabs, confiscating her shoes and clothing for forensic processing. Her clothing is replaced with a paper gown and booties and she is transported to the west valley police station for booking.

At the police station, booking photos and fingerprints are taken. Then she is given an opportunity to speak with her attorney before the police question her again. The unadorned pale grey room is claustrophobic with a rectangular small table separating the two women.

Feeling spent, her last tear shed she drinks some water, uses the bathroom, and eats some vending machine crackers making Maria-Teresa feel almost human again.

"Please tell me what happened," asks Ms. Tom. Maria-Teresa tells of her morning and ends with finding out that Fr. Santos is still alive.

Then, for the first time, Maria-Teresa asks, "I don't understand, who is lying dead in Fr. Santos' office?"

"From what I understand, the dead man is a visiting priest who is staying in the rectory in the back of the main church, do you know him?" asks her lawyer.

"No. I have never seen any priest other than Fr. Santos, but he looks so much like Fr. Santos," declares Maria-Teresa.

The interview at the west valley police station with her lawyer present ends pretty much the way it starts, with their only suspect vowing her innocence, unable to offer any information that might point the investigation toward someone other than herself, she gives the police no motive or a murder weapon. She rubs hard on the tense muscles in her neck before resting her head in her hands still unable to comprehend why anyone thinks she is a murderer. Only her friends know without a doubt that she's innocent.

The fact remains, someone wanted a priest dead and circumstantial evidence might put an innocent person behind bars. Can she rely on her faith, friends, or the law to save her?

4

The sun shone bright through the stain glass windows of the sacristy as if to plot out the horror inside the room. Detective Keating hangs in the doorway not wanting to impede the work of the forensic team as they photograph blood spatter papers on the desktop and follow the uninterrupted blood trail across the floor to the walls behind the oak desk.

The medical examiner's focus is on the body on the floor and comments, "That's an awful lot of blood for a stabbing victim." This statement causes Keating to take a few steps inside the room to peer at the body. Unable to see around the techs, he turns to his left and notices a piscina full of bloody water.

"Get prints from that basin thing, and check that briefcase beside the chair in front of the desk the murder weapon might be in there," yells Keating his orders met with annoying looks from the forensic team.

When the officers turn the dead body over, they realize that the priest's throat has been slashed in addition to a stab wound in his back under his left shoulder blade. The body is still warm and from what they can see, there are no defensive wounds on the victim. "He was probably surprised from behind," says the ME.

Without an autopsy report, it is clear that the victim probably bled to death from the slash to the right side of his throat. Small bloody footprints lead from the crime scene to the hallway where they suddenly stop. Maria-Teresa's shoes have been taken and will be matched to the prints at the crime scene, no other footprints are found leading in or out of the room.

Reluctantly, Keating leaves the crime scene in search of Fr. Santos and is directed toward the church nursery school on the lower floor. The detective walks the few steps down to the lower level and finds himself standing near the end of a well-lit corridor. To his left is a door leading to the outside and to his right is the expanse of the corridor with doors leading to the nursery and other rooms.

Keating is looking forward to hearing Fr. Santos' take on the morning's activities. Some questions come to mind as he walks down the corridor where a mixture of religious photos hangs in competition with preschooler's artwork. He peers into each room along the corridor until he finds Fr. Santos sitting in a room filled with miniature furniture, toys piled high in a large wooden box off to one side of the room, and crayon and Tempera paint drawings hung neatly on the walls.

"I didn't want to disrupt the children in the next room to get to the adult-size furniture," says Santos smiling good-naturedly while clutching a bible. He uncurls his long athletic legs allowing himself to exit from his perch in the tiny nursery school chair with the grace of a model. The young man's flawless butterscotch colored skin, his head full of dark brown slightly wavy hair worn long making the priest look more like a billboard model for religious vestments than an actual priest.

For the second time this morning, feelings of inadequacy flood Keating's thoughts, first by Hobbs' presence and now by the priest's striking good looks. Straightening his otherwise slumped shoulders Keating guesses the young man looks to be in his mid-twenties. *Too young to be a parish priest* he thinks, followed by *but no one is ever killed for being a young priest.*

A wry smile forms on the lips of Fr. Santos as he gazes at the detective reading the insecurity in his body language. His hazel eyes meet the detective's gaze and without a word, he flashes a bright welcoming smile dislodging any preconceived notions the detective initially has of him. The two men begin their discussion standing up.

"Where were you this morning Father between eight and nine-thirty?"

"I was here in the church nursery watching the children. Sister isn't feeling well you see, I was waiting for Lea, the young nursery assistant to show up, she usually comes in an hour early, but today she didn't come in at all. Then I had to phone one of the volunteer mothers to come in. At such short notice, it takes a while for someone to rearrange their affairs at home and get here."

Keating notes the priest provides a great deal of unsolicited information and writes one word in his notebook, why?

"Were you in your office at all this morning?"

"I was in my office an hour before six o'clock a.m. mass." The detective is writing in his small notebook when a woman in her early forties appears in the doorway. She brushes her hair off her face with one hand and fidgets like a giggly schoolgirl. In a soft voice she says, "Father, we're about to take the children outside, sister's office is free if you need to use it."

Again, Santos displays his model's smile, and the woman beams back, her eyes lingering on him before jerking her head toward the detective remembering his presence. Keating glances from the woman to Santos in time to see him wet his full lips while his bedroom eyes lock on her. Pink cheeked, she lowers her eyes and walks away.

As quickly as Santos displays flirtatious behavior, he becomes all business. The detective follows him into the next classroom while assessing all egresses, to the outside, and the upstairs. His eyes sweep over the modular triangular tables, brightly colored vinyl floor tiles in the classroom.

In one section of the room, the floor is covered by small colored mats laying in a circle, their colors fighting against the colors of the floor tiles. Standing along the wall behind the mats is a six-foot-long bookcase full of preschool books covering a range of subject matter.

The last of tiny feet can be heard shuffling softly out the side door. There is a momentary outburst of playful voices that become muffled as the kids move further away to play in the yard.

There is a stark difference between the classrooms and the office space where the two men will conduct the remainder of the interview.

The detective takes a quick look around the tired beige walls of the room noticing first the large crucifix on one wall, and a framed photo of the current Pope beside it. On the wall behind the plain metal desk are two long strips of paper. Under the watchful eye of Fr. Santos, Keating walks closer to read the list of names and corresponding phone numbers, he assumes are the parents of the students and their emergency contact numbers.

Taped beside the first list is a list of students' names and the various words like peanut allergy, vegan or vegetarian handwritten beside a couple of names. Then taking a seat on one of the two chairs opposite the desk he pulls it close to the small metal desk noticing the scraps, dents, and flecks of missing paint.

"Did you see the victim this morning?"

Seated in the chair behind the desk Fr. Santos takes a moment before answering. "No, I did not see Fr. Francisco this morning. I was about to go into my office after mass when Sister caught me in the hallway to inform me that she was not feeling well enough to stay with the nursery students. She didn't want to spread her cold to the children and suggested that I go immediately to the nursery because a few students have arrived," says Santos in one manic breath.

"What time was this, Father?"

"I am not sure exactly, sometime after seven," answers Santos in an even breath.

"Before then, where were you?"

Now much calmer he says, "I was just finishing up 6 o'clock mass which lasts an hour. I spoke for a while with a parishioner after mass and was walking back to the sacristy when I was grabbed by Sister."

"Did you leave a note for Maria-Teresa telling her you were in the nursery? You were expecting her this morning?" asks Keating looking over the rimless reading glasses perched on the tip of his narrow nose making him look very much like a cartoonish stork with glasses.

"No. I wasn't thinking, besides I didn't think I would be gone that long."

Keating fidgeted on the hard chair and crosses one boney leg over the other to fight off the numbness in his butt. In the florescent lighting, he notices his socks don't match, his color blindness always more apparent when he tries to match his dark-colored socks.

"What can you tell me about Maria-Teresa Rivera? How well do you know her?"

"I met her a couple of months ago. She invited me to join her mystery book club. She is co-owner of an engineering firm and she's gay."

"I assume she is a member of this church," says Keating again looking over his glasses. "I'll be blunt, do you think she is capable of murder, and has she ever voiced a reason to kill anyone?"

"She is a member along with several others who were casted out by the last priest for their sexual preferences." Santos pauses and studies his hands as if they will assist him in answering the second half of Keating's question. He raises his gaze to meet Keating's suspicious stare and says in a barely audible voice, "It has been my experience that mankind is capable of a great deal of acts both good and bad."

There is a long silence between the two men, Keating not sure what to make of the philosophical response from the priest.

"Ah, let's see now, Father," hastily uncrossing his leg. "What can you tell me about the victim," looking at his notes he adds, "uh Fr. Francisco?"

"I don't know that much really," says the confident Santos from his chair opposite the detective. Looking up to his left as if trying to draw knowledge from air Santos says, "He has been living in the rectory for just three days of a scheduled ten-day sabbatical. Fr. Francisco is from a parish somewhere in New Mexico, I think. He is, was in crisis," says Santos with an air of finality.

"What kind of crisis? Didn't he believe in God anymore or was there something else he was dealing with?"

Fr. Santos pauses before answering knowing full well what Keating is eluding too, but he shakes his head from side to side and says to the detective, "I have no idea."

"You have no idea? How can you help if you don't know what the problem is?"

"I, I well," he pauses. "I wasn't aware that he needed my help."

Keating twists his mouth to the side and bites the inside of his jaw. Scribbling in his notepad he brings his pen to rest then asks, "Did he have any visitors? Did he look concerned or worried?"

"I have been really busy. I only got to speak to him once, the day he came. I am sorry I can't be of more help, but I really didn't know the young man."

"Why is he here at your church if you don't know him that well? How do you know he's going through a crisis?"

"You'll have to ask Bishop O'Leary. He asked me if I had room at the rectory for a man in crisis. Maybe the Bishop can shed some light on your investigation."

"You have the bishop's contact information?"

"Yes, of course. May I text it to you, it's on my cell phone."

"Well, Father, if you think of anything else give me a call," says Keating handing Santos a business card before ascending the stairs to the outside.

5

By the time Grace and Sam arrive at the west valley police station, they know the gist of the situation from Hobbs, the high-powered attorney, and various television newscasters. The women can't help but spot the old four-story red brick building with its crumbling façade resembling a squat layer cake rising above the other low and long commercial buildings. The west valley police station is considerably older than its counterpart in the east valley.

Just yards away from the front door of the precinct building bedlam is brewing from a crowd unlike the stunned teary-eyed onlookers at the church. The west valley precinct services a heavy Catholic community. The idea of someone killing a priest is considered a cardinal sin. In the eyes of the community, the only thing worse than killing a priest is killing the pope.

The women make their way through the small but growing number of protesters holding hate placards milling behind portable barricades. As they pass through the crowd Sam reads with disbelief words like Lynch the killer, bring back the death penalty, Catholics united against murder, burn in hell, before turning with fearful eyes to a silent Grace.

"Sorry, what kind of business do you have in the station," asks a young detective holding out an arm blocking Grace and Sam's entrance to the building. Grace chats conspiratorially with the officer who consults with someone on his radio before allowing the two women to pass. Grace's law enforcement connection gets them five minutes with Maria-Teresa.

Inside the building, the sentiments of the protesters spill over. The police officer leading them to the room holding Maria-Teresa makes his view on the situation clear with a few nasty remarks uttered under his breath. When the door to the room opens, Maria-Teresa turns to stare at it with the anticipation of an ill patient seeing her doctor who has just come to impart a negative prognosis.

Their friend is huddled in a corner her tiny body swallowed up from neck to toe in a one size fits all paper garment. The paper sleeves and pant legs are rolled up several times to allow her hands and feet to show. Upon seeing her friends, Maria-Teresa's brows knit together in confusion, her tear-stained face crumbles and she turns her head away from her visitors putting the knuckles of one fist between her teeth expecting to hear the worst.

Conversely, Sam looks toward the ceiling to keep tears from spilling down her cheeks at the sight of her friend's distress. The blue cloudless sky peeks through a tiny window near the room's ceiling painting the promise of just another hot sunshiny day if not for the barely audible muffled chants signaling the unrest riding on the wind.

Sam makes a failed attempt at levity, "Umm girl, that is so not your color," referring to the chalk white of the paper outfit against Maria-Teresa's tan skin.

Grace gingerly approaches Maria-Teresa, "Honey, what happened?" As they get closer to her wide eyes and trembling body Grace asks, "Has anyone hurt you?" Followed by Sam first embracing her friend then vowing, "We came as quickly as we could."

Fresh tears threaten to spill from her already puffy red eyes. Maria-Teresa reaches up to give her friends a three-way hug and breaks down sobbing uncontrollably while simultaneously talking into their shoulders "I was," sobbing then sniffing. "And he," more sobbing and unintelligible words. "Oh god, I didn't," sobbing again. "Why?" to describe her morning. The remainder of their time together is spent consoling her never able to get a clear picture of what happened.

Exactly five minutes later they hear, "Time to go," from the surly young officer who led them to their friend his attitude toward Maria-Teresa unchanged. The ladies don't afford the officer an excuse to vent his anger on anyone and they promptly leave the room.

"What happens next?" asks Sam dabbing at her own tears once they reach the hallway.

"Well, she has to be arraigned. It will be up to the judge whether she can be released on bail or if she will be detained."

The west valley police want to rid themselves of the cause of the boisterous mob of protesters outside now hampering their normal activities. Removing Maria-Teresa from the west valley means further harassment from the protesters will possibly end.

Finding out when and where the arraignment will be Grace and Sam proceed to the adjacent courthouse. At the Mesa courthouse, the judge does not consider Maria-Teresa a flight risk because of her family ties, ownership in her engineering business, and her ties to the church. Thanks in part to the kind words from Fr. Santos and Grace's influence a rather high bail is set.

Maria-Teresa remains the only police suspect and at this point, unless circumstances drastically change, she will probably stand trial for murder based on circumstantial evidence.

Once she is released both women rush to their friend's side and Maria-Teresa's body sags like a rag doll in the arms of her friends.

"Let's get you home. Where is Danielle?" asks Sam referring to Maria-Teresa's life partner.

"Chicago, on business, don't call her. I'm all right. Can I stay with you 'til she comes back?"

"Of course! You don't have to ask. Grace will stay too." Without confirmation from Grace, they proceed directly to Sam's house at the opposite end of the valley.

6

Earlier that day, Hobbs fills his partner Turner in on the details of Maria-Teresa's early morning ordeal before they each work on separate tasks during the day. "You ready?" asks Hobbs poking his head in the doorway of Turner's office at the end of their shift.

"In a minute just need to close up."

Heavy impatient footsteps pace the hallway periodically interrupted by "Night, yeah you too, tomorrow," as Hobbs bids good night to his colleagues before Turner joins him in the hallway.

"You hear anything else?"

"No. Got me worried. Grace hasn't even returned my phone calls. I'll drive," says Hobbs forcing Turner to look at him with skepticism.

"My car's faster," says Turner referring to his sports car. "I know how you drive when you're distracted."

"I'm not distracted. What do you mean how I drive?" snorts Hobbs wishing he could make a good retort to this statement but is unable to think of one and climbs reluctantly into Turner's car. There is no doubt in either man's mind that all four of the mystery book club members will be present at Sam's house. The scenery blurs as the sports car weaves its way through town.

Quickly rounding the corner onto San Pedro Road Turner swerves violently nearly colliding with two cyclists. Seizing his opportunity to make a comeback Hobbs looks at his partner and says, "So what's that about my driving?"

Not rising to the bait Turner drives on before swinging out wide onto Sagebrush Lane where the lone dove grey single-family house with its lighter grey trim distinguishes itself from the earth tone homes surrounding it. Parking slightly askew in front of the three-car garage the men clamor out of the car, walk briskly up the winding paved walkway ignoring the brightly colored flowers lining both sides of it.

Reaching the Smokey Topaz-colored front door both men look up at the camera mounted above it and wave. Exterior cameras placed strategically around the house are a new addition following Sam's last encounter with dead bodies on her property. Aside from its color, the house itself bears the traditional stucco façade and arched framed portico. The sound of a remote click unlocks the front door.

The familiar well-lit hallway dumps them into the large bright open floor plan of the three-thousand-foot one-story house. The natural light streaming through the floor-to-ceiling windows that line the wall connecting the kitchen to the family room cast a long shadow of Grace on the terracotta tile as she quietly paces back and forth. Today, the wow factor of the massive granite counter tops, chef's kitchen, the pit sofa, and double-sided fireplace go unappreciated by the home's inhabitants.

Sam twists the ends of her grey-streaked braids while perching slightly hunched on the corner of the white U-shaped seating pit with the billowy cushions, her eyes trained on Maria-Teresa sitting inert in the opposite corner wearing borrowed workout pants and shirt.

Margot Towers the mystery book club's newest member sits on the edge of a stool at the kitchen island absentmindedly raking a hand through her thin shoulder-length greyish-blonde hair her alert pale blue eyes observing the inactivity. Margot's usual position at social gatherings is that of cautious observer on the peripheral of the action, head turning like an owl from person to person absorbing every nuance.

Margot receives a call from Sam to join her fellow sleuths just one hour before the detectives arrived. Absent from the group all morning tackling personal business she is not totally up to speed on this morning's activities.

When the detectives enter the room, three of the four senior women rise greeting them unemotionally in turn before returning to their original positions in the room. Noticing the stunned look on Margot's face Turner takes a seat next to her, "Everything will be alright."

Margot forces a smile, "What is it about this group and their attraction to murder?" she asks rhetorically remembering her only brush with murder also involved these three women.

"Listen, you've got to admit these women although falsely accused do know how to investigate to clear themselves while managing to find the real murderer."

"One solved crime does not an expert make," mumbles Margot. "If we investigate, can you guarantee we'll get out of this one on the right side of the law?" Turning her back on him to gaze at the backyard swimming pool indicating there is no need for Turner to respond.

Addressing Sam, the glue that binds the group and mother to them all, Hobbs asks, "How's she doing?" nodding toward the bedraggled Maria-Teresa, who sits on the sofa seemingly unaware of the other people in the room. Her dissociative behavior prompts Turner to ask, "Has a doctor looked at her?" Before anyone can answer a soft angry voice says, "Stop talking about me like I can't hear you. Please!"

Hobbs walks over to her and kneels to eye level, "Sorry, we're just worried about you. That was quite a shock finding that bloody body the way you did."

"Yeah, it was," she says resolutely. "They think I—I did it," she searches his eyes for answers, her eyes asking for help, and sighing deeply she turns toward the unlit two-sided fireplace beside her. Hobbs touches her hand and she returns her gaze to his face.

"I thought I was afraid a few months ago being held hostage at gun point but finding the dead body of a priest and being accused of his murder—" her voice trails off, her body shudders once before her right-hand touches her forehead, chest, left and right shoulder before continuing in a soft voice, "that could be me lying on the church floor had I turned up on time."

Margot pulls the collar of her shirt away from her throat and swallows hard to rid herself of the very real sensation of fear building in her throat. Turning away from the others she surreptitiously swipes at the tiny beads of sweat peppering her face. It's just a reaction, there's no reason to be afraid. I'm safe. She tells herself that every time she has a visceral reaction to some word, smell, or situation triggering the terror of the kidnapping incident she shared with Maria-Teresa.

Across the room, on the sofa, Maria-Teresa drops Hobbs' grasp, opens her mouth to speak then stops. She looks down at the box of tissue to her side pulls out a handful rips them like she's ripping the devil itself. Unfazed by the concerned looks from her friends, she silently continues to extract handfuls of tissues ripping each handful more violently than the last.

A grimaced angry look contorts her face. The onlookers exchange terrified glances conflicted as to whether to disturb her or leave her to her ripping. Sam, a retired child psychologist and mother to the group, knows it's best to have her lay down and call a physician. Maria-Teresa is in no mental state to assist their desire to absolve her of any suspicion.

"Honey, why don't you come with me and get some rest?" not expecting an answer and hoping to get no resistance to her suggestion, Sam gently ushers Maria-Teresa into a spare bedroom for a lie down.

"Anyone contact Danielle?" mouths Turner so as not to distract the two women slowly leaving the room.

"Maria-Teresa said not too. She's in Chicago, their firm is on the short list for some big engineering contract. So, we keep her in the dark if we can, periodic texts should work," says Grace. "Their firm needs the work. Danielle will only worry, and we can do that." Once the sound of Sam and Maria-Teresa's footsteps can no longer be heard conversation between the four swirls unchecked.

"I am surprised she's released on bail," whispers Margot looking over her shoulder at the hallway. Also, glancing at the hallway before practically talking over Margot Hobbs says, "Nonsense all the evidence is circumstantial. The coroner estimated time of death between 7:30 and 9:00 am. She didn't even get to the church until 9:40ish and was seen leaving the church ten minutes later. What killer in his right mind would stick around an extra thirty or forty minutes after committing a crime?"

Turner tries to solidify his partners theory, "The blood on her clothes clearly does not resemble any kind of splatter pattern resulting from committing that crime."

Twisting sharply on the island stool to face those in the room Margot says in a shrill voice, "Blood on her clothes, how did that happen? I thought she just saw a dead body," she searches each face in the room for an answer.

"Shh, keep your voice down." Moving her hand through the air gesturing that Margot's question is inconsequential Grace says, "She leans palms down on the desk that had splatter on it then wipes her hands on her clothes that's all. Simple explanation it could happen to anyone in the same situation. What concerns me are the angry protestors, they're forcing the police to find a killer or a scapegoat sooner rather than later. Right now, Maria-Teresa heads the top of the list for both."

They sit in companionable silence visibly worrying but not wanting to verbalize their fears. Instead, they just wait for Sam's return. The soft padding of Sam's footsteps entering the family room cause a uniform turn of heads.

"I phoned the doctor, he's sending over something to help her sleep. He wants to examine her tomorrow."

"Did she say anything?" asks Hobbs.

"Yeah, why is God punishing me?"

7

"If the evidence is just circumstantial as you all claim," says Margot now turning her body fully toward the group, "just leave it to the police to find the real culprit," a hint of finality in her voice. Her position is always the naysayer before quickly acquiescing to her friend's wishes which is and always will be that they can investigate a crime involving one of their own better than the police.

Quite familiar with her opposing views no one responds, instead the four of them sit facing each other on the parallel sides of the U-shaped sofa. Margot remains on the fringe of the huddle perched on the back of the sofa that connects the two sides. Looks of determination best describe the faces of the seated friends.

"How strong is this circumstantial evidence," asks the mildly curious Margot.

"Well, she was seen running from the crime scene covered in the victim's blood. There was no one else seen in or around the crime scene. There is still no murder weapon, but I'm sure the police will proceed with prosecuting Maria-Teresa anyway," announces Hobbs.

"What's her motive, she doesn't even know this priest, does she?" continues Margot.

"A simple case of mistaken identity. The police think she came to kill Fr. Santos and mistook this guy for him."

"Again, what's her motive for killing Santos? This just doesn't make any sense," echoes Sam.

"I don't know some church vendetta, you know payback for being kicked out by that old guy," says Turner.

"So, you take out your past grievance on the one person who accepts you back into the church? No way they can make that motive stick," responds Hobbs.

40

"They could say she used the acceptance to carry out her murder plot and not be a suspect," all heads turn toward Margot.

"Whose side are you on," they practically snarl in unison causing Margot's close set blue eyes to blink rapidly as she shrinks back. Everyone's attention turns to Grace who says, "What did they find at the murder scene, we need those crime scene photos," looking hopefully toward the two detectives.

"Keating's working the case and he hates me and Turner for the slap on the wrist we got for our behavior on our last case." Throwing his hands up in exasperation gesturing toward the kitchen, "You would have a better chance asking those damn whimsical mugs of yours than asking us to get our hands on those crime scene photos."

Sam Jones owns a collection of mugs with whimsical sayings on them. During the ladies last murder investigation, the sayings on the mugs appeared to correctly predict upcoming events or situations. As if a light bulb goes off, the ladies turn toward the kitchen cabinet that houses Sam's infamous mug collection. Without another word, Sam being the staunchest believer in the prophetic power of her mugs, strides confidently to the cabinet in search of truth.

Hobbs gives off a low guttural growl of disapproval, several well-timed eye rolls, and a smack with his palm to his forehead before saying, "Oh god no, I can't believe this again," as Sam reaches into the cabinet and extracts a mug. He gets up tromps off saying over his slumped shoulders, "Gotta pee."

The mug that Sam blindly pulls out simply has a rainbow painted on it with no phrase. "What's that doing in there with the sacred mugs. This is anything but a rainbow kinda day," yells Turner from across the room who secretly loves the predictions of the mugs. Shaking her head in disbelief Sam sets the mug to the side and reaches in the cabinet again.

"I first one doesn't count since it does not contain words," she announces before reading the second mug, *Do the right thing for the right reason at the right time—Harry Selfridge.*

"Guess that's settled then, we launch our own investigation," says Grace triumphantly as if she would have said anything different.

"Let's give our grey cells some nourishment," exclaims Sam now satisfied that the mug gods have given their blessing for them to investigate. Like any mother, Sam knows the body needs fuel to think and brings out the feast she prepared for this evening.

Hobbs returns from the bathroom and without even asking whether they intended to pursue an investigation, he says, "I guess asking you NOT to investigate this case is feudal," he says smiling because he knows this group never leaves the fate of a friend to the sometimes-incapable hands of the police.

Taking the comment as lighthearted as it was given Sam answers, "Why don't you have some dinner? You must be hungry otherwise you would never ask us not to investigate."

Everyone's attention returns to food. Hobbs and Turner eat with the appreciation of bachelors launching into the buffet like it's their last meal.

The ladies more interested in the investigation than the meal wait anxiously for the men to finish their first helping before asking, "What do we know about the dead priest?" asks Sam sincerely, directing her question to the officers.

The men are chewing, crunching, and swallowing when Turner manages to push his food to one side of his mouth and says, "Been busy all day, I don't even know the victim's name."

Hobbs follows up with, "I know that no weapon was found, and the name of the deceased is Fr. Hector Francisco from somewhere in New Mexico."

"That's it?" exclaims Margot in an accusing voice. This is not the first time the ladies have questioned Hobbs' information gathering skills.

Hobbs manages to answer Margot's accusatory tone as indignantly as he can muster with a mouth full of food, "You do know the crime didn't take place within my jurisdiction, don't you? I don't have access to all of the information concerning this case."

With that retort, Margot's back straightens and she shoots fiery looks in Hobbs' direction. Once again, its Sam to the rescue. "Calm down, you two. We've got important pressing work to do."

8

Once everyone has had their fill of food Sam rearranges items on the coffee table to make room for the computer. The detectives, now munching on third helpings, watch her bustle around the family room with mild curiosity. Then Sam takes a seat and gives a nod of her head signaling to Margot that she is ready to proceed.

"After our last investigation, Grace gifted us with the latest electronic equipment to make tracking murder clues and brain-storming easier," says Margot proudly. On cue, Sam presses a button on a remote and they all watch a clear reusable screen rise slowly from a credenza-like piece of furniture.

Hobbs' mouth opens as the screen becomes fully visible from the credenza, then he shakes his head in disbelief before saying, "Why am I not surprised," in that envious voice that he gets whenever wealth is hoisted in his face. He follows his first comment with, "Umph, this setup must have cost at least ten grand or more."

Grace gives Hobbs a sideways glance coupled with a condescending smile. Something about raising Hobbs' hackles with a show of her massive wealth gives Grace a morbid sense of pleasure. Turner interrupts Grace's secret musing when he jumps up and yells, "Damn girl! Look at you!" referring to the screen.

Then he does his version of a touch-down dance complete with knee wobbling and index fingers alternately pointing toward the ceiling while he yells, "Oh yeah, oh yeah, oh yeah." Turner's antics evoke raucous laughter from the ladies and even a smile from Hobbs. Once the levity stops, the ladies get down to business the screen wirelessly connects to Sam's computer, which allows her to write on the screen by typing on the computer.

Information can also be printed or emailed directly from the screen and all information written on it is saved in an electronic file for future use. At this point, the only thing the group knows about the murder is that a Fr. Hector

Francisco is dead, cause of death unknown, no murder weapon, and Maria-Teresa is the only suspect.

"What do we need to find out? We can list that on this side of the screen," points out Sam.

"First, we need to get a hold of that autopsy report and the crime scene photos, you can handle that can't you?" asks Margot once again glaring at the detectives. Each officer rolls his eyes at Margot.

Grace interrupts any response they plan to make to Margot and says, "Time of death is really important. Clearly, he died before Maria-Teresa arrived."

"Why was he in Fr. Santos' office?" muses Sam adding it to the list.

"How did he die and what is the motive," says Grace.

"Who the hell is this guy other than some priest from New Mexico? What the hell is he doing in Arizona?" asks Hobbs. The ladies eagerly write down all the questions that have been raised.

Grace finds it necessary to state the obvious and says, "Maria-Teresa is seen running from the crime scene covered in blood. Why would the police look anywhere else for another suspect? I guarantee she will be their only suspect."

"The fact that there is no other suspect is a pretty compelling reason for you ladies to do what you can to help Maria-Teresa. She is in no condition to help herself," concurs Turner.

"We have to prove she didn't kill that priest," says Sam while Margot goes a step further adding, "more importantly, we should find out who really did kill that priest."

Once everything they know and need to know is listed on the board Grace says, "Hobbs, you and Turner work on getting a copy of the police and autopsy reports."

"Grace, I am not going to be much help, sorry. I'll be away for a while," says Turner. "I was waiting to get my official notification before telling anyone, but I have an opportunity to get more military intelligence training at one of the Department of Defense's classified locations."

Eyes open wide and silence floods the room, then the women shower him with congratulatory words and hugs. Turner looks at Hobbs who remains seated and silent. The ladies follow Turner's gaze forcing the attention and spotlight on Hobbs who looks up and says, "What? Of course, I am happy for him. It's just that." He stops short and looks down at his lap, then continues in a voice that sounds like a hurt child, "You could've told me you were applying. You could've trusted me."

Sam turns to Hobbs and says, "We understand you'll miss your best bud." Turner gets exactly what Hobbs means and realizes that he should have trusted his partner with his secret. After all, it was just a few months ago that Hobbs trusted him with a secret of epic proportions. Turner looks pleadingly at Hobbs but Hobbs refuses to meet his gaze.

Grace is the only one of the women who knows and understands the unspoken feelings between the two men. In typical Grace fashion, she has learned to put feelings aside when it comes to completion of a mission. Not wanting sentiment to slow down the task at hand Grace says, "Well, now we're a person down. Let's get back to assignments."

9

"Wait, I can't really help either." All heads turn toward Margot everyone surprised to hear her say, "I need to clear up this mess with my family or I will never be able to move on with my life." Silence from her friends and looks of disappointment prompts her to add, "I'm available intermittently, just not all the time," says Margot resolutely jutting out her chin knowing that the reasons for estranging herself from every member of her real family needs mending or cutting.

"OK, anyone else bowing out?" asks Grace looking around the room from person to person. As her eyes reach the doorway, the sight of Maria-Teresa standing there silently forces the others to turn, "I can't help either," with tears welling in her eyes, she blurts out louder, "I just can't. I know you are doing this for me but—"

"It's OK, honey, we understand. I guess that leaves the three of us then, Sam, Hobbs, and myself."

Margot and Maria-Teresa bonded after their shared time as kidnappees during the groups' last murder investigation. The fragile condition of her friend solidifies the fact that she feels the bond they share is far more important than her own needs and immediately says, "On second thought, I can give a little more time to the investigation. I can only think of two motives for killing a priest."

Everyone leans forward to hear her motives, "Bad sermons and sexual abuse, but these are motive's a parishioner might have for murder. What if the killer is someone inside the church, like another priest or a nun?"

In the initial stages of the investigation, no theories are ruled out, so her theory is written on the murder board with the knowns and unknowns about the case. The rest of the night is spent doling out assignments, brainstorming motives, and means before everyone leaves for the night.

10

The archbishop of the archdiocese wants to remove the stigma of murder at the St. Francis de Sales Catholic Church from the public's eye as soon as possible. His fellow clergymen feel there is enough negative press surrounding the catholic church and killing a priest only leads everyone's mind to connect the murder to a revenge killing for sexual abuse.

The ladies have no evidence that Fr. Hector Francisco is or ever was a pedophile. Thanks to urges from the archdiocese the autopsy of the priest is pushed to the top of the medical examiner's list and it is performed the day after the body arrives at the morgue. Hobbs keeps his vow to check on the autopsy results and he calls his friend at the medical examiner's office.

"Hello Pete, it's Joe Hobbs, homicide east valley. Look, I need a favor. You got any information on that dead priest that was found over at the St. Francis de Sales Catholic church."

"Hey, Hobbs. Just finishing up. West valley's been calling all morning. Who is this guy?"

"Only know his name, well what have you got?"

"Why are you interested, this isn't even your jurisdiction?"

"Yeah, that's why I said I need a favor. A friend is involved in the case."

"Going off the reservation again? I can lose my job for helping you and I don't have friends in high places to keep me out of jams." Pete Simons refers to the friend(s) who prevented both Hobbs and Turner from getting fired for unauthorized policing in another state when they helped the book club ladies solve the swimming pool murder.

"Please help me out. I'll owe you big time," pleads Hobbs.

"You know I can't tell you anything or put anything in writing," says Pete.

Hobbs takes a leap and says, "Thanks anyway," and hangs up. Then he hops in his car and drives to the ME's office.

Hobbs enters Pete's office with Pete's favorite burritos, not so much a bribe but more like a thank you or a cheap date. "Hey, detective how's it going? Thanks, my favorite!" says Pete accepting the burritos. "I'll get something to wash these down with, going to get a cup of coffee can I get you one?"

"Thanks, Pete. I'd love a cup. I just hope your station coffee is better than mine," replies Hobbs with a lighthearted chuckle. Before leaving the office, Pete repositions his computer monitor that displays the complete autopsy report of the dead priest. Hobbs pulls out his phone to photo the report and takes the remainder of the time Pete is out to read it.

After reading the report, Hobbs leaves and races back to the office without waiting for Pete to return. Turner's phone alerts him to an incoming text from Sam, which says, what time are you coming for dinner? He is about to reply when Hobbs burst through his office door, sweaty and excited.

This time of year, the heat takes a toll on Hobbs' appearance, he pulls at his tie while undoing the top button of his wrinkled shirt, then still a little breathy he says, "I'm glad you're still here. I would have told you to meet me at Sam's house, but I wanted to run the results of the autopsy findings past you first."

"What did you find out, anything we can use?"

Hobbs pulls up a chair and opens the photo app on his phone, enlarges the screen which lays bare the medical examiner's findings. Aside from the victim being stabbed in the back and having his throat slit, there is something else about the body that disturbs Hobbs.

Turner reads through the pages in silence digesting each part making mental notes before he says, "You see this!" pointing to a particular section of the report that says an old bullet wound in one of the scars on the dead priest's body.

"Yeah, but I wanted to run it by you first. Glad you think it's as suspicious as I do. I'm starting to wonder if this crime goes beyond the church."

"I think we need to keep the bullet wound to ourselves for now. Agreed?" Turner gives an affirmative nod and asks, "Why would a Catholic priest have an old bullet wound? How did he get it?"

Hobbs picks up his phone and dials, in an exasperated voice Pete answers his phone, "Not you again. What's eating you this time?"

"Now, now, Pete that's no way to treat a friend. Didn't I bring you your favorite burritos?"

"OK, OK quit acting like you care. What do you want?"

"The autopsy report on the priest said he had an old bullet wound. Is there any way I can look at the body?"

"Sorry too late. He's gone."

"Gone where?"

"His body was released to a funeral home this morning. I signed the release slip myself."

"Which funeral home, where?" Asks Hobbs in a panic thinking his only lead is getting away.

Pete checks his computer for the file, "That's weird I entered the information in the computer myself." Hobbs hears computer keys clicking, harried breathing, papers rustling, and low groans coming from Pete's end of the phone.

"That's weird?"

"Talk to me Pete what's going on," asks Hobbs.

"His file is gone too. Oh god, if I erased the file, I'm in big trouble." Without so much as a see ya later, Pete slams down the phone.

The phone call with Pete Simons leaves both detectives wondering about the missing body, the bullet wound, and conclude that Francisco is not just some priest on sabbatical. Their recent experience with Grace's covert operatives has their minds racing to formulate reasons why a priest would have a bullet wound.

<h1 style="text-align:center">11</h1>

Meanwhile at Sam's house she, Margot and Grace sip coffee deciding how to proceed with their end of the investigation. The strong scent of lavender wafts through the open doors leading to the backyard oasis calming everyone inside the family room.

"I always say go back to the scene of the crime," mutters Grace looking unfocused into the horizon from her place at the kitchen island.

"I agree, let's head over to the church. Shall I call Fr. Santos and tell him we are coming," asks Sam reaching for her phone.

"No! It's better that he has no time to prepare if he is mixed up in this," says Grace shaking her head at Sam's lack of forethought. Catching sight of her friend on the sofa Grace asks, "Who's going to stay with Maria-Teresa?"

"I have tons of research to do, I'm sure tracking down a family I haven't seen in ten years is not going to be an easy task," says Margot agreeing to stay behind as the two women leave the house.

For at least an hour, Maria-Teresa alternates between sitting motionless on Sam's family room sofa or holding up in Sam's guest bedroom waiting anxiously to hear from the text she sent Danielle. The sound of the doorbell startles both women given the fervor with which it is continuously being pushed. "I'll get it," announces Margot rising from her chair.

The door opens, "Hello, Danni. How was your—," a red-faced Danielle brushes angrily against Margot's shoulder and passes her into the family room.

"What the hell is this about another murder? You arrested and suspected of killing a priest. A priest!" not giving Maria-Teresa an opportunity to respond, "and I hear about this shit from you in a text."

"I, I, I—" stutters Maria-Teresa, "don't be mad, it's not my fault."

"It's never your fault or the fault of your little band of wan-a-be detectives." Danni paces back and forth arms folded across her chest, suitcase beside her feet, "First, it's the kidnapping and now this. Do you even care how much I worry about you? Do you know the anguish I go through every time you voluntarily put yourself in danger? Well, do you?" ask Danni thrusting her face close to her partner.

A silence so intense falls over the room that Margot thinks it's possible to hear a pin drop on a carpet if Sam had carpet. "Uh, why don't I, um go outside and give you two some privacy," suggests Margot.

"You don't have to leave, we've had this particular conversation before," says Danni looking at MT, her nickname for Maria-Teresa. "I am leaving, are you coming home with me?" demands Danni obviously still enraged.

MT who has been unable to get a word in edgewise since Danni's stormy arrival looks pleadingly at her partner. "You know I can't abandon my friends, they are trying to help me. Even Margot is giving her time to help me. I need to help myself."

She wants to add surely you understand but she knows Danni never understood her loyalty to her friends or their loyalty to her. MT lowers her head, the tears and snot flow freely as Danni snatches up her belongings and like a tornado whipping up things in her path leaves the house as furious as her arrival.

Margot within sight of the two enters the room, "She's just a little upset; don't worry, she'll come around," assures Margot.

"No, she won't. Not this time," responds MT in a fait accompli voice head in her hands softly crying.

12

As Grace and Sam drive over to the church their conversation is peppered with concerns about Maria-Teresa's mental health unaware of Danni's visit. Pushing their concerns aside they focus on any little tidbit gleaned from her about the layout of the church and the inner workings of Catholicism.

Until the police release the crime scene Fr. Santos is unable to use the sacristy for his office. He is working out of an empty classroom near the nursery or any other available space he can find in the church. He is thinking of just going to the nearby public library for peace and quiet.

Grace and Sam get to the church and find no yellow crime scene tape at the front door, which they swing open and proceed to the lower level in search of Fr. Santos. They traverse the same corridor Keating used to find Santos and they too find him squished into a small child-size chair with his head down reading. Grace stops suddenly at the sight of Santos thinking to herself, *In jeans and a tee-shirt anyone might mistake him for a male model with his chiseled jaw and luxurious hair.*

He lifts his head and Grace looks into his hazel eyes, then quickly her gaze takes in his lean body that she imagines under his cassock. Gracefully extricating himself from his child-size chair, he stands up and strides confidently forward to greet them.

No wonder he catches the eye of every female in the congregation, probably all thinking what a waste to be celibate. The grumbling of Sam's stomach commands everyone's attention as Santos smiles at them.

"Hello, ladies. How is Maria-Teresa?"

Grace takes the lead and answers, "Hello, Father. She's doing as well as can be expected under the circumstances. If you have a minute, we have some questions."

"Well, you certainly sound official but I have told the police everything I know."

"Unfortunately, the police aren't sharing. You do want to help Maria-Teresa, don't you?"

Grace poses the question with a bit of uncertainty in her voice and stares intently at Santos gaging his reaction. He does not squirm or shy away from her stare. Grace is unaware that Fr. Joao Santos is not your ordinary man called to God. His colorful background and very possibly current lifestyle make him immune to even her trained scrutiny.

The sound of little footsteps running past the door followed by adult voices admonishing such behavior. "Come, let's stroll in the back garden, it's quieter there," suggest the priest.

Neither of the ladies has any idea how sprawling the church property actual is until they go through doors at the end of the corridor out to the nursery playground. Beyond the playground is a path that leads to a small serene garden. A row of tall hedges provides a square boundary for the garden with openings on opposite ends to enter and exit.

"How absolutely beautiful!" exclaims Sam as she makes a three-hundred-sixty-degree turn to admire every inch of the floral-laden garden. Grace, however, is struck by the seclusion the hedges give to anyone entering the church from the back garden. A person can easily go to and from the church without being seen.

She looks up and notices the only clear view of the entire church ground is from the bell tower in the main church but does not mention her discovery. Her surveillance of the property does not go unnoticed by the handsome young priest as he follows her gaze from the garden to the bell tower and to the back door of the church.

"What's over there?" asks Grace pointing toward the opening in the hedges on the opposite end of the garden.

"That path leads to the rectory," says Fr. Santos projecting a calm confidence but chooses not to add that the dead priest was living there. He has no idea until now how adept Grace's powers of observation are.

"You said you have questions?" says the priest looking from Grace to Sam before continuing, "how may I help?" in a soothing, comforting voice with an even cadence that oozes concern.

His demeanor resembles that of every actor who has ever played a priest on stage and screen with his hands clasped in a prayer position at his solar plexus, his Mona Lisa smile, and the tilt of his head slightly to one side as he leans his body toward them.

This gesture gives the appearance of being fully engaged with the ladies. *He's good,* thinks Grace, while Sam grins at him like a schoolgirl with a romantic crush. Most of the women in the parish, old and young alike, react the same way Sam does whenever they are around him. There is something about this man, other than his devastatingly good looks, that is just not right, thinks Grace.

Sure, there have been other good-looking, attractive, and even handsome men called to the priesthood but this guy, no this guy, doesn't feel like one of those men. A bit tongue in cheek and taking a stab in the dark Grace remarks, "I understand the female attendance in the church has increased quite a lot since you came. Why do you think that is?"

Fr. Santos quickly says, "The Lord works in mysterious ways." Before he can complete his sentence, Grace finds herself thinking, *He did not just give me that old cliché.* Fr. Santos is about to continue when they hear an adult voice yell, "Come back here, give me that." The three of them turn just in time to see a small child running toward them, his head swallowed up by an adult size baseball cap.

Quick as lightning, Fr. Santos takes one step in front of the moving child, bends down, and scoops him up in his right arm, while grabbing the yellow and green cap by the crown with his left hand and whips it from the child's head.

"Sorry, Father, he's been on the move all morning," says a rather shy, out-of-breath, young woman from the nursery as she takes the wriggling child from the arms of the priest. Fr. Santos smiles and assures her no harm is done but he hangs on to the ball cap with his hand still obscuring the logo.

"Father, may we see your office?" asks Grace.

"I am afraid the police still have it cordoned off. I can show you the hallway outside my office and how to get to that hallway from the nave."

"Thank you, that will be very helpful," says Sam almost apologetically. Looking at the hallway leading to his office is not the least bit helpful to their investigation. They thank him and head back toward the nave. He watches them with a quizzical expression on his face clearly wondering how much of a problem they will be.

As they go outside Grace absentmindedly says to no one in particular, "Something about that young woman chasing the child that seems so familiar to me."

"It should, she looks like a younger version of Maria-Teresa," responds Sam, just after popping something edible in her mouth that she mysteriously grabs from either her purse or a pocket. On the way home from the church, Grace can't help but think there is more than meets the eye with this murder and they have to work fast if they want to keep Maria-Teresa out of prison.

13

At the east valley police station, Hobbs puts away some things on his desk, gathers his briefcase before asking his partner, "Did you copy the arrest and crime scene reports?" Turner nods in the affirmative and they head out for Sam's house and their usual evening debriefing meeting. In the car, their discussion turns to a subject they share, food.

"Wonder what she's serving tonight?" asks Turner.

"Yeah, I kind-a feel like eating a juicy tenderloin with all the trimmings," says Hobbs as a slow smile creases the laugh lines around his mouth, "umm, the thought of a sumptuous dinner makes my mouth water. I just have to make one stop for my beer."

"You know they will serve a great wine, why drink beer when the wine is excellent and free," asks Turner.

"Don't want to spoil my taste buds with habits I can't continue. I am still reeling from my lack of Grace's Macallan 25 whiskey." Hobbs makes his purchase of beer and jerky for his midnight treat and they continue to Sam's.

Sam's door is opened promptly by Margot who by the sour look on her face is annoyed with someone or something. She turns to strut back toward the family room and the guys pass a look between them that says we are in for a bumpy ride. When Margot gets annoyed, it ripples out to everyone she encounters.

Stepping into the open plan kitchen family room the smell of a home-cooked meal wafts up their nostrils and floods their brains with endorphins. "What smells so good?" asks Turner.

"I thought you hard-working men might like a hearty meal, so I fixed a tenderloin complete with all the trimmings," says Sam.

Hobbs throws his arms around Sam squeezing tight enough to labor her breathing, "Let go of me, you crazy man," gasps Sam wriggling out of his grasp with a smile. Turner shakes his head in disbelief when he hears the evening's menu.

"There is something mystical and spooky about this group's relationship," says Turner referring to the fact that on more than one occasion there have been instances of mental telepathy passing between members of the group.

"You might be right we do seem to be on the same wavelength," admits Sam. Turner grabs a glass and fills it from the open bottle of wine on the table. With a teasing grin, Sam grabs Hobbs' loosely hanging tie leading him into the kitchen. Hobbs puts up no resistance as he places his hands on her waist to gently push her along in front of him.

Beer and Hobbs always come as one for dinner and she reaches in a cabinet to get him a drinking glass, she notices one of her novelty mugs is on the wrong shelf. Sam places it on the counter with the intent to return it to its rightful place when she is stopped by the following words printed on the mug, Pray Now's the Time.

Superstition is familiar to Turner a Southern transplant who grew up in a household of strong Black women obeying every superstition known to mankind. Turner halfheartedly regards Sam's whimsical mug collection as her very own version of Tarot cards. Turner comes into the kitchen and follows Sam's gaze to the mug sitting on the counter. Reading its wording he says in an ominous voice, "Here we go again."

Margot turns to observe the three in the kitchen searching their faces for the source of the sudden quiet that swallows the room. Slowly Margot rises and enters the kitchen only to catch sight of the ominous mug on the counter.

"Pray for who, for what?" She turns to the others, "is this about Maria-Teresa or something else?"

14

"Are you there? Hello? Hello?" the words seem to emanate from a faraway place. It is only when Grace hears her name does the voice on the other end of the phone bring her back to reality.

"Grace, we have not located his body but there is every indication that Rhys is dead—" Grace does not remember any words after hearing Rhys is dead.

Flopping down hard in her library chair, Grace stares at the phone in her hand but she has no idea for how long. How does a man as careful as Rhys just suddenly die and no one knows how, why, or where his body is? Grace tries to regulate her uneven breathing while digesting the news that her covert handler, friend, and long time off and on-again lover is dead.

The pain rips at her heart and drags her mind into a temporary downward spiral. She has been taught to compartmentalize her feelings, but this pain is too raw, too real, too much a part of her to push aside. They met when they were a lot younger before the horrors of their profession in the covert world of spying turned their opinion of the world on its heels.

Like so much of her life's story she cannot share with anyone, so too must she bear this pain alone. She takes a couple of hours to work through her feelings before leaving her house to go to Sam's. To the outside world, Grace has neither changed her demeanor nor her purpose in life. Inside, her feelings are running as deep and wide as the Grand Canyon.

Grace will be herself because she must because he would want her to. With all that needs to be done to keep Maria-Teresa from going to prison, she will have to grieve her loss a little later. Forty-five minutes later she pulls into Sam's driveway exhales and walks to the front door. Margot, the self-appointed official greeter lets her irritation show once more when she greets Grace at the door.

"Where have you been? Everybody's waiting." Margot knows the pecking order of this group and she is not at the top; however, she doesn't hide her displeasure with Grace's tardiness. So, there is no surprise to her when Grace brushes past her and heads to the family room without answering or acknowledging her question.

"I see the gangs all here," says Grace with one of those fake but convincing smiles plastered on her face. "What have I missed?" continues Grace in an upbeat voice indicating she is eager to get started.

"We are waiting for you, are you hungry?" asks Sam.

"Hey guys," Grace says addressing the detectives. "Sure, I'm feeling a little peckish, Sam. What's for dinner?"

Grace grabs her plate, puts just enough food on it to satisfy the rules of etiquette. Then she takes a seat in the family room before saying, "OK spill, what's going on?"

Turner says, "It's the damn mugs forecasting doom and the fact that we found out nothing significant about the priest."

"Which one? Looks of confusion pass among the others, is she asking about the mug or the priests?" Picking up on their confusion, Grace clarifies, "I mean which priest."

"We thought we'd start with the dead one," adds Turner. Neither detective mentions the concerning information found in the autopsy report, why add to the already somber mood.

"Don't feel bad. Sam and I didn't get very far today either. Something will break, we just need a clue, a good lead," adds Grace feeling an overwhelming need to immerse herself in something other than her feelings. She looks over at Margot squirming in her chair fiddling with her napkin, "What's wrong with you, why are you so antsy?"

"This whole thing about dead priests just gives me the willies. It's like killing God or something. The devil's got his hand in this I'm sure and it just makes me nervous is all."

"Never picked you for the evangelical type," says Hobbs while he absentmindedly fixes another plate of food. He is also wondering why no one is asking about the autopsy report. He knows why he doesn't bring it up because it clearly shows that someone about Maria-Teresa's height stabbed the victim, and slit his throat, not to mention the victim's old bullet wound.

As if Grace can read Hobbs's thoughts, without warning she turns to the detectives and says, "Let's stop pussy footing around the bad news. What does the autopsy report say?"

The detectives look at each other wondering how she even knows the report is complete. Turner launches in, "Well from the angle and depth of the wounds, a person about the same height and strength of Maria-Teresa cannot be ruled out as the killer," Hobbs continues with the fact that the priest's throat was slit.

"How can someone as short as Maria-Teresa slit the throat of a man over six feet tall. He is not going to let her stand in front of him, reach up and slit his throat without overpowering her," asks Margot.

"If the perpetrator stabs him in the back and he falls to his knees that will put him at just the correct height to have the perpetrator still standing behind him to follow up with a slash of his throat," says Turner eloquently.

A hush falls over the room and they sit contemplating what was just explained to them. Perhaps it is time to pray like the mug says.

<h1 style="text-align:center">15</h1>

The bell tower at the St. Francis de Sales Catholic church is a small square platform that sits just below the church steeple. There has not been a bell in the tower for some decades, but everyone refers to it by its original purpose name.

Determined to find a clue that instinctively Grace knows must be at the church, she and Sam get an early start the morning after the disappointing evening and head to the St. Francis de Sales Catholic church. Their mission this morning is a secret one so entering the church by the front door is not an option. The ladies find a small pathway leading from the street to the back garden which they follow and find themselves at the entrance to the bell tower.

Grace grabs Sam's arm and they begin climbing the winding staircase to the square room with arch-shaped openings exposing the outside world from all sides of the tower.

"Why are we going up here?" gasps Sam after tackling the first half dozen stairs.

"Sometimes, I think better when I can get a macro view," answers Grace while she stealthy takes on the narrow winding stairs the scarf around her neck barely moving as she climbs.

"I'm starting an exercise regime tomorrow," vows Sam breathing hard holding on to the thin black rail to pull herself up one step at a time while palming the wall with her other hand. Grace has heard Sam make an exercise declaration so many times it means less than nothing.

"What," whew "what if someone sees us?" gasps out Sam stopping to rest and ease her burning thigh muscles. Once she catches her breath, "We don't exactly have permission to be here, and besides the murder took place indoors which is nearer to the ground," says Sam with more of a soft whine in her voice than conviction. She continues with, "The solid ground that I love to feel under my feet."

Grace reaches the top of the stairs first and walks onto the platform ignoring Sam's chattering. Leaning over the side she concentrates on the grounds below as she stands in one place looking down for several minutes before moving in a circular manner around the small platform.

From one vantage point in the tower, she can see the nursery school playground equipment, moving around on the tower platform, she sees the back garden with its paths leading past the backside of the nursery door. Her eyes move past the multi-purpose room, to the tall hedges surrounding the mostly green garden. If she continues her gaze around, she will look out over the front of the church and the two news vehicles still parked there.

Her instincts bring her attention back to the path and exit at the back side of the garden. As she gazes at the path leading from the garden to the rectory building, something shiny on top of one of the hedges leading out of the garden glints in the morning sun.

"Sam, come here. Look over there is that something metal?" Sam steps closer to Grace careful not to get too close to either the edge of the tower wall or to the spiral staircase behind her. Grace eagerly grabs Sam's arm guiding her to a spot where she can see.

"See there on top of that hedge," Grace says pointing to the object lying half-hidden in a hedge below.

"What is that?" asks Sam as she squints to see. "How can we get to it, those hedges are at least six feet tall?" asks Sam, not knowing what role that question will play in her near future.

"Come on we've got to see what that is, suppose it's the murder weapon," says Grace excitedly scrambling down the winding staircase with Sam moving at a much slower pace behind her. Once they reach ground level, Grace stops to get her bearing giving Sam time to catch up. Then Grace rushes over to the row of hedges at the end of the garden nearest to the path to the rectory.

Grace surveys the height of the hedge and announces, "You're right we need a ladder to get to the top." Without missing a beat Grace says, "Come here, hold my purse and give me a lift up?"

Sam looks around the garden for the person Grace must be talking to. "I know you didn't just ask me to hold your purse while simultaneously lifting you in the air." Ignoring Sam's protests, "Well, don't just stand there," says Grace already holding her leg in the air waiting for Sam to cup her hands under her foot to hoist her to the top of the hedge.

"Lay your purse on the ground. I'm not capable of holding and lifting at the same time," says Sam. Wishing she can come up with a reason not to participate at all Sam reluctantly cups her hands under Grace's foot.

After a couple of tries, Grace shimmies to the top of the hedge, and with just the tips of her fingernails she dislodges the object. The object is flicked out of the hedge and falls with a soft thud to the grass below just in time for them to hear someone say, "Sam, Grace, is that you? What are you two doing?"

Startled by the voice, Sam unclasps her hands with a snap of her wrists as she twists her body around toward the sound of the voice. Sam's sudden movement leaves Grace to fall unladylike on top of the shiny object on the ground as Fr. Santos walks toward them.

On her knees with her back to the approaching priest, Grace quickly takes off the decorative scarf from her neck and throws it over the shiny object. Then like a magician, she stuffs the object in her purse that is laying on the ground near her.

Sam sees Grace's attempt at being an illusionist and steps in front of her to block the priest's view while the object is being hidden. While on the ground, Grace replaces the scarf around her neck leaving Sam to help Grace to her feet and they both turn to greet the priest.

"Oh Father, I was just getting my scarf that somehow got tangled in the hedge." The priest looks at the height of the hedge and the scarf around Grace's neck before saying, "Next time come and ask, we have a maintenance person, I am sure he has a ladder. What are you two doing out here?" asks the priest casting suspicious glances at the two women. Given the ladies' reputations for snooping he predicts a second visit but their appearance this morning is far sooner than he expected. The surprise shows on his face.

"We were in the neighborhood and thought we'd tell you the title of this month's book club novel," blurts out Sam nervously trying to give a good reason for their presence at the church.

"Yes, and the garden is so lovely we thought we'd take a minute of solitude," chimes in Grace with a smile. The priest looks skeptically at first one face then the other before saying, "Well?"

Confused glances pass between the ladies and Grace is the first to voice her confusion, "Sorry?"

"What is the name of the book?" asks the priest in a tone he reserves for dullards.

"Oh yes, the book." Sam searches her mind for a book title and oddly enough remembers a recent book review she read. She blurts out, we are reading A Truth for a Truth by Emilie Richards. "Can't wait to discuss it," pipes up Sam grinning like a Cheshire cat. Grace thinks Sam looks like a schoolgirl caught hiding something from the teacher.

Carefully watching his face Grace notices the momentary narrowing of his eyes as if he doesn't buy their story but the priest doesn't push further. Before the Fr. Santos can respond to their choice in reading material, a loud familiar voice shouts, "Come back here!"

The young nursery school worker rounds the corner close on the heels of a little boy who is giggling and running in a zig-zag pattern in an effort to thwart his pursuer. "Sorry Father, he got away again," says the nursery assistant as she runs past them yelling, "don't you dare, come back here I mean it."

Fr. Santos' attention turns to the truant student as he helps the nursery school worker round up the little boy and take him back inside. This break in the conversation gives the ladies the opportunity they need to vacate the premises. They quickly do just that running down the garden path to the street.

Reaching the car, Grace carefully uses her scarf to lift the shiny item retrieved off the hedge from her purse. She handles the item carefully not to leave her fingerprints or smudge any fingerprints that might be on what looks like a letter opener with a carved wood handle.

"Is that blood near the hilt?" asks Sam spotting a dark reddish-brown color.

"Oh my God, I think this might be the murder weapon."

Their first thought is never to contact the police, relinquish crucial evidence, or leave things where they find them, no, they rush back to Sam's house without hesitation. This is not their first rodeo so there is little need for them to rationalize their actions with such phrases like, how do we know if this little trinket is important or even connected to the case? Nor does the fact that they are not trained detectives ever stop them from their pursuit of justice.

16

Back at the east valley police station the morning is proving to be routine for everyone except Detective Dwayne Turner who is rereading a letter from the Department of Homeland Security, and he is hardly able to contain his joy. The official letter contains several paragraphs, but he only rereads one of them. It says—we are pleased to inform you that you are selected to participate in the advanced cyber intelligence training program—

No matter how many times he reads the letter he still can't believe it is real. The smile fades from his face when he wrestles with how to tell Hobbs that his departure is official, and he is leaving the east valley police department. Detective Turner, the other half of the crime-solving duo Hobbs and Turner will shortly find himself at the Mountain, short for Mount Weather.

Mount Weather Special Facility is an unacknowledged Continuity of Government Facility on the east coast. While at the Mountain, Turner will sharpen his intelligence skills. He will be shut off from any communication with friends in the outside world. He will remain cocooned until his required simulation training time is over.

The captain at the east valley police station is riding Hobbs really hard now and Turner will not be available to buffer the craziness for his partner. Turner is thinking of how to inform his partner that he is leaving in three days when his office door opens so hard it bangs against the wall behind it.

"You're not going to believe what that incompetent, no good, dust for brains son of a bitch has me doing?" yells Hobbs. Turner looks at his partner and smiles, there is something about this brash, bear of a guy that makes him glad Hobbs is in his life.

"What's up partner?" asks Turner in that calm smooth voice that compliments his dapper exterior.

"Why the hell are you looking so pleased?" asks Hobbs slumping down in one of the two chairs facing Turner's metal desk. At that moment, he notices the order of the office, how the internal memos are pinned with care to a large cork board. There are even a couple of framed pictures on the wall behind Turner's desk.

Turner's stomach flip flops once knowing Hobbs is bound to see the letter but any action to hide the letter only delays the inevitable. Turner watches his friend taking in the interior of his office like he's viewing it for the first time. Quickly Hobbs' eye travels to his friend's computer monitor which is free of post-it notes dangling off the edges then dropping his eyes to the desktop where neat piles of paper are stacked and the very official letterhead catches his eye.

He looks into Turner's eyes and there is no need for words, he just turns his head toward the office window in silence. Swallowing hard to force down the lump in his throat. Hobbs' jerks his head around to face Turner and says, "Congratulations, I am happy for you man," his words say one thing yet the disappointment in his face says something different.

Turner understands the effect his leaving is having on his partner, but he is much too excited to have his mood changed by anything. The only thing he feels now is sheer exhilaration.

"I do wish you the best you know that, right?" says Hobbs before getting up from his chair extending his hand to Turner who grabs it and pulls Hobbs in close for a hug.

"So, when do you leave?"

"In three days, but today is my last day at the station. I'll use vacation time for the next two days; I have a ton of things to do before I fly out."

"Just like the government not to give you much time to get your affairs in order."

"You can help me out though if you don't mind, there are some things I can't get around to."

"Glad to help, maybe you better write me a list. I've got so many shit things to do around here I might forget," says Hobbs.

"No problem. Take care of yourself big guy," they shake hands again. Hobbs' gripe about the brass seems minuscule and inconsequential at this point. He knows his life in the police department will drastically change when Turner leaves.

"Just hurry back! I'll try to get off the shit list by the time you return." They both chuckle and Hobbs leaves Turner for his own office.

17

After leaving the church with the shiny object secured in Grace's purse, Sam drives her car toward home as fast as a shopaholic racing to a one-hour sale.

"Damn Sam, why are you driving like you just stole something."

"Because we did, Grace," answers Sam with all the guilt of a get-a-way driver. Grace doesn't bother to explain that the object was out in the open and that it wasn't theft as much as finding something, she just hangs on to the dashboard to brace herself against Sam's fast erratic driving.

In the family room, the object is lifted from Grace's purse shrouded in her scarf. Grace does not want to handle the object too much before securing it in a large zip-lock plastic bag. Sam runs down the hall to get Maria-Teresa.

Once the object is placed in the plastic bag, Grace holds it up for closer scrutiny and confirms it is a letter opener with a carved Teak handle. She lays the plastic bag out on the coffee table in the family room and looks toward Maria-Teresa for identification who recoils at the sight of the letter opener, then flops down on the sofa.

"Maria-Teresa does this look familiar?" Without hesitation Maria-Teresa says, "Yes, Fr. Santos has one just like it. We use it open the bids for the nursery addition construction." She reaches for the plastic bag while asking, "Is this his? why do you have it?"

Grace grabs Maria-Teresa's hand preventing her from touching the plastic bag. "Never mind how or where we got it," not wanting to reveal their trespassing or the falling off the hedge incident.

"If this is the murder weapon, it lets me know the murder was a spur-of-the-moment decision. The killer used what was available, nothing was brought to the scene for the purpose of killing the priest. Not premeditated."

The thought of whose fingerprints might be on the letter opener occurs to Sam and she asks Maria-Teresa, "The last time you and Fr. Santos met, did you touch the letter opener?"

Her friend's small hands ball into fists that she raises to place on either side of her head, her eyes squeezed close reminding Sam of a cartoon the only thing missing is smoke billowing from Maria-Teresa's ears as she tries to recall. Lowering her shoulders looking defeated she blurts, "I, I can't remember. Maybe this whole thing is an accident?"

Grace does an exaggerated eye roll before saying, "His throat was slit, and he was stabbed in the back, that's no accident. The question is why THIS priest?"

"We need to find a crackerjack computer person to thoroughly check out the priest's background," suggests Sam.

"I believe Turner mentioned he does computer work for military intelligence," offers Maria-Teresa as she perks up trying to be of assistance in her defense. In a forced calm voice Sam says, "Yes honey but he is unavailable, remember he texted this morning. He is leaving town for a while."

This statement and Sam's tone make Maria-Teresa's body once again sag against the sofa, not only is she about to be convicted she can't even remember important things anymore. Her unfocused eyes look toward Sam's backyard swimming pool and her thoughts flash to Danni.

Sam says to Grace, "We have no choice we have to access all of the search engines we can for information about Fr. Hector Francisco, then you and I can compile what we have and go from there."

"Sounds like a plan." They both set up their computers on the table opposite each other resembling the dueling pianos and commence their searches while Maria-Teresa wonders if she will ever hear from Danni again. The women search for an hour and turn up a few Hectors who may have Francisco in their last names but their ages and photos make them older or considerably younger than the dead man.

No other information can be found regarding where and when Fr. Francisco joined the priesthood. They can find no personal information, no churches he may have been affiliated with, no status of his movement before he died, there is no mention in any publication of his death, nothing.

"Umm, looks like our dead priest is hiding something," says Grace.

"He's like a ghost," adds Sam. Grace knows all too well about ghosts and sits silently wondering who this priest works for while Sam continues to say, "Yeah, do you think that's even his real name? What does he do for the Catholic Church?"

Unfortunately, Maria-Teresa can't answer anyone's questions not thinking of herself, but the agony Danni and her family must be going through. Grace wonders if he has any connection to anyone she might know in her secret world.

18

At Sam's later that evening, Margot has been brought up to speed concerning the computer search and the lack of information about the dead priest purposely leaving out the most important discovery. Hobbs shows up looking like a lost puppy already missing his friend and exhausted from his doghouse detail at work. When he enters the family room, the ladies are sitting quietly.

He looks at Sam first, and she gives him that child-like innocence before turning away.

Quickly glancing at the others who also fail to meet his gaze he knows from experience that this evasive behavior means they have been up to something. The most he can hope for is that whatever they have done doesn't get him fired.

He sucks in a deep breath before reluctantly saying, "OK, spill it, what's going on? What have you been up to?"

Like a magician, the plastic bag containing the letter opener is pulled from the pillow behind Sam and put on the coffee table. Hobbs takes one look at the plastic bag and immediately feels a ray of sunshine replacing the rest of the day's gloom.

"Don't tell me that's the murder weapon. Where did you get it?" says Hobbs grinning at Maria-Teresa, all the while hoping she has nothing to do with hiding it or knowing where it was.

"Don't look at her. Grace found it at the church," says Sam wanting to make sure their skills get the proper recognition.

"Spill it, where, how, and when," demands Hobbs before grabbing a beer and taking a seat on a section of the U-shaped seating group that will allow him to see all the ladies. Sam and Grace take turns relaying the events of the morning at the church.

"I think the killer must be someone connected to the church," says Grace.

"What? They are priests and nuns! Don't even think that!" cries out Maria-Teresa who knows thinking such a thing will dismantle her lifelong beliefs a thought she cannot bear. Grace gives her friend a sidelong glance before explaining her theory.

"If the killer is not connected to the church, he/she would take the weapon and discard it away from the church. Someone connected to the church would not have time to get rid of the weapon away from the church and have enough time to return to the church establishing an alibi."

Her theory about the weapon is mulled over by the group and even a couple of other possibilities are bandied about before all agree that Grace's theory makes the most sense. "So right now, everyone connected to the church is a potential suspect," voices Sam.

Maria-Teresa chews her bottom lip and looks anxiously at her friends before dropping her shoulders and looking out the floor-to-ceiling windows. Discussions of the weapon and how to proceed with the next step in their investigation occupies conversation for another thirty minutes.

"You know we have to turn the opener over immediately. Give it to me I'll get it to detective Keating," says Hobbs, now grinning just a little too much causing Sam to ask, "why are you so eager to see Keating, I thought you two don't mesh?"

Grace squints her eyes at Hobbs trying to understand his eagerness and then he makes everything clear.

"Oh, it's not him I want to see, it's the expression on his face when I hand him a linchpin to his case. I don't like that guy. I want to show him I'm a better detective than he is."

The ladies glance at each other before Grace shakes her head realizing how juvenile men can be sometimes and remarks, "Just what we need a pissing contest."

Hobbs ignores her remark, feeling his chest inflate with a false sense of achievement. He carefully lifts the plastic bag from the table with a calculating smile and puts the item in his suit jacket. The find of the possible murder weapon invigorates his appetite, "So what's for dinner ladies?"

19

Fr. Santos strides confidently down the familiar dimly lit hallway to his sacristy three days after the murder. Stopping just outside the doorway he remembers administering last rites to the victim through a zipped black vinyl bag in this very spot. Peering into the dark room he is aware that the sun, just beginning its ascent in the sky, doesn't fully illuminate the room through the stained-glass windows.

With a flick of the light switch inside the room near the door, he surveys his office space, the space the professional cleaners finished with yesterday. The floor and walls look brighter than before the murder that's to be expected. Stepping inside he runs his fingers along his carved desk first the sides then the top concluding that it too feels and looks the same as before the murder.

He is quite familiar with the sight and smell of human blood, but he has never experienced a murder scene once it has been professionally cleaned and wonders how long the smell of the industrial cleaning solvent will last. How long will it be before he forgets violence was recently here.

The folders stacked neatly on the corner of his desk, still damp from the cleaning fluid's effort to remove the blood makes him wonder if he should discard them. After a couple of hours of thinking and aimlessly touching items unable to settle himself in his antiseptic surroundings, he pulls out his diary from the aumbry where he keeps it from prying eyes.

His recurring 9 a.m. Monday, Wednesday, and Friday appointments jump off the page, and he smiles. Circled for today at 11 a.m. is the monthly mystery book club meeting at Sam Jones' house. It was Maria-Teresa who insists he joins her mystery book club an invitation she extends without consulting the other members of the book club.

A month ago, at his first meeting, he arrives at Sam's house greeted by Margot.

"Yes, can I help you?"

"I'm here for the mystery book club meeting," announces Fr. Santos with a dazzling white smile. Margot smiles back at the sight of this tall tanned athletic young man. His jeans, sneakers, and green and yellow ball cap don't give her any idea that he is clergy. Just a damn good-looking man.

"Is he here," shouts Maria-Teresa advancing to the door interrupting further conversation between the stranger and Margot.

"You made it! Please come in. I'll introduce you." Grabbing his hand and leading him forward Margot closes the door and follows them down the well-lit hallway into the family room. Sam's mouth opens but no words come out as Maria-Teresa says beaming with pride, "Everybody this is Fr. Santos, my parish priest."

Margot's lascivious grin morphs into a face of embarrassment, while Sam's hopeful eyes look down at her lap. Grace's eyes narrow with suspicion as she gazes upon his form-fitting tee-shirt bearing a small logo of the archdioceses. Maria-Teresa's face falls into disappointment with the reception her guest is receiving.

"Sorry Father, we just weren't expecting such a, a, uh—" utters Sam failing to find a non-offensive way to end her apology. They all wonder how much of their vocabulary they will have to sensor as they sit like chastised children regretting their less than pious thoughts about this beautiful young priest.

Fr. Santos remembers his first meeting was packed with long silences, stilted conversation, and palpable tension. Silently he vows not to return to the all-female forum but since the murder and hearing of their inability to keep out of an investigation, he suspects the ladies will have crucial information. He needs to know what they know and how they know it.

Glad he will have something to take him out of his sterile office Fr. Santos readies himself for his second mystery book club meeting taking particular care to look and smell as physically appealing as he can without being obvious. On the drive over, he checks his face in the rearview mirror several times while he rehearses his tone and various facial expressions that will be most helpful in getting him the answers he desires.

Standing at Sam's door with the confidence of a well-prepared actor the priest smiles pleasantly when she opens the door. The alluring scent of his body wash both precedes and follows him as he makes his way down Sam's hallway.

His choice of a body-hugging tee-shirt sporting the flag of Brazil hanging loosely over jeans that accentuate his thighs and buttocks cause the women to fight their desire to be lulled into euphoria by his looks. Their goal is to find out what involvement if any he has in the murder.

Maria-Teresa, Margot, and Sam are seated in the family room just waiting for Grace's arrival. The atmosphere is highly charged with suspicion, sexual tension, and piety on Maria-Teresa's part.

"Maria-Teresa, you look so much better. Has anyone found any evidence to clear you?" asks the priest thinking it's best to get straight to the point.

"I feel better, Father, thanks," answers Maria-Teresa but she does not offer any other information instead lowering her eyes in embarrassment for thinking of him as a suspect in the murder. The other women slyly look at the priest careful to avoid direct contact with his dazzling hazel eyes which could reduce them to uncontrollably grinning idiots.

They still scrutinize his behavior over the rims of their drinking glass as they sip liquids and over open books held up to their faces. He is about to launch into more questions when the sound of the doorbell startles everyone. Sam jumps up nervously to answer the door giving everyone a chance to relax their shoulders, loosen tightly clenched jaws while replenishing drinks and food.

She fully expects to see Grace breeze into the house in her usual fashion with no explanation for her lateness swirling an air of mystery about her prior movements. The front door swings open and there stands a tall fair-haired young man in his twenties. He is holding a piece of paper which he consults before meeting Sam's perplexed gaze.

Smiling warily, he asks, "Is this the mystery book club meeting?"

"Yes," still confused Sam says, "why are you asking?"

"I saw your meet-up notice." Sam's face registers uncertainty and the young man says, "Sorry guess I should have replied online. I can leave."

The word online jogs Sam's memory back to that brief period of time just after their last murder investigation. A feeling of restlessness permeated the members. They missed the rush of adrenaline, the surprises at every turn that comes with danger. Responding to a dare Grace advertised online for additional book group members.

Sam plasters a smile on her face, steps to the side, and says, "Non-sense you're here so come in and welcome."

The young man follows Sam through to the family room. His entrance into the room is met with stares and confusion, he is certainly not Grace.

"Come in and sit down anywhere," says Sam. Just as the young man's butt is about to hit the sofa, Maria-Teresa yells, "Not there! Grace sits there." The young man obeys and selects another spot on the sofa with all the confidence of a new kid entering a new school mid-way through the school year.

All eyes peruse the tall thin person who made some effort in his dress evidenced by starched white shirt tucked neatly into his very skinny blue jeans making him look very much like a pencil with clothes. Once seated the newcomer's beady eyes flick past the probing faces of the women as he scans the kitchen stopping momentarily on the food laid out neatly on platters on the island.

The mid-morning sun casts warm yellow streams of light in the room through the floor-to-ceiling windows giving the room a technicolor feel. Sweeping a complete three-sixty examination of his surroundings he rests his gaze on Fr. Santos. In that moment, Sam who has noticed how silly the stranger's large sneakers look at the ends of his stringy legs, looks up in time to see the men share a fleeting look of recognition.

Dismissing that thought as her imagination she is about to make introductions when she hears, "Hey guys, sorry I'm late can you believe it, a traffic jam in Arizona. Whose strange car is parked in the driveway?" Grace stops full tilt seeing the young man.

Her eyes narrow suspiciously, "Who are you?" she asks in a cold matter-of-fact voice.

Feeling her obvious lack of warmth toward him, the young man nervously stutters, "Ja, James, I'm, I'm James," now questioning his choice to join the group.

Quickly Sam adds, "Grace, he answered our meet-up invitation, remember that online thing?" Grace's face tightens as she remembers giving in to one of Sam's not well-thought-out ideas. Then before taking her seat, she looks the interloper up and down causing him to fidget uncomfortably, near the spot on the couch that Maria-Teresa designates as Grace's.

The members introduce themselves Sam gives a brief history of the club, sans their involvement in murder investigations. All eyes turn to James who feels the sofa cushion beneath him warm throwing his mind into thinking he is literally on a hot seat. For the next several minutes, James twists and turns his head and or body on the sofa to address the barrage of questions from the group.

"How is it a young man like yourself is not at work?" asks Margot.

"I work night shift so I'm available to come once a month to a mid-morning book club meeting," answers the young man now pulling himself up tall confident feeling he responded correctly.

"What kind of work do you do?" inquires Sam.

"I work at an airpark nearby," answers James swinging his head around to face the next person asking:

"I want to know does James have a last name?" asks Grace her voice thick with distrust.

"Wilding, James Wilding."

"Do you read much?" Followed rapidly by, "Who's your favorite author?" As James looks from person to person deciding which one to answer first, Fr. Santos lets out a long sigh finding the inquiry tedious and the interloper a hindrance to his plan to grill the ladies for information. The priest says irritably, "Can we get on with the book discussion, please. Some of us have other things to do."

The women are surprised by Fr. Santos' lack of patience while James innocently says, "You sound like a man with a hot date," then he laughs.

Maria-Teresa stares at James in disbelief at his obvious lack of reverence for a man of the cloth. Is he inferring something untoward about Fr. Santos? No one follows up on James' comment, instead everyone settles down to discuss the book.

To ensure a robust discussion and for those who have not read A Truth for a Truth by Emilie Richards, Sam brings everyone up to speed by reading the online summary of the book's plot and main characters. James offers some interesting insights about the protagonist who just happens to be a priest. James analyzes the actions of the priest protagonist always tying his actions back to his personal devotion to the word marriage.

In James' opinion, the protagonist uses the word marriage to explain relationships to each other, as well as the vows he made to God. Each time the newcomer expresses his view on vows or marriage he shoots a hard look at Fr. Santos. Does James want Fr. Santos' approval of his views, or does he want the priest to openly disagree with him?

The ladies look from James to Fr. Santos, only getting silence and a hard stare from the priest as James continues to spout his views.

20

Grace's Bentley pulls up in the circular driveway in front of her palatial home making a mental note to tell the landscaper to pay more attention to the topiary. Her thoughts in a fog she finds herself at her massive white front door opened by Mr. Smith.

"Hello Ms. Liu, let me take your things," says Smith before disappearing allowing his employer a moment to herself.

"Hi, Smith, thanks," as she places her purse on the foyer table and kicks off her shoes accidentally knocking the table, spilling the purses contents to floor. The first thing that catches her eye is the sight of a cell phone. Not her personal cell phone but the one she uses, used to use, to communicate with him. Rhys.

She stares at the phone and thinks fondly of him and of them. *Could the report of his death be a mistake?* Grace remembers all too well the phone call that changed her life. She replays the dialogue over and over in her mind. On her routine check-in calls to her handler, she dials in, and an officious voice on the other end of the line says, "Code in."

Momentarily, taken aback by the unfamiliar voice she manages to respond with her secret code. The voice asking for the information is not his. This is unusual for him to go away without letting Grace know he is going to be out of pocket.

He always provides a safe place, number, or person she can contact if he is going to be away. Her thoughts are shaken by the officious voice asking for the one word indicating she is not in danger.

The voice repeatedly says, "Yellow," pauses then repeats, "yellow."

"Yes, yes, yellow." All the time she thinks where can he be? She asks, "where is," before she can complete her sentence, the officious voice interrupts with the word 'indisposed'.

Grace's body reacts in a shudder to the word indisposed. In her covert world, this word does not mean he is in the bathroom, away from his desk, or getting coffee. She sucks in a breath and asks the question she fears hearing the answer too.

"Dead or alive?" Without skipping a beat, the voice with no name or face says, "Dead." She is hoping to hear 'alive', which means he is embedded with the enemy but still alive. Hearing the word 'dead' announced without emotion resounds in her ear.

She sinks to her knees. He can't be, what happened, how can he be. Grace lingers in her thoughts for an undetermined length of time and the only thing that brings her back to her present reality is the sound of the dial tone buzzing in her hand.

Grace collects the contents of her purse from the floor and walks into her study. Her mind cloaked in the past. Those days in Europe when they were the hottest extraction team working for the United States government. They look good together as a couple, they work well together, the Bonnie and Clyde of the spy world, sans the dying in a hail of bullets part.

Then you age. Slowly, so slowly that the only signal you get is when you can't run as fast or as long, when your trigger finger gets a little slower, and when you ache a lot longer after your body is battered. But even these little signs don't deter you from your mission.

It is only when you are lying in the hospital bed taking twice as long to recover from a concussion, gunshot, a knife wound, or just extreme internal bruising that reality hits you. The end of your active days as a field operative is near. Her end, their end came way too quickly for her.

The end of their work together and the end of their personal relationship fizzled about the same time. They are taken off active status and he becomes her handler for the occasional secret jobs she performs for the off-the-books government agency. Now even that occasional contact with him ends. Can she accept presumed dead as the truth? In any other line of work presumed dead is final but in her secret world, presumed dead can mean any number of things.

<h1 style="text-align:center">21</h1>

Hobbs greets the morning with a smile on his face and a song on his lips with the plastic bag in his hand. He makes a special trip to the west valley police department first thing in the morning to personally hand over the possible murder weapon. As suspected, Keating is less than thrilled to see Hobbs bounce into his office still grinning like the cat who swallowed the mouse.

"What are you doing here?" snarls Keating putting special emphasis on the word you.

"I brought you a gift." Before Keating can respond, Hobbs holds up his hands, palms facing out to interrupt what he is sure is the beginning of an angry rant from Keating.

"You don't have to thank me, it's all in the name of brotherhood," says Hobbs as he lays the letter opener on the desk and watches Keating's slack jaw expression. With a smirk and sense of self-satisfaction Hobbs says, "I may have just solved your case."

Keating picks up the plastic bag and scowls, the corners of his mouth turn down before yelling, "Where the hell did you get this? Have you been monkeying with my crime scene?"

"No. Got this from an anonymous source." Hobbs crosses his heart and says, "I swear I have not been back to the church." Giving a final smirk of amusement, he leaves the office as Keating's swear words fade into the ether behind him.

The weapon is immediately sent to forensics for testing. The size and shape of the blade and the residual blood match both the victim's wounds and blood type. There is one small fingerprint found on the blade of the letter opener.

Compared to the fingerprints belonging to their prime suspect Maria-Teresa, there is no match. The introduction of an unknown fingerprint presents a break in the case but without a match, in any law enforcement database, the case just becomes more convoluted.

After getting the results from forensics, Keating paces his office still seething from his early morning faceoff with Hobbs. He barks out the following order to a junior grade detective, "Get over there and take fingerprints of all the church staff and anybody living in that rectory out back. Oh yeah, show the photo of the murder weapon and see if the letter opener belongs to anyone at that church."

"But Sir, I can't fingerprint nuns and priests, ain't that sacrilege or something."

"Just because they live and or worship in a church don't make them Jesus. Get over there. Now!"

22

At crime solving central, Sam's family room, Grace takes the lead in the morning's discussion, "We need to search that church. I'm sure more clues can be found on the church grounds."

Sam says, "I'm inclined to agree with you our book reading priest is very likely harboring useful information."

Margot adds, "Whether he knows it or not," her way of lessening the priest's involvement and impact on Maria-Teresa whimpering at the thought of her favorite priest's committing a sin.

Margot remembers Sam is scheduled to have a potluck meal in lieu of another book club meeting and says nonchalantly, "Why don't you call Fr. Santos and find out if he is coming to the potluck. While he's at the potluck, one of us can search the church."

"Duh, keep it simple stupid," says Grace as she picks up the phone to dial Fr. Santos. "Father, just calling to make sure you don't forget the upcoming potluck at Sam's."

"Oh, I'm sorry I won't be able to come. We are losing nursery staff because of the murder, suddenly everyone's afraid to work here. I must say the murder has had the opposite effect on Sunday Mass attendance," says Fr. Santos with a sardonic chuckle.

"You're in luck. I know just the person to help you out. Sam just loves children and she's available to start this morning."

"Are you sure, it's not too much trouble?" he says smiling hoping to get information from her about their investigation.

"No problem, I'll send her right over," says Grace ending the call elated that she'll have a spy on the inside.

Sam who has been half-listening says, "What do mean send me right over, don't I get a say in all this. Who do you think you are?"

"I am the person who is trying to get into that church to have a look around. I am the person who is trying to solve a crime and save a friend, I—"

"Alright enough," protests Sam holding up her hands in a gesture of surrender. "Let me get my purse."

Before leaving for the church, Grace equips Sam with a pair of earbuds. "Now, remember I will be able to hear and talk to you. I need you to tell me everything that's going on in that church," says Grace.

The drive over to the church is spent with Sam nervously asking, "Can you hear me," driving a mile or so and asking again, "can you hear me now?"

"Sam, don't talk to me anymore until you reach the church," replies Grace in a frustrated tone.

Sam ascends the church stairs, stops at the huge wooden door looks around, and says, "Grace? Grace you there? I'm here at the church."

All she gets in response is a grunt. Sam makes her way to the ground floor where she heads for the nursery room. She finds herself outside the room next to the nursery in time to see standing in the room a young man engaged in intense conversation with a nun and Fr. Santos.

The room is set up like a classroom with elementary school-size tables and chairs facing the front. She peeks in the room and notices a large adult size desk and chair pushed off to the corner of the room, the set-up she promptly whispers to Grace. No one acknowledges her presence as she quietly enters the room.

Sam keeps her back to the group pretending an interest in the posters exulting the first holy communion and Eucharist that decorate the side walls of the room. She slowly moves across the rear wall that contains three rectangle windows about eighteen inches from the ceiling. On the next side wall, there is a bank of four-foot-high bookcases above them the walls are painted a pale yellow and the floor is covered in speckled grey industrial-grade tile, which she mutters quietly to Grace.

Sam who is now standing within ear shot of the conversation; with a quick glance toward them, she can see that the young detective is uncomfortable. She listens to the conversation the detective is having with Fr. Santos and the Nun in charge of the nursery who is referred to simply as Sister.

She is about to pick up the book laying on top of the bookcase when she hears Fr. Santos say, "That looks like the one I use," holding a photo. "I can't say that it's mine because I can't get into my office to confirm it's missing."

"You do have a similar letter opener," confirms the young detective making a note pad then dropping his head, squirming for a few seconds, he looks up apologetically and says, "detective Keating wants fingerprints of all the staff," dread clouds his face and he follows quickly with, "you know, just to rule you all out as suspects."

"Some, someone can, can always return at a more convenient time," stutters the officer hoping to pass the fingerprinting task off to someone else.

"Nonsense, the sooner we clear this up the sooner things can get back to normal," instructs Fr. Santos.

Sam gives Grace a play-by-play account of the conversation between the junior detective and Fr. Santos putting her hand up to her face, turning to the side to hide the fact that she is talking. "Grace, why are the police just fingerprinting them?"

"They just found the murder weapon they must have found a fingerprint on it. Everyone connected with the church are suspect," answers Grace unalarmed by the junior detective's presence.

Sam's fingerprints are already in the police database from a past investigation. Perspiration and heart palpations grip her body as she wonders if Maria-Teresa's, Grace's, or her own prints are on the letter opener? Grace hears a fast string of unintelligible words in her earbud.

"Slow down Sam what about my fingerprints?" asks Grace. Sam turns her back to the small group and in a panicked slower voice says, "Did you touch the letter opener, did I touch it, I can't remember, oh god. I can't go back to jail."

In a very stern, almost angry voice Grace says, "Calm down! Nobody touched the letter opener. I need you to get your head back in the game." The next thing Grace hears is a blood-curdling scream.

Grace yells in Sam's ear, "What's happening? What's the matter are you alright? Answer me?" She is about to grab her purse and rush to the St. Francis de Sales Catholic Church when she hears the faint voice of Fr. Santos say, "Oh God, I am so sorry I didn't mean to frighten you."

Sam grabs at her ear which is still ringing from Grace's screams but realizes she can't pull the device out and places her hand over her heart to calm her breathing. "It's not your fault, Father, I guess I am just a little jumpy." The others in the room turn in her direction.

The junior detective walks over to her glad for any distraction from his unwelcomed task, "What's the problem? Is everything alright?"

"Detective, this is Sam Jones. I am afraid I startled her. I called her this morning to fill in for our regular nursery school attendant." Explaining further he says, "Sam was not here when the murder occurred, and she doesn't even attend this church. I don't think she needs to be fingerprinted."

The junior detective eagerly agrees with him, still under the impression that conducting police investigations of any sort within the confines of a church must violate some religious law.

23

Sam smiles broadly and excuses herself while the junior detective completes his task. Sister finishes first and leads Sam next door to a bright yellow room with a rainbow painted on one wall. On the opposite wall is a well-executed mural of Beatrice Potter's beloved animal characters frolicking.

Unlike the floor where the police duties are being conducted, the nursery floor is covered with colorful interlocking rubber tiles that give Sam a spongy feel under foot. A large blue oval comprises half the width of the floor with white lines dividing the oval into equal segments of alternating yellow and red letters and numbers painted on the segments. The center of the oval contains a white duck with a bright yellow bill and feet.

Sam continues her report of the nursery layout, "Oh, what a lovely three-foot-high bookcase lining this wall. I notice the subject matter of its contents differs from the Eucharists classroom."

Sister turns to face Sam and raises an eyebrow, "Do you always speak aloud, describing your surroundings like a news commentator?"

Giving Sam a stern look causes the latter to fidget avoiding eye contact with Sister while in her ear she hears, "For god's sake Sam stop being so obvious."

"You told me to tell you everything I see," says Sam irritation prevalent in her whispered voice.

"What did you say?"

"Sorry, Sister, was talking to myself. I'm just a little nervous, this is my first time—" her voice trails off. Her apology is made more for Grace than Sister.

"Well, give me a few minutes to get the kids down for their naps and we'll have some time to talk," says Sister as she strides off to take charge of the kids.

While the kids' nap, Sister explains how the reading nook is to be used by no more than three kids at a time. Sam did not relay to Grace that there is one small yellow rocker, one small blue armchair, and one small green bean bag chair, learning her lesson from her last transmitted description.

Sister continues to fill Sam in on the rules of the water play area, where and how the toys are housed, and finally the day's activity plan for the nursery students. Sam's training concludes with Sister explaining the importance of Sam's role at the church nursery.

"You're about to embark on a very precious responsibility," says Sister slipping each hand across into the opening of the opposite long black sleeve so that no skin on her arms or hands show. "Contrary to popular belief, this is not just a babysitting job. You are responsible for shaping and molding young lives," stresses Sister. Then giving Sam a doubtful stare, she adds with some emphasis, "They depend on you."

Feeling quite confident that she knows kids, Sam finds it difficult to suppress a smile considering her pre-retirement occupation is a child psychologist.

"Let me show you what you mean to them," Sister says taking Sam by the hand, grabbing a scarf hanging on her office coat rack as she leads Sam outside past the row of cubby's housing extra clothing and lunches for the children. They walk toward the garden and Sister stops just inside the doorway and blindfolds Sam with the scarf.

"What are you doing?" asks Sam with her hands already prying the blindfold up so she can see.

"Relax your anxiety is what a small child feels like being left in the care of strangers," explains Sister as she leads Sam blindfolded in and around the garden with just Sister to protect her from any pitfalls in the garden such as steps, divots, or other impediments to her safety. "This is the kind of trust the kids have in you."

The trust exercise that she has experienced leaves Sam with an overwhelming desire to protect her little charges and can't wait to make the little darlings feel loved and protected. Her first opportunity to show off her newly acquired insight is at afternoon story time. Sister is called away for about ten minutes leaving Sam in-charge. In-charge is probably the wrong way to describe what happens next.

Seated on the floor Sam announces to the class, "Lets everyone grab a seat on your mats and sit around the blue oval, it's story time. Who wants to select today's book?" A flurry of tiny hands dots the air complete with voices talking over each other as they shout out book titles. Diplomatically, Sam lets the kids select the book, diplomatically with a show of hands for a choice of titles, which takes more time than she expected.

Everyone is seated and mostly quiet when a tiny bright red car magically appears in the hands of little Oscar. Sight of the car causes little Erica to yell, "He has a toy. You're not to have toys during story time," and Erica tries to take it from him with some difficulty. Little Peter seated on the other side of the oval sees Erica's struggle and jumps up to help, creating a three-way tug of war over the car.

Those kids who were engaged in conversations or fidgeting now become fully aware of the problem between the three tiny hands. Loud voices erupt into something akin to boisterous fans at a football game, "Give it to Peter," "no it's Oscar's, I saw him with it," "pull hard Erica."

Little Peter overpowers his classmates, snatches the car, and takes off running full speed around the classroom, causing little Oscar to wail loudly in protest while Erica gives chase. Sam knows instinctively that she has lost control of the situation watching the two kids run around her as she yells, "Stop, give me that car. Come back here."

Grace has a pretty good idea what's going on and laughs. Sam takes a few minutes to get to her knees then uses a nearby chair to help herself reach a standing position. By this time, half the class is running around the room and the other half is cheering them on. Sam takes chase after little Peter who is now ducking and dodging around chairs, tables, and other impediments in the room.

Little Oscar still crying decides he needs the comforting arms of Sam and somehow manages to clamp both his arms around her leg as she runs past him. Oscar's unexpected grip on Sam's leg causes her to lose her balance and crash with a thud to the floor as the word shit softly escapes her mouth followed by a loud groan.

The rest of the class thinks this is a game where you run as fast as you can and then fall on a person. In the blink of an eye, Sam is lying on her back under a pile of small kids as she yells, "Give me that car. Get off me and sit down now!"

Sister walks back into the room just in time to see chaos in its full glory. With just a few loud taps of a ruler on the top of the bookcase, all the children scatter to their places on the mats leaving Sam to look very much like a bug stuck on its back her arms and legs flailing. Rolling to one side, then to her knees she can finally bring herself to stand.

Sam straightens her clothes, her chin juts out she turns to Sister, "I though you said they felt frightened and needed my help. I'm the one who needs help," she says indignantly before striding out of the room dragging her tattered pride. Sister laughs, takes a seat on a small chair, and begins the afternoon story time.

Grace anxiously waits in the family room for Sam to get home. "What did you find out? You didn't talk to me the rest of the afternoon."

Sam just plops down on the sofa, grabs a cushion, and lays down. Grace curiously watches as Sam, fully clothed, adjusts her position on the sofa. First, moving her head around on the cushion to find the most comfortable spot. Then she adjusts her hips drawing her knees up in a fetal position and closes her eyes.

Grace stands over her still waiting for a response, she gently jostles Sam's shoulder and is amazed with Sam's ability to block out her existence.

"Grace, I need a minute I've had a hard day," whispers Sam. "I want a hot bath, a glass of wine, and some sleep. Not necessarily in that order," she says sinking her head further into the billowy sofa cushions.

"How hard can the job be, Sam? They are little kids who range in age from two to four years old," remarks Grace. This statement is made by a person who does not have any children and has probably never spent more than a few minutes in the same room with children.

"I think I broke something," says Sam rubbing her lower back first then an arm. "I definitely dislocated something I ache all over." Sam falls off to sleep muttering over and over, "Don't make me go back."

Grace looks over at Sam's closed eyes. Sam's soft rhythmic breathing is followed by light snoring. "A bath, wine, and sleep not necessarily in that order," says Grace grabbing a lightweight throw to cover Sam then she quietly leaves the house.

24

Hobbs tiny office is a welcoming site after delivering Keating a plate of crow served on the blade of wood handle letter opener. Even the fact that his desk is piled high with cold case files and his best friend is gone he's still in a good mood. Stories of Hobbs' little stunt in Keating's office with the murder weapon quickly get back to his Captain.

He sits down at his metal desk smirking as he takes one of the files from the pile and turns to face his computer. The note sticking to his computer monitor stands out among the rest of the notes dangling from his monitor because it's white not yellow and it's stuck to the middle of the screen as opposed to the sides with the rest of his reminders. The note simply says, See Me Now!

Recognizing the handwriting he crumbles the note and heads to his Captain's office mumbling, "Somebody up there hates my guts," knocking lightly on the door.

"Come in," yells the voice of his overweight perpetually red-faced superior. Opening the door, Hobbs finds the captain seated behind his large wooden desk, jerking his hands out of the half dozen strands of grey hair confirming he has been absentmindedly grabbing at them. Some might describe his actions as literally pulling his hair out.

Not inviting Hobbs to sit down the captain launches into an unusually loud tirade, which is a shift for the otherwise mild-mannered man.

"Where have you been?"

"I was—"

Talking over Hobbs the Captain says, "I get a call from the west valley that you been over there messing with their investigation."

"Sir—"

"I'm not having a repeat of that swimming pool murder."

"But I—"

"I don't know what you've done this time but you better keep your nose out of things that don't concern you. Is that clear?"

"Yes, sir."

"Here, take this stack of cases and follow up."

"But I already have," again the captain talks over him, "With Turner gone for two weeks for that military thing, I don't trust you on your own."

Leaving the captain's office Hobbs looks straight ahead avoiding eye contact with his fellow officers as he plods back to his desk arms full of more unsolved cases. For ten minutes, he sits at his desk like a man with a death sentence hanging over his head surrounded by case files. His thoughts drift to his dead father also a police officer and wonder if he made a mistake following his father's footsteps.

"Protect and serve and play by the rules," his father always told him.

Hobbs watched his father play by the rules over and over for twenty-plus years. His dad was a good enough officer, unfortunately his efforts yielded him only one promotion during his service with the department. Less than a month after his father retired from the force, Hobbs watched his father die of what Hobbs knew was a broken heart that he had not achieved more in life. The mixture of shame and pain he recognized in his father's eyes told Hobbs everything he needed to know regarding playing by the rules.

For the remainder of the day, Hobbs contemplates his future in and out of the police force.

For now, he must try his damnedest to fit in in the east valley police station even if it means doing grunt work.

25

The sun rises hot on Sam's second day of volunteer work at the nursery, and she makes the less than enthusiastic drive back to the church. Mounting the front stairs of the church she opens the door entering the vestibule. Making the sign of cross, even though she isn't Catholic, but feeling the need for fortification she straightens her back and marches off down to the lower level.

Sam stands in the doorway of the classroom when Sister catches sight of her, "Oh you came back, thought we'd lost you." Sister says with a smile, "Well, don't just stand there; here's the lesson plan for today," unceremoniously she thrusts the daily lesson plan at Sam.

The beginning of the day starts better than Sam's first day and her confidence is boosted when Sister says, "You are great with the kids, they really like you. You need a sense of humor sometimes, they get a little silly."

"Thanks, I like them too," remarks Sam and on some level, she means it. "Although they do have more energy than I am used to," confesses Sam.

"You'll get used to it. The noise level got me at first."

The kids arrived one after the other and the morning's activities starts. The next time Sam and Sister can have an uninterrupted conversation Sam asks, "What happened to the regular nursery attendant?"

"She called yesterday morning to say she has a family emergency."

"Does she have a lot of family in Arizona?"

Sister takes a moment looking to one side in thought, "I think there's some family. She was enrolled in a local Mesa university and as far as I know, she stays with extended family in the west valley."

"Was she working on the day of the murder?"

"No, she called in sick that's why I asked Fr. Santos to fill in until one of the neighborhood volunteers can relieve him. I was sick and didn't want to spread my germs to the children." Sister looks off into the distance frowning, fingering her rosary beads while quietly thinking, before exclaiming, "Umm, until the day of the murder the nursery attendant never missed a day of work, and most times, came early.”

“How long has she worked here?”

“She started to work here right after Fr. Santos became the priest here. Just popped up and father told me to hire her.”

“Did you know Fr. Francisco?”

“No not before he came here. I didn’t see him but once he spent a great deal of time in the rectory out back. Why do you ask?” says Sister searching Sam’s face.

“Oh, I just think it’s odd that no one knows very much about a man who lives on the grounds.” With that statement, a silence fills the air between them.

While Sam tries to find out as much as she can from Sister, Grace is trying to figure out how to infiltrate the rectory. Grace knows she needs to see Fr. Francisco’s living quarters. She requests via Sam’s earbud to find out Fr. Santos’ schedule.

“Sister, does Fr. Santos conduct all of his business from the church?” asks Sam as casually as she can.

“Let’s see, today is Friday, he will be attending a lunch meeting off the church grounds.” Turning to look at Sam, Sister says, “You ask an awful lot of questions.”

“Sorry, I don’t mean to appear noisy, but I guess everyone wants to know who is responsible for such a horrible thing.”

“And you think Fr. Santos is guilty? You should look at the person who hasn’t been to work since the murder,” and Sister walks off.

Sam whispers to Grace, “I have a two-hour lunch break when the kids go down for their nap, we can sneak over to the rectory then.”

“Great, I’ll meet you in the garden,” and Grace gets ready for her drive into town. Once she arrives at the church Grace takes the same path that they used to enter the bell tower the day that they found the murder weapon. In the garden at the back of the church, she waits as inconspicuously as she can for Sam.

When Sam gets the text that Grace is waiting outside, she excuses herself under the pretext of self-reflective time and heads toward the garden with no push back from Sister. The architecture of the rectory that sits beyond the secluded hedged garden is clearly inspired by Benedictine buildings from the past.

The ladies round the hedge to find arch shaped pillars supporting the roof of a walkway extending around the exterior of the rectangular rectory.

"Sister says this building serves as a domicile for the groundskeeper, for Fr. Santos, and visiting clergy."

"This building was originally built for the monks who ran the church in the nineteen sixties and seventies," adds Grace as they bypass the front quickly walking around the back of the building vigilantly looking around to avoid unwanted company. A neglected patch of overgrown weeds nearly covers another path leading to an interior courtyard.

Stepping over brambles Grace says, "I think they need to fire the groundskeeper," heading back to the front of the building after not finding an easy access to the rooms. They enter through an unlocked double door and are immediately met with a cold dank smell. Sam holds Grace's arm as they make their way through dimly lit walkways and eerie silence.

"Didn't Fr. Santos say he had not seen Fr. Francisco but once since his arrival?" asks Grace.

"Yes?" answers Sam as the ladies stop in front of two closed doors.

"Look, the door to their bedrooms are only twenty feet apart," says Grace pointing to slips of paper with their names on them stuck in a small slot on doors that are next to each other.

"Umm, in three days you think they might run into each other at some point. What about meals, did they eat together?" asks Sam thinking about missing her lunch to conduct this investigation.

"Umm, you have a very valid point. We need to quickly search each room. You take one room and I'll take the other," suggests Grace even though she would like to search each room herself.

Grace opens the door to Fr. Santos' room to find it quite monastic. Simple single bed made neatly, crucifixion hanging on the wall over the bed, one table and chair complete with a small lamp under the high window, one wall shelf containing a bible, and one double door wardrobe. She opens the wardrobe to find one side has drawers from top to bottom for folded items like sweaters, collars, underwear, and socks.

The other side is the place for hanging jackets, pants, shirts, and cassocks. There is a shelf above the hanging items in the wardrobe that contains the yellow and green baseball cap that the ladies saw Fr. Santos take from the child's head the other morning. Grace looks at the cap to find it is a Brazil soccer team hat. *No law against being a sports fan.*

In the floor of the wardrobe is a line of black shoes, and one pair of sneakers and she gently searches the inside of each shoe for anything that might be hidden there. She pushes the clothes aside and finds in the corner against the back wall a riding crop. *Perhaps he rode horses in his home country.*

She turns her attention to the rest of the room. As a matter of habit, she bends down to sweep the underside of the table and finds nothing. She puts everything she touches back in place, finding nothing she leaves the room to find Sam. Opening the door to Fr. Francisco's former room, she leans her head inside and whispers, "Sam it's me," before quietly entering the room. The victim's room is set up the same as Fr. Santos' room but not nearly as tidy.

"I thought priests were neat," says Sam standing in the middle of a room in complete disarray. The mattress is slid to one side, the bed linen pulled back, the wardrobe doors are open, and the clothes inside shoved to one side or thrown to the floor.

"Someone's been looking for something. The question is what are they looking for and did they find it?" announces Grace as she critically scans the room not touching anything. A growl of Sam's stomach diverts Grace's attention and she turns to give Sam an annoyed look.

"I can't help it," says Sam defending her body demands. Sam is about to wring her hands together when she realizes she forgot to mention the small key in her hand. In typical Sam fashion never getting to the point without a back story she launches in, "You know I like tidiness and cooking. So, without thinking, when I see this mess my first instinct is to tidy up and I bend down to pick up clothes on the floor and I notice this key." She gives it to Grace who instantly knows it's a bank safe deposit box key.

"I think we have what someone is looking for, a safe deposit box."

"Why would a priest need a safe deposit box?" asks Sam.

"Why indeed," remarks Grace.

Just then, Sam's stomach lets out another cry for food and Grace knows the growling can only be quelled by ingesting food.

"I guess we need to feed the monster, let's get out of here," says Grace satisfied that she has found her first lead in the case. As the ladies sneak out of the rectory, they just reach the hedged garden when they see Fr. Santos strolling in their direction.

A jaunty stride and self-satisfied smile turn instantly into narrowed eyes, pursed lips, and a stiffening of his athletic body once he sees Sam and Grace coming toward him. His jaw muscles tense even though his lips maintain his fake smile. Getting closer to the ladies he says, "What are you two doing back here?"

"We noticed the abandoned vegetable garden behind the rectory and Sam thinks a garden restoration project will be great for the kids," blurts out Grace hoping she correctly remembers someone mentioning the former priests grew their own food in an old vegetable garden.

She must have been correct in her assumption because Fr. Santos counters her suggestion with, "These kids are two to four years old, I hardly think they are capable of restoring a garden."

"Well, yes obviously, not the weeding part, but they can plant the seeds, water, and help pick the veggies," offers Sam in a cheery nursery school voice. Fr. Santos does not change his harden facial expression nor does he respond. Instead, he sidesteps around them and continues toward the rectory without another word.

His once carefree stride is now fraught with determination as he practically jogs off looking back at them over his shoulder wondering what they discovered.

26

Grace feels jubilant as she drives to the Grand Prairie Bank knowing the key, she has will open a box giving them another clue to solving the priest's murder. The lavender and green colored Grand Prairie Bank is a small one-story building that sits adjacent to a strip mall housing an Asian eatery, a dollar store, and a Mexican café. The beginning of the bank's small parking lot faces the street and surrounds the building with its one-way driving lane culminating at the drive-through services at the back of the bank.

Grace exits her car and walks up to the doors where an ATM machine pokes out from the wall in a glass enclosed foyer and off to the left is the door to the bank lobby. Grace pulls open the lobby door where a couple of people are seated waiting their turn to speak with bank personnel. She cast her gaze behind them to the maze roped area leading to the teller windows and it is off to the right of them tucked in the corner that she finds the entrance to the safe deposit boxes.

The Grand Prairie Bank has no numbering access code like Swiss banks. Here your handprint on a screen standing outside the safe deposit box area gives you access to it. Once inside, a customer has access to any box bearing the same number they have imprinted on their key. Grace locates the box that matches the number on her key.

She takes a deep breath before inserting the key that turns easily in the lock. Extracting the metal rectangle box from the wall she carries it to a private room and pauses a minute as her mind flits through possible contents of the box. She whispers to herself her fingers poised on the lid, "It doesn't feel heavy enough to contain a gun, perhaps a written confession, worse comes to worst, I'll find another key," and with that last thought she lets out "Ugh."

Grace flips open the lid of the metal box and stares down at a small hardcover journal about five by seven inches with its front cover adorned in gold fleurs reminding Grace of the time she spent in New Orleans. Grace lifts the two-inch-thick book from the box noticing it feels lighter than a baggy full of cotton balls. Without opening the journal, the fluttering in her stomach tells her she'll find something useful.

Methodically giving way to her spy training, she runs her hand along the spine of the journal searching for any unusual thickness. Next, she double checks the journal for any imperfections, abnormalities, or something hidden in the journal's gutter, the space on the inside margin of the pages where the book is bound. Finding nothing, she instinctively suspects what she is looking for will be found written on the pages of the journal.

Eagerly, she opens the first page of the journal and finds it blank. Grace uses her thumb and forefinger to give the book a quick flip through fanning the pages from front to back. All the pages are blank. She smiles ruefully and a tingle of excitement tickles her spine as her smile broadens. This little book requires special attention to extract its secrets, the kind of attention that she is not prepared to perform in the bank.

Grace stuffs the journal into her purse, exiting the private room she replaces the box in its designated slot on the wall. In a gesture of excitement, she tosses the key in the air and catches it like a child playing with a ball. If grace was the kind of person to show emotion, one might say walking out of the bank Grace's gait has a bit of a bounce. One thought plagues Grace, how does a journal this size and thickness have virtually no weight?

27

Every house has its own creeks and groans and houses that you don't live in have unnerving creeks and groans. Sam is volunteering, Margot is dealing with her family issues and Grace's actions are always a mystery. Maria-Teresa walks from room to room in Sam's house desperately trying to feel useful. Most of all she tries not to think of the disagreement she had with Danni.

Try as she may, she fails to make herself feel useful to the investigation or to Danni and her business. Maria-Teresa knows she must return home and leaves a note for Sam. Returning to her home she is greeted with a chilly reception.

The two women tiptoe around each other one finding no reason to apologize and the other expecting an apology.

"There you are. I wondered where you had gone off to," says Danni in a fake cheerful voice. The curtains are drawn in the small sitting area off the bedroom but the Stubben lamp on the side of the divan gives the room a soft evening glow even though it's early morning.

"MT, are you getting up today I can use your help on the new job," asks Danni crossing the room to the divan where MT sits with her knees drawn tightly together rigidity visible throughout her body.

"I just need some time to think," whispers MT refusing to meet her partner's gaze.

"What's there to think about? I thought we were past the whole investigation thing or were you lying? I thought that's why you came home," asks Danni raising MT's chin, forcing their eyes to meet. Tears tumble from MT's eyes and her lower lip trembles as she blurts out forcefully, "Everybody thinks I'm too fragile to help myself. Well, I'm not!"

"Don't tell me you're getting involved with the murder investigation. I thought we agreed you would give up the investigation."

"I never agreed to anything. I've thought about it, and I can't just sit on the sidelines playing the victim." Stunned but not surprised by MT's newest declaration, Danni stands and walks away head down shoulders slumped displaying the rejection she feels.

MT says to her partner's back as she leaves the room, "I can't let my friends put themselves in danger and I sit around being afraid of my own shadow. I need to be helpful in my own defense. I have deductive skills I'm good at it."

"You call being frightened speechless good at it." Danni turns to face MT, "Go on, do whatever the hell you want. I don't care anymore. Know this, I won't stand by waiting for the next horrible thing to happen to you." Her words carry with them a hurt that stabs them both but for different reasons.

Drawing in a deep breath knowing now more than ever she must prove herself, she straightens her posture and grabs a pad and pencil from the table near the divan. She writes down her strengths and announces them aloud while she writes. "I am familiar with the church, familiar with the people in the neighborhood, and I speak Spanish. Surely that accounts for something." She writes down exactly how she wants to proceed.

Picking up the phone she calls Margot. Based on the alliance formed during the last murder investigation she is sure Margot will agree to help with her plan.

28

Sam ends her second day at the nursery school reaching some startling truths about her newfound volunteer position. First, chasing young children all day is far more tiring than she ever imagined. Second, her stamina is not what it used to be. Third, her toleration of the loud level of noise created by these little ones is wearing thin.

After Grace runs a few errands, she and Sam pull into Sam's driveway right behind each other. When Sam notices Grace's car pull into the driveway behind her, she knows her plans for a quiet evening are on hold. Grace jumps out of her vehicle too excited to wait until they get in the house. She rushes over to Sam's car grinning from ear to ear and opens the car door.

Tired and hungry Sam munches on tiny crispy cheese filled crackers which Grace notices upon entering the car, "Where did you get those?" quickly followed by, "I swear, you should be a magician you can produce food out of thin air."

Moving the crackers to one side of her mouth, "Well, did you find anything?" ask Sam ignoring Grace's hurtful comment. Grace produces the blank book with all the majesty and triumph of a gold medalist at the finish line. Sam reaches for the book with her cheese coated fingers and Grace snatches it out of her reach at lightning speed.

Grace holds the book up so Sam can see as she fans the blank pages triumphantly. Seeing nothing on the pages Sam closes her tired eyes barely whispering, "Who the hell locks a blank book in a safe deposit box?"

"Exactly! Why go to such lengths to hide this book?" Hearing light snoring Grace says, "Sam, are you listening to me?"

"Yeah, yeah, secret book. Grace can I just go inside and rest," asks Sam nestling into her leather car seat as Grace continues to rant about the book. Sam dozes off into light sleep while in the distance she hears the entire book is made from limestone, not wood and water.

One word finds its way into Sam's tired brain, limestone. She opens one eye and says, "You mean like the rock. How can you even make a book out of rock? Besides, if that's true shouldn't the book be too heavy for you to be waving in the air like that?"

"I don't know how it's made. I just remember reading about some Japanese company marketing lightweight paper made from limestone." They both jerk around as a car pulls into the driveway behind them. Hobbs emerges from his vehicle like a newborn bird breaking from its shell stretching out his arms and legs before joining the women as they walk toward the front door.

Since Sam's undercover assignment at the church, the meals at their evening debriefing sessions consist of individual carry out food supplied by the attendee. Gathered around the island as they put their meals on plates and garner cutlery Grace looks at Hobbs' plate, "Nothing like two beef burgers loaded with bacon, cheese, onion rings, and chili sauce on a brioche bun to preamble a heart attack."

Mouth full of beef chewing not nearly long enough before swallowing he mumbles, "A big man needs a big meal." Sam settles for a milkshake mainly because chewing anything will require energy she doesn't have.

All eyes turn to Grace with nothing in front of her except the journal, "Don't worry about me, I've already eaten," she explains to the onlookers.

For the next five minutes, Hobbs chumps, Sam slurps and Grace thumps the outside of the journal waiting for either of them to come up for air. Hobbs eats enough of his meal to take the edge off his hunger and looks at Grace, "Looks like you got something you want to share, well spit it out."

Grace tells of their exploits at the church at nap time then she launches into her find from the safe deposit box that she suspects belongs to the murder victim.

Sam, who by this time, has lost interest in this entire blank rock book kicks off her shoes and sits down on the sofa. Hobbs picks up the journal, fans the pages, "I see what you mean about the light weight. The pages are blank what's your theory on that?"

"Old ways work best. No one will expect him to use a technique that dates back to George Washington's time."

Hearing George Washington's name interjected in Grace's mad ravings, Sam says, "Grace honey, you do know we as a civilization has progressed since

Washington's time. Why on earth use something most everyone forgot or never knew?"

Grace ignores Sam, reaches in her purse and pulls out a pen that resembles an ordinary yellow plastic highlighter. When Grace removes the cap of the pen, on one end is a writing tip and the other end is a small UV light. This is the item she picked up after leaving the bank.

29

All Sam wants to do is rest yet seeing the UV light pen she's up on her feet at the island with renewed vigor. Grace slowly moves the pen over the first page and writing appears.

"Well, what do you know. How did you do that?" asks Sam who is now fully on board with Grace's madness. Grace is too busy analyzing her clue to respond to Sam.

The first thing that stands out to Grace is not the message but the writing itself. Clearly, two different people wrote in this journal. The cursive on the first line of writing slants to the left. Grace thinks to herself, *Perhaps a left-handed person wrote this.*

She also remembers from her government handwriting analysis training that a person who writes with a left slant prefers to work alone. More than likely the person who wrote this is an introvert. Might be why the writer chose to communicate in this fashion.

Then she concentrates on the message which is dated three days before Fr. Francisco's death. *First day, things are quiet. SMM is major to this case.* Under that writing on the same page is a message written in a smaller more carefully constructed handwriting. The second message clearly shows a right slant that says, *Proceed with caution. Dangerous.*

On the second page, following the same sequence as the first page is written first in the left-hand slant saying, *Second day, noticed one other interesting person.* Just like on the first page, underneath the first statement is written in a right-hand slant, *Go forth with both. Confirm outcome.*

The third page is blank the day Fr. Francisco dies. Hobbs who has been silent all this time comes to life, "Is Fr. Francisco the person writing with the left-handed slant or right-handed slant? He is obviously using the safe deposit box to communicate with someone, but with who."

Grace starts to pace the room while posing a string of questions to no one in particular. "Fr. Francisco is investigating something or someone at the church. SMM is either the subject of the investigation or is another clue for additional information."

Spinning on her heels she says, "If the key belongs to Fr. Francisco, and he is an investigator who is he working for?"

"An investigator will explain the old bullet wounds," says Hobbs aloud. The two women jerk toward Hobbs with confused, expectant looks. "I didn't want to tell you about that until I had something else to piece it with," says Hobbs.

Ignoring his reasoning for withholding information Sam says, "Is Fr. Francisco a real priest?"

Grace jumps ahead asking, "Does this Bishop O'Leary have insight, information, and knowledge of Fr. Francisco's purpose? Did Fr. Santos verify that O'Leary sent Fr. Francisco, or did he just take the dead man's word that the bishop sent him?"

30

The Budding Branch Tiffany table lamp perched on the oversized desk in Grace's home study emits a subtle glow to the room competing with the garish dimmer controlled recessed lights that punctuate the high ceiling. Grace paces back and forth in front of her desk her bare feet sinking into the silk rug covering the floor under and around the desk. The nagging feeling that she is missing something critical to prove Maria-Teresa's innocence grips her mind like a vice.

Even with the information in the limestone journal Grace still needs clear-cut evidence that Maria-Teresa did not kill the priest. Absentmindedly, she fingers the delicate dark brown tree branches filling the spaces on the Tiffany lampshade and her mind fills with all the facts of the case. That logical imaginary voice in her head screams, "Always go back to the scene of the crime, always go back to the scene of the crime."

Following her own excellent advice, she peruses the crime scene photos again. Staring at the photo of the bloody footprints found in Fr. Santos' office, "What am I missing," she asks the challenging voice in her head.

"Look closer," responds the imaginary voice after a few minutes of viewing the photos. She grabs the magnifying glass zeroing in on the wear pattern of the bloody shoe prints and makes some notes. Next, her attention is drawn to the victim's autopsy report.

The nonlethal stab wound was probably first inflicted in an upward motion in Fr. Francisco's back under his right scapular. The fatal wound was administered to the left jugular also in an upward motion.

Vocalizing a possible scenario of the murder, she says aloud, "The wound to his back indicates that the perpetrator is probably shorter in height and right-handed. If the victim falls to his knees after the first stab, the shorter person would be on a level with the victim to complete the final blow slitting his throat in an upward motion from left to right."

Whipping her body around with the force of a bolt of lightning her palms slap her forehead then she hastily shuffles through her scribbled notes, gathers up the crime scene photos, and dashes out the door to her car where she places a call to detective Hobbs.

"Hobbs, it's Grace. I think I might have a possible breakthrough, can you sneak out? There is something I need to check out, meet me at Maria-Teresa's."

Hobbs hangs up the phone before Grace completes her sentence, and heads for his office door. Grace is trying very hard to contain her excitement before confirming a few things. In her car, she dials Maria-Teresa's cell.

"Hey, Grace," answers Maria-Teresa glad to have someone to talk too.

"Hi, how're you holding up?"

"The press has been calling and I just started receiving email threats," her voice cracks. "I am not sure how much longer—"

"I think I can help," says Grace interrupting her friend. "This will sound weird, but I need to examine a few pairs of your well-worn shoes."

"What?" Maria-Teresa's mind races thinking she did not hear Grace correctly. "Why do need my shoes?"

"No time to explain. I am on my way."

Everyone knows Grace is unorthodox, even so this request pushes the boundaries of weird yet intrigues Maria-Teresa enough to immediately send her rummaging through her closet floor. Standing in the doorway unmistakable signs of tension shadow Danni's face as she fingers the hummingbird dangling from the gold chain around her neck.

Her Anguish is evident in her voice, "So was that one of your book club friends enticing you back into their foolish investigation."

MT emotionally exhausted steadies herself looking up from her position on the floor, "Danni, I don't want to fight." Since her return home, she and Danni alternate between fighting, making up, fighting, not speaking to each other, making up, and whatever this is that they are going through today.

"Grace is on her way over with some news," then feeling the need to offer an explanation Maria-Teresa continues in a quiet inflexible voice, "they're my friends, they just want to help. I know you don't like them," lowering her head she cuts short her explanation fearing she is treading on the fringe of another massive fight.

Hobbs committed a dozen traffic violations arriving at Maria-Teresa's fifteen minutes before Grace. To Danni Hobbs' arrival lends more credibility to Grace's visit, her request, and any possible news she may have.

Hobbs, Danni, and Maria-Teresa sit silently in a smallish room jammed pack with books crammed into two wall-length built-in bookcases. Wondering what the array of Maria-Teresa's old shoes has to do with anything all eyes remain fixated on them lying there in the background of a light blue carpeted floor.

The doorbell rings jolting thoughts and bodies into the present. Danni and Hobbs jump up shoulder to shoulder jockeying to be the first to open the door. Grace peers into four expectant eyes when the door opens, and she gives her welcoming committee a wry smile in response to their looks of confusion and anticipation.

"Come in, the things you want are in the living room," says Danni stepping aside to let Grace enter leaving the lumbering Hobbs to bring up the rear. Making their way down the hall Danni quickly adds, "You didn't specify, so she has flat shoes, heels, and sneakers."

"Great!" Grace sits down on the floor in front of Maria-Teresa's sofa and examines the wear patterns of the soles then comparing the pattern to those in the crime scene photos. After a few minutes, Grace says triumphantly, "Gotcha."

"What is it?" asks Danni while Hobbs leans over Grace's shoulder reviewing the photos hoping to spot the answer before Grace explains.

"I just want to confirm one other thing. Maria-Teresa you're left-handed, correct?"

"Yes, you know that Grace, why are you asking?"

"The killer is definitely right-handed and these footprints although about the same size as Maria-Teresa's definitely do not belong to her," says Grace with finality. Hobbs agrees the killer might be right-handed but is still confused regarding the shoe prints.

"How can you be so sure?" asks Hobbs again hoping that Grace will give some clue so he can skip to her conclusion before his companions.

"Look," says Grace in the tone of a patient teacher explaining a new concept to fledgling students pointing to all the shoe soles lined up on the floor. "Maria-Teresa wears her shoes down on the outside of the sole, see." She points out the shoes soles and heels are worn more on the outer side than the inner side.

"Maria-Teresa is an under-pronation walker," they all look at each other in awe mixed with confusion. "This means when she walks her weight shifts or rolls onto the outer edges of her feet causing more wear to the outer sides of her shoes than to the inside." Grace continues, "But in the crime scene photo, the footprint is worn on the inner side of the shoe, see; the person puts more weight on the big toe and inner heel." She pulls out her magnifying glass so each of them can get a close look at the pattern she is referring to.

"The blood from the victim's body is more pronounced on the inner side of the footprint, this is clearly not Maria-Teresa's footprint."

Danni delivers a loud incredulous gasp, "Why didn't the police notice this? That's a dereliction of duty and untold emotional stress on MT."

Hobbs folds his arms across his chest, "Footprints hump, who the hell even knows such an innocuous tidbit of information?" using the word innocuous at least makes him sound intelligent even though he himself did not find the clue. "The police are trying to wrap this case up quickly to satisfy the Archdiocese and since Maria-Teresa is their only apparent suspect, why look any further."

"Well, don't just sit there, we have to tell the police or somebody," says Maria-Teresa excitedly. Suddenly, feeling invigorated.

"I'll call her lawyer, she'll take it from here," says Grace smiling.

"Thank you, Grace," says Maria-Teresa through tears of joy as she hugs her. The evidence is sent to the prosecutor's office, there is a meeting held between the defense attorney, the prosecuting attorney, and the presiding judge. All charges are dropped against Maria-Teresa. While that mystery is cleared up, there is still the mystery of why someone wants to harm a priest who had only been in the area for three days.

<h1 align="center">31</h1>

Sam knows first-hand what it is like to be a murder suspect. She is delighted to hear that Maria-Teresa is no longer a suspect and decides a celebration is in order. Sam invites the usual guests minus Turner who is still off on his classified military intelligence training.

Hobbs arrives first grinning brandishing his usual offering of a cold six-pack of beer, "Can't let my taste buds get used to that fancy wine you serve can't afford to continue the habit."

Margot arrives with a bouquet of flowers for the table and a smile that she didn't have the last time they all met.

Maria-Teresa and Danni arrive bringing thank you trinkets for everyone. Grace is last to complete the group when she arrives not with gifts and smiles but with questions. After dinner, Grace does not hesitate to launch into the issues about the murder that still troubles her.

"Who knew Fr. Francisco was at the church, why was he there, what do we know about him?" asks Grace just as Sam is about to serve coffee in small dainty cups along with dessert. No one answers Grace. They don't look in her direction because those questions also nag each one of them and they just want to forget they have no answers.

Maria-Teresa goes to the kitchen to grab a mug for her coffee. The small cups don't give her comfort when she wraps her hands around them. Without looking she chooses a mug from Sam's whimsical sayings collection. The first mug she grabs has the word TROUBLES on it which will fade into NO PROBLEM when the cup is filled with hot liquid.

Reading the word trouble her eyes open wide in surprise, her expression quickly followed by fear. Involuntarily, her fingers open releasing the mug, allowing it to crash on the counter chipping the handle off. The other dinner quests turn in the direction of the clatter just in time to see Maria-Teresa take a few steps backward as her face goes pale.

All at once, everyone jumps up. Despite Hobbs' bulk he reaches Maria-Teresa first, his voice slightly panicky and he asks, "What's the matter?" as the rest of them rush to her side in the kitchen. She is still looking at the mug and they follow her gaze to the now chipped mug laying on the counter. After reading the saying on the mug, Hobbs forcefully says, "Not this shit again." Of the group, he is the only nonbeliever in the prophetic mugs.

To end this harebrained tradition Hobbs adds, "I'll grab another one to prove you have nothing to worry about." Closing his eyes, as is the custom, he reaches into the cabinet and pulls out a mug that says, DIG DEEP over a cartoon of a dog lying beside an open hole enjoying a bone.

The messages on the mugs turn the mood of the entire evening from jubilant to somber with overtones of intrigue. The one-word ringing in everyone's thoughts is Why. Why kill the priest, why isn't this over, why can't they stay out of the investigation, why is the nursery assistant suddenly gone?

Hobbs returns to his chair, strokes his bushy mustache distracted. Sam busies herself in the kitchen not wanting to give in to her thoughts. Grace paces the room before saying aloud, "Just clearing Maria-Teresa is not enough, we must find out who and why Fr. Francisco was killed. We have to quell our curiosity. This means, Sam, you have to continue working at the church nursery."

Hobbs turns a confused gaze toward Sam, "Why are you working at the church nursery?"

This time Sam fields the question, "Well, my good friend Grace," pointing to Grace and rolling her eyes, "volunteers me to take the place of the young nursery assistant who suddenly abandoned her duties."

"What?" still not comprehending how the volunteer assignment came about he asks, "how does Grace even know there's a need at the church, or is this another one of her super-powers," stated sarcastically making air quotes when he says super-powers.

Grace answers in a level voice clearly unphased by the inference that she can be overbearing. "Just dumb luck, I'm afraid," admits Grace. "We made a call to invite Fr. Santos to the monthly potluck." Hobbs's body straightens, his face optimistic and his eyes alert at the mention of food, "The potluck is for the book club members only," clarifies Grace, "one thing leads to another and Sam has a volunteer job, we need a person on the inside to find the answers at the church."

Everyone is brought up to speed on the evidence they have before they list the following questions: What is the real reason for Fr. Francisco's visit to the church? Does the sudden departure of the nursery assistant have anything to do with the murder? Who has the balls to kill a priest and why?

Let's list the relevant players suggests Grace, "Sister, Bishop O'Leary, nursery assistant, Fr. Francisco, and Fr. Santos."

Hobbs asks, "Sister, is that like the woman's name or her title?"

"Sam, you work with the woman every day, answer the man," says Grace emphatically also waiting for the answer.

"Let me think," Sam stops talking and puts her fingers to her chin, and looks up toward the ceiling. Then she twists her mouth to one side. The waiting audience makes loud throat-clearing sounds and light coughing.

"Well?" asks Hobbs tired of waiting.

"Don't rush me," says Sam. "Everyone calls her sister but I—"

Grace who is often impatient flicks her hand dismissively, "Never mind, Sam, just find out tomorrow," turning away, both her body language and facial expression leaves no question to anyone that the subject is closed.

A final discussion of the people present at the church on the morning of the crime and their alibis are summed up before the next day's assignments are given out. Sam is to speak with Sister about that morning Fr. Francisco was murdered and of course, find out her name. Hobbs is told to check all the law enforcement databases for further information on Fr. Francisco while Grace checks her unnamed sources.

"I know Margot is working on her family thing and Maria-Teresa, I am not sure you're up for investigating," says Grace turning to face Margot and Maria-Teresa searching their faces for input. Neither object to Grace's assumptions wishing to secretly pursue their own plan to prove their usefulness in the investigation.

"Well, I think that's that then, we'll meet here tomorrow to compare notes."

32

"You look lovely," he says his eyes wide with pleasurable surprise as he moves across the room his gaze never leaving her Emerald green evening dress.

"Glad you find me pleasing," she teases as his outstretched hand touches hers and their fingers intertwine. Drawing her close his hand now on the small of her back his lips brush lightly on hers before his full deep kiss causes tiny shudders through her body.

Grace's body responds just as it had then only now, she is alone. Remembering. Grace's bare feet nestle in the various silk rugs that cover her study floor as she walks around the room. She likes the different patterned rugs each telling its own story of love, origin, a mission failed or complete. This is her place to be alone with her thoughts, her memories, without judgment or explanations.

A near-replica of her late father's study filled with classic books, heavy leather furniture a wet bar, and his portrait hanging majestically over the gas fireplace while smaller photos of the two of them dot the surfaces of tables, bookcases, and the desk.

Slowly making her way from the tall windows to the Chesterfield sofa, she curls up staring down at the phone clutched at her breasts her mind flicks back through those times with him. Rhys and Grace worked as agents for the same off-the-book black ops agency whose funding can be traced to line items found on different government agencies' budgets.

Although sanctioned by the Defense Department, they never worked directly for any of the well-known three-letter federal government agencies. Their assignments consisted mostly of undercover work to clean up or initiate an action. Their unpredictable schedules require them to leave at a moment's notice going to God knows where for God knows how long making a normal family life impossible contrary to some on-screen portrayals of their kind of work.

It is inevitable that prolonged proximity breeds either contempt or love, for them a love that is forbidden by the agency but ironically expected. The distractions of the last couple of days give her a reason not to think of missing Rhys, rumors of his death, and any circumstances surrounding it. She clutches a phone not just any phone the one she and Rhys use to communicate.

The thought of dialing THAT number and not hearing HIS voice on the other end makes her sad beyond words. The inability to share her grief and heal is sadder than his death. In life, their love was forbidden, hidden, and now grieving him is the same.

Compartmentalizing is what she does best and with that thought she dials the number and requests a dossier on one Father Hector Francisco.

33

His belly full his thirst about to be quenched with another beer from his apartment fridge Hobbs begins his computer search. The opportunity to be part of real detective work spurs him on to spend half the night searching for information on the murder victim, Fr. Francisco. There are several Francisco's but none of them meet either the age, the looks, or the occupation of the victim.

Four beers under his belt, Hobbs is not quite sure if his inebriated state has caused missteps in his search. He rises from his kitchen chair that doubles as an office chair, he massages his neck and shoulders, catching his reflection in his toaster his red rim eyes and day-old beard stare back at him evoking an 'ugh'.

Searching unsuccessfully for another beer he sits down recalling his conversation with Pete Simons the medical examiner. Surely, the quick release of Fr. Francisco's body from the morgue and the victim's old bullet wound means someone higher up in the church wants to keep this quiet. Afraid to lay down for fear of sleeping through the day, Hobbs showers dousing himself in mouthwash and cologne before paying the local diocese a friendly visit.

The diocese, located just off a busy thoroughfare, sticks out like a sore thumb amid the fast-food chains whose signs tout world-famous burgers, best tacos, and those two-for-one specials. He parks in front of the one-story beige stucco building the arch-shaped windows trimmed in dark wood sit just below a mini steeple.

He is surprised that the inside color looks very much like the outside of the building down to dark wood floors and trim. It is the quiet that makes an impression on Hobbs where only the sound of his shoes indicates activity within its walls. Down a long bare hall, he locates a door marked Bishop O'Leary.

The bishop's office resembles a monastic principal's office complete with a row of chairs lined against the wall in his outer office. He approaches the male receptionist whose stern face makes him feel like he should apologize or ask forgiveness for something. Hobbs too takes on a stern official persona flashing his badge, "Here to see the bishop."

Giving the policeman and his badge a sidelong glance, the receptionist types something on his computer. Hobbs remains standing expecting acknowledgement of his request, instead the receptionist continues typing alternating that with shuffling papers on his desk. At the sound of a little ding from his computer, he says, "Please have a seat, the Bishop will be with you shortly," then he busies himself with what looks to Hobbs like a lot of nothing.

Hobbs sits down in one of the half dozen wooden chairs against the wall to the side of the reception desk and peruses his choice of reading material. From the small table at the end of the row, he shuffles through titles of unfamiliar magazines like Catholic Digest, Inside the Vatican, and a copy of the Catholic Sun newspaper.

The titles of the magazines and newspapers garner a disapproving shake of his head and he mutters under his breath, "Not even a copy of Reader's Digest." With a derisive snort, he plops the magazines back on the table. Five minutes go by no one enters or leaves the Bishop's office. A few minutes later, Hobbs starts to squirm shifting his body on his hard-wooden chair. The unpadded chairs must be designed specifically to inflict untold numbness on the occupant's behind.

First, Hobbs crosses left knee over right, then right knee over left, then he places his feet flat on the floor and drums his fingers on his thighs. These actions accompany audible snorts and exhalations which are met with a smirk from the receptionist. After a little more than ten minutes of waiting, it is clear to Hobbs that he is being left to wait on purpose.

He stands up, strides to the receptionist; his bulky body now directly in front of the receptionist's desk, the heat rising from his collar when the man looks up with his familiar smirk and says, "The bishop will see you now," pointing toward a large oak panel door just behind him.

Finally, an audience with the head collar wearer in charge thinks Hobbs. He opens the door and enters the large inner office. Flashing his police badge briefly he sputters "Detective Hobbs, sorry to bother you, Sir." Unsure of the appropriate greeting for someone of Bishop O'Leary's holy stature. On the way over to the diocese, Hobbs toys with using titles like his royal-ness, or his bishop-ness but settles instead on sir.

"Have you found the murderer?" the bishop asks with dull impatience already bored with his uninvited guest.

"No, not yet. That's why I am here. I understand you suggested Fr. Francisco stay at the St. Francis de Sales rectory."

The bishop's face reddens with anger at the implication that he may be somehow responsible for sending a young priest to his death. He suddenly stands, eyes wide, perusing Hobbs closely, "I know about you, you're that cop always sticking your nose in where it doesn't belong." Pointing his index finger at Hobbs, O'Leary continues, "Keating told me not to talk to you, get out, now!"

"Are you trying to hide something, Bishop? Why are you afraid to speak with me?"

Now stepping around his desk to position himself two feet from Hobbs's face, "You'll hear from our lawyers. You don't know what you've stepped into," threatens Bishop O'Leary. The telepathic receptionist enters the room just at that moment accompanied by two security guards. Hobbs holds up his hands showing he surrenders and heads for the door.

34

Grace sits at home contemplating the complexities of the church murder. Perhaps, if she has a better understanding of the catholic religion, she can see a way forward in the investigation. She phones Maria-Teresa for insight into the Catholic hierarchal structure.

Sam has the opportunity for uninterrupted conversation with Sister during nap time. They choose to sit in the Eucharist room next door to the nursery. Sam remembers the posters exalting the holy communion, the Eucharist, and the novena from her first day volunteering at the church. Sam perches on the edge of the adult desk while Sister comfortably settles into a small chair.

A secretive smile turns the corners of Sister's mouth upward as she dips her hand into one of the deep pockets in her habit and takes out a tiny box with candy in it. "My guilty pleasure," she says taking the lid off the sample size box and pops a small chocolate-covered turtle in her mouth savoring it with an audible "mmm."

Looking skeptically at Sam, "Sorry you want one," tentatively holding out the box to her.

"No," says Sam then whiffing the aroma of chocolate she says just as Sister retracts the box, "well, maybe just one."

Both sit in silence enjoying the gooey caramel, chocolate, and pecans, and Sam asks in earnest, "Sister, is that your full name?"

Sister throws her head back and chortles then she shakes her head smiling at Sam's lack of knowledge of the Catholic religion. "No, Sister Mary Margaret is my full name. It is easier for the children to just call me Sister," she says reaching for another candy. "You must feel good that Maria-Teresa is cleared of any wrongdoing?"

"Oh God, yes," says Sam immediately wondering about her use of god's name in vain. She presses on quickly not giving Sister an opportunity to scold her if she did make a faux pas. "There is still a killer out there?" contemplating

117

this truth they both look concerned. "Can you tell me more about that morning?"

"Well, like I told the police," says Sister euphoric from the chocolate rendering her in a cooperative mood. "I woke up feeling ill, so I called the nursery office phone about six-thirty a.m. to tell the nursery assistant, the person you're filling in for, that I would not be in."

"Why did you call the nursery and not Fr. Santos?"

"Because Lea, the nursery assistant, is always at the nursery at least an hour early, so I was hoping to speak with her and not have to bother Fr. Santos. I tried Lea's cell phone too, but the call went straight to voice mail."

"Go on," encourages Sam trying her best to sound mildly curious.

"Well, I phoned Fr. Santos next and got no answer on his cell phone either. That's when I decided to walk over to the church to find someone. The order I belong to has a convent three blocks away."

"Was it odd that you couldn't contact either person by phone?" asks Sam drawing the conclusion that they might be together.

"Yes but, I knew Fr. Santos had his early morning mass, so I thought maybe he had turned off his phone. But Lea was different, she was always so conscientious about coming to work."

"Did Lea come into work that day?" asks Sam.

"No, we didn't see her until the next day. She said her phone died and that she had a family emergency."

"Where is she now, why did she leave again so suddenly?"

"The same reason, a family emergency. She is really great with the little ones." Sister looks off into the distance a sad smile creeping across on her lips making Sam wonder if she was crashing from all the sugar.

"I think I saw Lea chasing little Peter in the garden," adds Sam remembering the time she and Grace spoke with Fr. Santos. "Doesn't she bear a striking resemblance to Maria-Teresa. I mean size, height, and all. At lot younger though."

"Yes, that sounds like her," says Sister through a mouthful of candy. "She has the energy to do the chasing."

Sister pops the last piece of candy in her mouth, "Now that I think about it, I thought I saw Lea upstairs when I came in. I called out to her, the person didn't respond so naturally I felt I was mistaken."

Sucking on her last piece of candy with a faraway look her forehead frowns and she says, "There's another strange thing about that morning, I called Lea's relatives to find out when she would return to work, and they didn't know where she was."

"That is odd," says Sam needing the answer to one more question. "What is her relationship with Fr. Santos like?"

Sister's face clouds her eyes cast downward, "Oh, you know like most of the females in the parish." She pauses, blushing slightly and fidgeting a little in her chair still avoiding Sam's scrutiny. Then regaining her composure, she says softly, "We all Love him."

35

The three sleuths meet later that evening laying out all the information they have found. Hobbs is the first to speak mainly because he wants to eat his meal uninterrupted. He regurgitates his encounter with the bishop adding the fact that he finds nothing related to Fr. Francisco's name in any law enforcement database. He proceeds to eat his dinner with vigor.

Sam is very excited as she relays information regarding the sudden departure of Rosalea Cardenas, the young nursery assistant. She also reveals Sister Mary Margaret's name. Grace is last but probably gives the most important clue.

"I spoke with Maria-Teresa and found out there are annual reports published for each state that list all the priests in that state. The report indicates whether they are active, inactive, and which parish they are assigned to."

"Well, did you find Fr. Francisco?" asks Hobbs raising his folk to his mouth and leaning in so as not to miss anything.

"He is not listed in any church publication going back for the last three years in Arizona or New Mexico," this statement takes the wind out of everyone's sails agreeing something fishy is going on.

"Where the hell did this guy come from, what does the bishop know about him?" asks Hobbs shifting food around in his mouth to speak.

"I think if we find out who Fr. Francisco is, that might lead us to the motive for his death," announces Grace, the rest of the team too stunned to speak. The sleek new screen rises from the credenza and the following information is listed:

1   The bishop is hiding something.

2   Is the sudden disappearance of Lea Cardenas connected to murder?

3   No record of Fr. Francisco as a priest—who is he?

4   Is Sister Mary Margaret the SMM from the journal?

Even though Maria-Teresa is not active in the evening meetings, she is kept in the loop regarding the investigation. Hearing about the oddness surrounding nursery assistant, she and Margot agree to find out all they can about Lea Cardenas.

36

The next day during nursery nap time Sam decides to go up to the nave and possibly visit the sacristy to have a look around. Without telling Sister her destination she climbs the stairs to the main level arriving at the entry to the nave. The majesty of the stain glass windows, the relief carvings of the apostles that line the side walls and the beamed cathedral ceiling is breathtaking.

Sam stops on the red carpet that covers the length of the center aisle and the altar. Her eyes take in the large gold crucifix, fresh-cut flowers, and candelabra on the altar not expecting to see a little boy dressed in a white long-sleeve surplice staring back at her from the altar. She smiles at him and wonders why he's not in school his sweet face and eager smile make it easy for Sam to approach him.

There is a searching look in the little boy's eyes his arms hang loosely at his sides. He stares at her curiously, head tilted to one side sizing her up as she approaches, he lets his full smile morph into a half-smile not yet trusting this stranger. He locks his gaze on her and takes one hesitant step backward before deciding instead to maintain his position on the altar.

Sam makes the first move donning her friendliest smile and he walks down from the altar, as she reaches him and leans down to his level, he in turn lowers his gaze, "Hello, my name is Sam. What's yours?" she says holding out her hand.

The little boy of about ten-years-old looks at his sneakers before meeting her eyes, extending his hand, and answering, "Cameron."

"By the way you're dressed, you must be one of the altar boys," a proud smile crinkles the eyes of the young man. "Yes, Fr. Santos chose me. He says I am special."

"You seem special to me too, Cameron," says Sam smiling back. "I bet you have a great memory too," continues Sam wanting to know if he was around on the morning of the murder. The little boy beams, puffs out his chest before shaking his head enthusiastically in agreement with her comment.

"Can I let you in on a secret, Cameron?" asks Sam as she takes a seat on the front pew to remain on his level without continually bending down and feeling the sharp pain in her sciatic nerve. "Me and my friends are helping the police solve the murder of the priest."

Cameron's eyes light up at the possibility of helping the police. He solidifies his trustworthiness by putting his finger to his closed lips, then makes a twisting motion on the side of his mouth indicating his lips are locked and sealed.

"Were you serving as altar boy the day of the murder?"

He shakes his head yes.

"Did you see or hear anything unusual that day."

Eager to show off his recollection skills, Cameron launches into the events of that morning gesticulating for emphasis.

"I was about to put out the wafers on the altar before early morning mass and I remembered I left the tray in the sacristy," says Cameron slapping his hand to his forehead, "duh I start to walk down the hallway toward the sacristy, and I hear loud angry voices coming from Fr. Santos office," says Cameron sitting down beside Sam. "I start to tip toe because I was wearing my brown Sunday shoes and they squeak if I walk normal."

"Could you hear what the angry voices were saying?" This time he shakes his head no.

"What else happened can you remember?"

Now, pleased that the information he delivers is of interest to Sam he continues, "just before I get to the door, Lea comes running out of the sacristy."

"You're sure it was Lea?" with this question Cameron immediately looks offended. Then with an exasperated sigh, "Yes, I'm sure it was her," looking past Sam momentarily and tapping his foot.

Realizing Cameroon has taken offense to her last question she says, "I'm sorry; of course, you know what she looks like."

Feeling her apology was satisfactory he continues rapidly not wanting to be interrupted again or doubted, "She was wearing jeans, white top, and pink and white sneakers. She didn't look around, so she never noticed I was standing against the wall. She looked really mad and ran out the side door. I just thought it was strange that Lea and Fr. Santos were yelling at each other because once

I caught them kissing." He relaxes his shoulders and looks up with eyes that ask did I help.

"What makes you think she was mad?"

"Cause she looks like this," says Cameron purses his lips together forming his mouth into a small round shape, he knits his eyebrows together and narrows his eyes. "My mom gets the scary look when she's mad, that's how I know. My mom wants everybody to leave her alone, so I went back to the nave."

"What about after the mass, what did you do?"

"Fr. Santos said he would clear up and put things away, so I left for school."

"How do you remember all these details?"

"Mom says I have a gift, but Dad thinks it's just creepy."

"Thank you, Cameron, you have been a big help." A full grin fills the little boy's face. Sam smiles back and is about to walk away when she turns back, "Did you tell the police any of this?"

"No, nobody asked me any questions."

"Thanks again," says Sam giving Cameron a big hug and he leaves the nave.

Sam sits down thinking about the fact that Lea had a lover's tiff with somebody in the sacristy early that morning, which also means that Sister was right when she thought she saw Lea in the church that morning.

Deciding not to wait for the evening information exchange, she texts out her news to the team.

37

Maria-Teresa and Margot shared a kidnapping experience during their last investigation that forever forged their deep friendship. That is to say that Margot is closer to Maria-Teresa than any other member of the investigative team. The others take Margot's prickly exterior and antagonistic attitude at face value, but Maria-Teresa sees it as a façade.

The two commence their secret plan by canvassing the neighborhood surrounding the church for information about Lea. Remembering an old family friend of Maria-Teresa's lives across the street from the church the ladies pay her a visit indulging in cups of coffee and polite conversation before the family friend gives them a phone number where Lea can be reached. Maria-Teresa dials the number, Lea answers and after some persuasion agrees to meet her.

"Did you read this? It says here," pointing to the text on her cell phone screen, "Sam thinks Lea might have something to do with the priest's death."

"If she is guilty and hiding, why agree to meet with you," asks Margot. "Perhaps we should call off the meeting she could be a killer."

"We just found somebody that everyone is looking for, we have to see this through." Like any good friend Margot accompanies Maria-Teresa to her clandestine meeting in a bookstore near the church.

The drive is a short four blocks to the strip mall where the bookstore is located between a coffee shop and an organic food market. A sign touting new and used books shares window space with adverts for new releases.

"Are you sure you want to go through with this?" asks Margot turning to face her friend who has been quiet since she got into the car. Margot clasps Maria-Teresa's hand, "You don't have to do this you know."

Exhaling and forcing a weak smile, "I can do this. It's a public place and we have no evidence that we are walking into danger," blurts out Maria-Teresa.

"I'll go in first," says Margot getting out of the car advancing to the sidewalk where two racks of books line either side of the path to the store's front door demanding passersby to at least glance at the contents of the racks.

Bookstores have a particular air of mystery, anticipation, and knowledge regardless of their size. A bell on the door tingles as Margot walks into the small privately-owned bookstore first to survey the space for exits or potential ambushes. Walking around the three tables set up displaying new paperback and hardcover releases Margot looks to her right at another entrance to a coffee shop.

The store is well lit with rows of five feet tall bookcases ending in cozy reading nooks where Margot positions herself near the middle of the store enabling her to see the front and side door traffic. Margot knows Lea looks like a younger version of Maria-Teresa even though the older doesn't agree with her friend's description.

Margot's senses heighten and her body tenses when she spots a person meeting Lea's description browsing at the rear of the store. If Lea intends to cause harm what better place to carry out the deed than in the back of the store where there are currently no customers. Margot texts Maria-Teresa who enters the bookstore, stops just inside the door placing her hand lightly on her abdomen to quell the flutter.

Lea locks eyes on Maria-Teresa weaving her way toward the back merely glancing at Margot as she walks past. Much like Sam's prophetic mugs, she takes the signage, religion, indicating the books found in that aisle as a good omen. Lea thumbs through a book as Maria-Teresa stands next to her pretending to read the spines of the books on the shelf.

"Hello Lea, I'm Maria-Teresa." Standing this close to the young woman looking into her wide chocolate brown eyes, seeing the way her long brown loosely curled hair falls around her face Maria-Teresa can indeed see herself.

In a barely audible voice Lea says, "Thanks for coming, I need to talk to someone." There is part desperation, part fear, and part relief in Lea's eyes that tug at Maria-Teresa's heart.

"Why are you hiding?"

"I made a mistake and now everyone is looking for me."

"What are you talking about? Who is after you? What mistake?"

Lea looks around for other people before walking to the nearest reading nook pulling two chairs in an alcove flanked by floor-to-ceiling bookcases minimizing chances of being overheard.

Margot steps a little closer to the two carefully gauging Lea's body language.

"You mentioned a mistake. What kind of a mistake?"

"I was there in Fr. Santos' office the morning that other priest was killed, but I didn't kill him." Lea leans closer tears welling in her eyes. This movement triggers Margot to lean in closer from her position not far away.

"Why were you there?"

"I went to confront Fr. Santos. You see, we were lovers and I found out that he was seeing someone else. I was angry, but I didn't kill anyone."

"Was Fr. Santos in the office? Who was the other woman?"

"No, but from behind, I mistook Fr. Francisco for Santos. We had words and then I left."

"How long have you known Fr. Santos?"

"We are both from the same poor town in Brazil. He had a troubled childhood, we all did. We met on the streets, became friends," her voice falters she looks down, "then lovers."

Maria-Teresa is shaken to the core with the revelation that a priest is having an affair and for a few minutes rendered speechless. "Don't judge us too harshly," pleads Lea reading the disappointment on her face.

"I'm not judging you," lies Maria-Teresa unable to meet the girl's gaze, "you want to go someplace where we can talk freely?"

"I can't. I have to get back. Please, don't follow me I might be in contact."

She jumps up causing Margot to lurch forward ready to intervene but stops when Lea turns toward the door not Maria-Teresa and dashes out of the bookstore, leaving both the women to wonder if they will ever hear from her again.

38

Sam's text about the altar boy reaches Grace who rushes over to the church to have a word with Sister and finds her in the small office space off the main playroom completing some paperwork. Sam enters the room leaving Grace to linger at the doorway.

"Sister, sorry to bother you. I was wondering if you have heard from Lea or if you know where she is." Looking up from her desk her reading glasses perched on her nose bridge Sister says with a pleased smile, "Funny you should ask about her. I was shocked to see her this morning at breakfast. Apparently, she joined my convent as a novice," says Sister unphased by Sam's inquiry.

"Wow," not expecting to hear that, "are you surprised at her decision?"

"Yes and no," Sister drops her pen on the desk and takes off her glasses, "with the murder and other tragedies people automatically get closer to God. Even the non-believers."

"You think she's at the convent now?"

"Most of the nuns in our order work outside the convent, at catholic charities and the like. I don't know if she is there now. I didn't speak with her," says Sister in a distracted tone.

"So, can she accept visitors, if she is there I mean?" asks Sam, trying not to appear too eager but before she gets an answer Grace leans in grabbing Sam by the arm, "thanks Sister, she won't be long. Come on Sam." Grace maintains her firm grip on Sam's arm as they practically run out of the church Sam says, "Why are you dragging me, where are we going?"

"To the convent, we don't want Lea to take off again."

39

Sam and Grace pull up in front of a Spanish inspired stucco building that looks more like a retreat than a convent with tall palm trees lining the walkway to the front door. The exterior stucco is painted a pinkish beige color trimmed in dark brown. A three-foot iron fence encloses the grounds of the building.

The women leave their car and rush toward the four wide flat steps leading from the walkway to the front door. There is a center door made of dark wood with ornate stucco relief columns on either side. Above the center of the door recessed is a statue of Mother Mary on a pedestal.

"How do we get in? Can we visit?" Sam's questions are answered when Grace walks up to the front door turns the doorknob, finds it unlocked, and opens it wide enough to peek in. Seeing no one else in the inner foyer, they slip inside.

Grace and Sam are surprised to find that the interior of the convent is much brighter than the interior of the rectory behind St. Francis de Sales church. By using the center door, they are able to view the main nave which has a high arch-shaped ceiling with decorative tiles and recess lighting over the altar area.

Three ornately carved chairs sit recessed just below a life-size crucifix that sits above the middle chair. A biblical mural finishes off the walls in the altar area. The altar itself is comprised of a long dark wooden table with hand a carved four-foot-tall candle holder on either end.

The sight is breathtaking and Grace has to pull Sam away as they walk quickly and quietly down another hallway off to the side of the nave. The sound of female voices echoes off the cathedral ceilings as nuns and novices walk the halls in other parts of the building.

Sam notices the highly polished floors and she envisions poor nuns on their hands and knees scrubbing and waxing until they can see their reflection on the floors. Portraits of priests, saints, and nuns hang on the walls lining the hallway as they walk toward an undetermined destination.

"Where are we going?" whispers Sam as she looks side to side taking in the beauty of the building.

"To find Lea but we need to blend in so keep your eyes open for some clothes," whispers Grace.

This edict is met with a frown from Sam as she says, "Grace this is not a department store. Habits won't just be hang—" she stops in the hallway and mid-sentence causing Grace to turn in her direction.

Sam stares like a deer caught in the headlights her mouth agape because through the glass of a door beside her she spots a rack full of freshly cleaned habits still in their see-through cleaner bags. Once she composes herself, Sam mutters, "Seek and ye shall find, ask and ye shall receive. Wow, this really is a place of God." Sam grabs Grace by the arm and they duck inside the room throwing on a habit over their street clothes.

Then they set out again to find Lea. Halfway down one corridor, they see a young woman bearing an uncanny resemblance to Maria-Teresa coming toward them accompanied by an older Nun. Peering through the glass door of what looks like an empty room, yet another gift from God, Grace yanks Sam into the room as anguished-faced Lea and the older nun approaches.

Once inside the empty room, resembling a mini chapel the female voices outside the room get louder and clearer as the women approach. Sam and Grace frantically look for someplace to hide and realize that the safest place is in the confessional booth sitting off to one side. They listen as the door to the chapel opens then closes.

Sam and Grace strain to hear the conversation between Lea and the nun that is being conducted from a pew, "Stay and pray ask for God to show you the way. Remember the visiting priest is due today to hear confessions," the nun looks around the room and sees the light lit above the confessional, "he may have already arrived," says the older nun.

Grace sits on the confessional chair and leans back so that her face is not visible through the grated partition separating her from the confessor while Sam finds herself on the floor at Grace's knees and feet. Just when they think they are in the clear, the voices get even closer so that now Lea and the nun are standing outside of the confessional.

The two people continue talking until the older one bids farewell to the other. In the confessional, the two women carefully crack the door open enough to see Lea kneeling in one of the pews in prayer lasting ten minutes. A cramp in Sam's ham string causes her to wince in pain.

She lays her head in Grace's lap mouthing another prayer to God that they get out of the cramped booth soon. Unlike the other times, the ladies requested help this time they will have to wait for her prayer to be answered. The door to the other side of the confessional opens suddenly and Rosalea Cardenas takes a seat.

"Why is she on the other side?" whispers Sam looking curiously up at Grace. "The outside light on our side of the booth must be on to indicate the priest is available to hear confessions," answers Grace. Sam's eyes wide in panic she mouths, "What do we do?"

Grace smashed against the back of the confessional and Sam squished on the floor they hold their breath hoping Lea will leave but she sits in silence for a few minutes before clearing her throat. The cramp in Sam's ham string is now a raging pain to distract herself she reaches up and slides the partition open separating the two booths and in her deepest voice she says, "Yes, my child."

It's Grace's turn to look panicky glaring down at Sam vigorously shaking her head side to side and mouthing, "No." Unfortunately, it's too late, Lea starts in a tense voice, "Bless me, father, for I have sinned it has been four days since my last confession and during that time there has been a murder."

"Did you say murder, my child?" asks Sam in her deep voice while Grace maneuvers her hand under her habit to press record on her cell phone hoping the rest of the confession is captured. When Lea is finished, Sam gives a version of absolution that she remembers hearing from the movies and television shows.

When they are sure the young woman is gone, Grace opens the confessional door putting her left out and lifting her right leg over Sam's head she wriggles out of the booth. After stretching and bending, she turns to see Sam still on her knees face down on the chair just extricated by Grace. She walks over to the confessional, reaches down grabbing Sam by the arms dragging her out of the booth and turns away.

Sam's whimpering causes Grace to turn around to find Sam laying on her stomach arms stretched in front of her, her habit yanked above her legs that are still bent heels touching her butt. "Just roll on your back," snickers Grace.

Wincing in pain, "I would if I could help me," pleads Sam. Grace walks over to straighten her legs then says, "Get up, we don't have time to sit around we have to get out of here."

"A little sympathy goes a long way Grace you weren't on your knees for twenty minutes." Grace sheds her habit then helps Sam to do the same as they flee the convent without further incident.

Outside Sam says, "We are going to burn in hell. Listening to a confession under false pretenses."

"What do you mean 'we', you started talking to her not me, besides I think we have just cracked the Fr. Francisco murder."

40

Sam hobbles along still trying to regain full circulation in her legs as they race back to their car. They make a mad dash over to Hobbs' office to share their recorded confession.

"I want this done immediately, no excuses," yells the plump man sitting behind the desk in the captain's office.

"Yes sir," says Hobbs backing out of his superior's office heading back to his own office.

Hobbs' desk phone rings simultaneously with his butt connecting to his chair. He lifts the receiver, "Detective Hobbs," he says his fingers rubbing his temples preparing himself for more demands from his captain.

"A Jones and Liu are here to see you, Hobbs," says the front desk officer, Hobbs' eyes brighten, "hmm, send them back," he says hiding his excitement pretending their visit is strictly business. Once the ladies close the door to his office, he grins at them like a drowning man at a rescue boat.

"What have you got? It must be great because you never visit me here."

"We just came from the convent," starts Sam. Confusion clouds Hobbs' face, "Wait don't tell me you two joined up," asks Hobbs fully expecting them to say yes.

"Don't be silly," says Grace, letting out a dismissive snort and turning her back to him she continues, "I take that as a personal affront." Sam snickers thinking Grace can't get accepted into a convent if she paid them.

"Why the hell were you at a convent?" asks Hobbs in all seriousness.

"We found Rosalea Cardenas. She is a novice at the convent where Sister Mary Margaret lives." Hobbs is still not making any connection from the convent to the murder. Furthermore, he is not convinced that Rosa Carda whatsit has anything to do with any murder.

Showing how unimpressed he is, so far, he points his index finger toward the ceiling and twirls it in a circular motion.

"Can you just stop being such an ass for one minute," says Grace rolling her eyes. She looks him squarely in the face and says, "She confessed."

"To what?"

"She confessed to the murder of Fr. Hector Francisco," says Sam glaring at him in disbelief.

"So, the two of you just stroll into a convent and this Rosa whatsit just slides up to you and spills her guts. Why would she tell you she committed a crime, the convent is not some sort of sacred or hallowed ground, doesn't she know she can go to jail?"

"OK, let me start at the beginning," says Sam.

Hobbs folds his arms across his massive chest his skeptical face waiting to be impressed. Nothing about Sam's long-winded story garners his attention until he hears the part about Lea having an affair with Fr. Santos. He leans forward elbows on his desk now more interested in their story.

Then Sam tells him that Lea was angry with Santos the morning of the murder and went to the sacristy to confront him.

"What about the stabbing and throat-slashing part did she confess to that too?"

"Not exactly," admits Grace disappointed that their evidence is not airtight. "She was crying pretty hard during most of the confession."

"We couldn't very well ask her to speak clearer or ask her any questions then she would realize she was not talking to a priest."

"Hold up, why would she think she was talking to a priest?" asks Hobbs falling back in his chair and pushing away from his desk afraid that the ladies might have broken the law again.

"Don't worry about that," says Sam not wanting to relive how and why they wound up in the confessional impersonating a priest. Sam continues, "Lea never mentions Fr. Francisco by name, but we can surmise that maybe she killed him by mistake. What do you think?" she asks, hopeful that Hobbs will buy into their theory.

"So, sex, a woman scorned, and perhaps a case of mistaken identity sums up this case," retorts Hobbs sarcastically, "the only thing missing is the money. Church sure has changed since I last attended," he says still not sold.

Maybe this will convince you says Grace as she pulls out her cell phone recording and they all listen to it intently for the first time. Unfortunately, the phone was hidden under Grace's habit and not close enough to Lea to obtain a clear confession. Sadly, most of the confession is barely audible.

At the end of the recording, Hobbs says, "Even if it is audible this is inadmissible in court. Plus, the recording is taken illegally under fraudulent circumstances, and you bring it to me, an officer of the law," says Hobbs incensed.

"Since when have you cared about being on the right side of the law if it means you get to catch a criminal?" asks Grace referring to their antics during a past investigation.

"Since I nearly lost my job a few months ago," says Hobbs raising his voice a little and glaring at Grace he turns away to calm down before saying, "even guardian angels get tired of helping a fool who won't learn a lesson."

"You're no fool just a passionate crusader for justice who knows we have to find the best way to turn this evidence over to the police," says Grace trying to smooth his feathers but their debate on the pros and cons of the recording continues.

41

At the convent, Lea is just finishing her class and walks out into the hallway with her fellow novices when she overhears a fellow student say, "Did you hear the visiting priest was unable to come this morning to hear confessions. He will be here tomorrow morning instead."

Hearing that tidbit of news Lea recounts her early morning experience in the confessional booth and breaks out in a cold sweat. *Who was I talking to in the confessional?*

Her stomach lurches, her face drains of color. "Are you OK," asks a few classmates noticing her distressed look.

"I'm not feeling well. I have to lay down," and she stumbles off in the direction of her room. Instead of going to her room she pushes open the door to the nearest exit where the sudden impact of the oppressing heat bends her at the waist. Leaning with one clammy hand against the side of the convent to maintain her balance she clutches at the large wooden cross dangling from her neck.

Perspiration lightly peppers her forehead her tongue thick in her mouth as the calm of the morning's absolution fades into panic. The realization that one slip of her tongue in a confession to God knows who sends shivers through her quickly followed by a wave of nausea complete with reflexive dry heaves. Her peace of mind is gone. Lea's heart pumps fast and hard against her chest as she staggers away from the convent desperate to find a place to hide.

42

Margot and Maria-Teresa sit together in the Sundial coffee shop next to the bookstore after Lea leaves. Maria-Teresa muses, "How can she lead a priest astray, a priest," she repeats. "Has she no dignity."

Margot sips her coffee remembering her own failed marriage and solemnly says, "It takes two to tango. I am sure she didn't have to do too much leading he's just a man."

"Uhm I still think she's at fault," says Maria-Teresa holding on to her belief in the sanctity of the vows of the catholic church. Margot knows a continuation of this conversation will not budge either from her position and lets a companionable silence settle between them.

Maria-Teresa absentmindedly passes her spoon between her fingers, "You know I wonder where she ran off to in such a hurry." She bits her fingernail fidgets in her seat her doleful eyes look pensively into the distance before she snatches up her phone and dials.

"Who are you calling?" asks Margot startled by the sudden movement of her friend.

"Lea," Margot turns to Maria-Teresa with a puzzling look on her face as the blaring cell phone in Lea's Habit pocket stops her aimless journey. After the fourth ring, she hesitantly answers with, "Ye yes."

"This is Maria-Teresa." The voice on the other end of the line breaks into uncontrollable sobbing garnering looks from those in her vicinity. Between sobs, the sound of terror in Lea's voice is perceptible prompting Maria-Teresa to invite her back to the Sundial coffee shop.

"You just can't help it can you?" says Margot, "one minute you blame her for the affair and the next minute you want to help her."

"What? what's wrong with me wanting to help her?" asks Maria-Teresa sticking out her chin defensively. Margot says with a chuckle, "I bet you take in strays." The statement hangs in the air without a response.

"I think we need to find out more about that Fr. Santos. He may be hiding information about the murder," says Margot looking up from her cup.

"That's absurd Fr. Santos can't be a suspect in this investigation," protests Maria-Teresa in his defense.

"I think you might be a little too close to Fr. Santos. Keep an open mind."

The ladies sip their drinks half expecting Lea to be a no-show. Maria-Teresa's position in the booth faces the front door. Every time the bell over the door tinkles to indicate the arrival of a new person she looks up. The third time the bell sounds Maria-Teresa rises from her seat in slow motion her mouth open squinting her eyes and frowning in confusion.

"What's the matter," asks Margot turning around to follow Maria-Teresa's gaze to the front door, "who the hell is that?"

Lea rushes over still dressed in her habit taking both ladies by surprise. Expecting to meet just Maria-Teresa the sight of Margot causes her to recoil, turn and try to flee. Margot quickly reaches out grabbing her wrist firmly pulling her gently beside her into the booth.

There is no further resistance from Lea her shoulders slump as she sits in resignation to her circumstances. Tired drained and scared Lea's eyes wildly search the wall posters of classic cars, the red and yellow vinyl booths nearly full of patrons before settling her gaze on Maria-Teresa.

"Why are you dressed like a nun?"

"I am a nun well I mean a novice." The word novice hangs in the air like a dripping faucet it's always there but you choose to ignore it. As shocking as this news is the ladies prefer to leave Lea's reason for becoming a nun for another time.

"What has you so upset?" asks Maria-Teresa noticing Lea is still twitchy, moving her hands from the tabletop to her lap to her face finally resting them on her rosary beads. Her lips tremble preparing to speak, "Umm," then she presses them together before saying, "I think I'm in trouble. Someone might have the wrong idea," says Lea her eyes pleading for help as she recounts the events of her morning in the confessional.

As if literally saved by the bell the tone announcing a text stops the proceedings. Margot reads the news from Grace about the confession then shoves her phone across the table to Maria-Teresa. Lea's gaze falls on the cell phone sliding back and forth across the table unable to see the screen she focuses on the unreadable faces of her companions.

Margot and Maria-Teresa exchange fleeting glances as Margot presses two fingers to her lips indicating silence. "I don't think you need to worry about the confession trust us. Let's order lunch," says Margot authoritatively leaning in toward the other two.

Lea blinks anxiously searching the women's faces for an explanation, receiving none she says, "What uhm?" unable to form her question she exhales and starts again, "how can you be so sure I don't have to worry?"

The restaurant fills with customers their voices increasing the noise level as they compete to engage in conversation. The ladies not wanting to be overheard huddle closer together in the booth. The waiter approaches their table arms laden with burgers, fries, and shakes for three that were ordered in haste without the aid of a menu.

"Let's just say we know a little something about the people who heard your confession," says Maria-Teresa her explanation fosters more suspicion than confidence.

"Tell us everything you know about the morning of the murder. Start with how you know Fr. Francisco."

"Fr. Francisco?" asks Lea through a mouthful of burger and fries her hunger catching up with her. Wide-eyed she looks from one woman to the other, "I don't know him at all I already told you that," says Lea.

A toddler who escaped his occupied mom approaches their table giggling his tiny fingers gripping the edge of their table. On his tip toes, his eyes are barely seen over the table where he engages Lea in an impromptu game of hide and seek. First on his toes then off entertaining Lea with his antics leaving the other two women unmoved.

An adult hand grabs his shoulder and yanks him away without any mention of an apology to the ladies at the table. This momentary diversion allows Lea to regain control of her nerves.

"When did you first meet Fr. Francisco?"

"The morning he died was the first, only, and last time I ever saw him."

"We know you exchanged angry words with someone in the sacristy. Who was it and why?"

Sheepishly looking at the women inhaling deeply, "Well if you must know I walked into the sacristy and a priest stands with his back to me I thought it was Joao, uh Fr. Santos." Looking at the ceiling then down at her rosary she hesitates.

"What happened?"

"From the back, they look so much alike I had no idea there was another priest on the grounds. I put my arms around him from behind. Joao has been pulling away from me for some time I was desperate to hang on to what we had. I said some very intimate things to him before he turns around."

Margot swallows hard wondering but not wanting to ask what Lea said to Fr. Francisco. Maria-Teresa tries to accept the fact that the priest she most admires is involved in a sexual affair.

"I yelled who are you? how dare you, identify yourself," says Lea. She pauses her face screws up as she reminisces her unpleasant ordeal. Sighing and shaking her head her face now showing disbelief she says, "He just stands there grinning at me like he just confirmed the world is round."

Their waiter deposits the bill on the table, "Can I clear anything away?" he asks surreptitiously glancing at the line of customers forming at the door waiting to be seated. Ignoring him Maria-Teresa asks, "Did you see a letter opener on the desk? Did you handle it?"

"Letter opener?" asks Lea confused. "Why do I care about a letter opener?" she adds with a dismissive wave of her hand. "I just ran out humiliated. He was alive when I left him, I swear," proclaims Lea.

43

Fr. Santos rises from his restful sleep bathed in a glow of confidence. Leaving his room in the rectory he pauses in front of the room that Fr. Francisco used and the worry lines on his forehead and around his eyes soften at the thought of the empty room. A satisfied smile lifts the corners of his mouth as he raises his hand giving a farewell salute to the closed door.

He crosses from the rectory through the garden to the church the morning wind gently nudging the hem of his cassock. The quiet night gives way to the early morning sounds of rumbling vehicles, foot traffic and an occasional raised voice as the neighborhood surrounding the church wakes. From his cassock pocket, he produces an old fashion skeleton key to open the wooden door where once inside the beep, beep, beep of the newly installed alarm invites him to enter the code to silence it.

Slipping the key back in his pocket he stands at the door listening to the cracking sound of an old building settling its groans resounding throughout its walls. Flicking on the dimmer switch next to the alarm control panel he surveys the ancient wood paneled hallway displaying photos of the last ten Popes inter laced with photos of Mother Mary and Jesus in various reposes.

Shoulders back chin lifted Santos' purposeful footsteps echo off the wooden floor his smile broadening. The sound of his solitary footsteps down the hallway versus the back stairs to the nave gives him time to appreciate every nook and cranny of an empire he snatched from the clutches of Fr. Francisco.

Rounding the corner to the entry of the nave the red-carpet center aisle gives the room a regal air as his steps soften to muted thuds. The apostles on the carved reliefs that line the side walls whose eyes cast downward; their lips carved in pious smiles give their blessing to his reign.

Even the creaking pews announce the arrival of the ruler the muted lighting showing off the gold crucifix, gilded statues of Mother Mary and baby Jesus against the backdrop of stained-glass figures on the windows. His chest swells with pride remembering the boy rising from the poverty-stricken streets of Brazil to rule his own kingdom with god's approval. He recalls that ill-fated message of a week ago, "Hump, ah yes, Santos this is Bishop O'Leary. I'm sending over a priest from New Mexico, show him the ropes. Thanks."

The first time Santos lies eyes on the visiting priest, he knows he is sent to disrupt his life. He can ill afford to tolerate any upset to his well-ordered existence. A wave of relief floods his body when the priest dies yet another sign that he has the approval of heaven for his work. Now that the visiting priest is out of the way, he can continue with his sainted life.

It is with joy in his heart, mind and soon to be body that he begins his day with the lighting of frankincense and myrrh he prepares for his morning devotion before mass.

Dropping to his knees clasping his hands together in prayer his thoughts are not with the dead priest's salvation or even his own, instead he prays that his Brazilian soccer team has a better season than last year.

Without contrition he adds in a whisper, "Please, let the diocese find enough money to provide me with a new cassock, mine is getting frayed around the edges." With those final words, he rises straightens his cassock his eyes linger on his hems and sleeves before turning around leaving the nave. He makes the sign of the cross, genuflects and hums his favorite hymn as he starts his day.

44

That evening in the nave of St. Francis de Sales Catholic church, candles are lit, the overhead lights are dimmed and the heavy scent of incenses waft through the air creating a meditative atmosphere. A few parishioners sit quietly their physical bodies appear relaxed, but anxiety is clearly present in the worry lines on their faces. Their eyes dart around the nave scanning their surroundings alert for any unwelcomed intruder in view of the recent death.

They are left waiting longer than usual for vespers to start anxiety building as they fidget in their pews while they listen to the organist play softly. When a seminarian enters the nave, the congregation sits up straight in their seats but to their surprise, he doesn't walk to the ambo or lectern to start the evening prayers. He heads straight for the organist, leans down and whispers in the organist ear.

Initially when the seminarian begins to whisper in the ear of the organist, he continues to play softly then without warning a loud crescendo emanating from the organ jerks heads toward the sound and the two men. The two men, eyes widen, faces pale, and their mouths gape open before they jump up and suddenly run from the nave, some parishioners stand up peering after them. Those who remain seated turn toward their fellow parishioners and exchange concerned whispers breaking the silence in the room.

Downstairs in the nursery Sam tidies up after the last child is gone, gathers up her purse and turns to say good night to Sister Mary Margaret. Unable to find Sister in the small office connected to the nursery, Sam heads upstairs to leave.

It isn't the loud resounding noise of that cord on the organ, or the fact that she can't find Sister Mary Margaret that catches Sam's attention. It is the rustle of the black cassocks as they attain warp speed running pass her. The swishing sound of the two men running is only overshadowed by their loud praying as they make their way along the hallway to the sacristy.

45

The pained faces of the two men in the black cassocks signal to Sam that something serious and possibly sinister is going on. She takes off down the hallway behind the two men. A million thoughts run through her mind as she heads toward the sacristy. Has something happened to Sister Mary Margaret thinks Sam?

Just as the thought enters Sam's mind, she sees Sister Mary Margaret running up the hallway from the opposite. The nun is approaching the three of them in a full gallop causing her rosary to swing violently across her chest. Sam steps in front of her and grabs the distraught nun by the shoulders asking, "What's the matter, what's happened?"

Sister Mary Margaret drops to her knees making the sign of the cross while uttering what sounds to Sam like a prayer. Tears stream down her face, she looks up with fear in her eyes, and says, "Oh God, he's dead. Help us all, who's next?"

"Who's dead?" asks Sam looking behind the nun down the hallway but not wanting to run into the unknown to affirm what she has just been told. The organist and the seminarian reach the doorway of the sacristy breathless stopping in the doorway and gazing down at a lifeless body.

Lying face up on the floor near the door to the sacristy, mouth open slightly, the wide hazel eyes of the body stare up at nothing. The head is turned slightly to one side, the color is still in the cheeks and one hand is on his chest amid spilled wafers and wine. The other hand palm up rests on the floor close beside his body.

Blood pools around the body from the gunshot wounds to the chest. The arrangement of the bullets appears in a close grouping consisting of three holes on the left side of the dead man's chest. The seminarian and the organist stand transfixed at the horrific sight in front of them. Their hands automatically fly to their chests and clutch the crucifixes hanging around their necks.

The seminarian is the first to return to the hallway followed closely by the organist. The blood has drained from their faces. The organist staggers back from the doorway to take his place in the hallway next to the seminarian who drops to the floor with his back against the wall.

Sam makes her way pass the organist who is clutching his stomach with one hand and palming the wall just beneath the portrait of the church's first priest with his other hand. Sam watches as the seminarian's body involuntarily slides slowly down the wall until he reaches a squat position on the floor.

Sam stops just outside the open sacristy door and peers in. Not wanting to disturb any evidence in the room, she shines her cell phone flashlight around the dimly lit room. No blood splatter appears to be on the sacristy walls. Thank god! Then Sam shines the light on the floor, that's when she sees Fr. Santos lying face up.

Someone must take charge of the situation, clearly none of the staff is in any position to do so. Sam, being a veteran of viewing murder victims, runs down the hall to the nave and announces to the parishioners that vespers will not take place this evening because of an emergency plumbing situation.

Offers of assistance are fended off by Sam with thank you but no thank you because of liability issues in case of injury, the church cannot cover lay personnel working in the church.

46

After dismissing the congregation, Sam rushes back to the hallway outside the sacristy and finds the other three pretty much where she left them huddled together in silence except for incoherent mumbling of prayers. The scene is reminiscent of something from the Blair Witch project. Scared people loudly praying gripped by fear unable to remove themselves from their location.

Sam immediately wonders why Sister is coming from the direction of the crime scene. How long has Sister been away from the nursery. Did she kill Fr. Santos? Did her controlled crush on the handsome young priest reduce her to murder?

"OK, listen up," says Sam in a commanding voice. "Everybody, stand up, grab each other's hand and follow me out to the nave to wait for the police." Obediently, they follow Sam like nursery school kids in a line holding each other's hand resembling a herd of elephants marching trunks to tails.

Reaching the nave Sam dials the police thinking, here we go again. Her next call is to Grace. She tells her the important thing first, "Grace, Fr. Santos is dead."

"You've got to be kidding me. What is this open season on priests at St. Francis de Sales?"

"Get back to that sacristy and take as many photos as you can. We have got to find the connection between these two murders," says Grace in a determined voice.

The address of the crime scene is still fresh in the minds of local law enforcement and emergency personnel, so when the nine-one-one operator hears the address of the church she immediately routes Sam's call to Detective Keating.

"What the fu—" the rest of his response is cut short. The expletives he is thinking he doesn't say aloud because all the calls at the police station are recorded. Instead, he says to the operator, "Are you sure?"

"The caller says that Fr. Santos has been shot and appears non-responsive in his office," says the nine-one-one operator.

"Call the ambulance. I'm heading over to the church now." Already stymied by the lack of a perpetrator for the death of one priest at that location, homicide detective Keating finds himself faced with another priest's death in that very same sacristy.

These two deaths must be connected, says Keating to himself as he speeds through the evening rush hour traffic in the west valley of Mesa, Arizona. Who kills priests? Is there a vigilante in the community?

47

Once again, the majesty of the nave strikes Keating as he steps into the foyer of the church. The vivid colors of gold, reds and purple, and the relief statues present quite the contrast from the modern whitewashed walls of his Baptist church. His eyes roam over to the four people huddled on the first pew.

"Hold it, what are you doing here?" Keating says to Sam with furrowed brow.

"I work in the nursery alongside Sister Mary Margaret," answers Sam proudly.

Turning to the rest of the group Keating says sharply, "Where is the crime scene?"

"I'll show you," pipes up Sam.

Keating addresses the three-church staff, "Don't go far I have questions." His command wasted on them since they are still in the grips of shock unable to move from the pew. He grabs Sam by the arm and heads off to the sacristy.

"Is this hallway always so dimly lit?" asks Keating straining to take in his surroundings while struggling to detect any changes since his last visit. Sam doesn't respond her mind focused on the gruesome scene she is about to relive.

Reaching the sacristy doorway Sam stops, Keating peers in first. Sam turned on the lights earlier when she photographed the crime scene. There on the floor is Fr. Santos with three bullet holes in his chest and a startled yet very dead look in his eyes. The rest of the evening at the church goes pretty much as expected with extensive police questioning.

The forensic team brush past Sam to join Keating in the sacristy. Sam pulls out her cell and texts Grace an update of the situation including crime scene photos before returning to the nave to wait with the others. Some thirty minutes later, Keating appears in the nave his gray hair in disarray, his face lined with worry.

"Who found the body?" asks Keating looking intently at the array of potential suspects.

The seminarian his lower lip trembling says, "I came over to the church from the rectory. I moved into the rectory this morning," moving his head up and down before continuing, "I can't believe this is real, who is killing us?" he stuffs the knuckles from his right hand between his teeth and bites down.

"Is this unusual to have the lights in the hallway off," asks Keating still addressing the seminarian.

"Yes, no, I don't know," flustered his face flushes red, "when I entered the church, I flipped on the hall lights and noticed the sacristy was also dark. I wondered if Fr. Santos was already in the nave."

He stops talking and sits eyes glazed for such a long-time that it prompts Keating to asks, "What did you do next?"

The seminarian bends slightly at the waist and rocks back and forth before holding out his arm to reenact his movements, "I reach my arm around the open sacristy door," he stops again his chest heaves up and down. "I, ugh, oh God," reliving the trauma his breathing quickens to the point of near hyperventilation.

"Take it easy, Father," says Keating resting a hand on the young man's shoulder to comfort him. The passage of three minutes calms the seminarian enough to continue, "I feel for the wall switch and turn on the office lights." He turns his head away from detective Keating as warm tears escape his already moist eyes.

The seminarian inhales deeply and uses the sleeve of his cassock to wipe his face. "That's when I, I, I see him lying on the floor in a pool of blood," he immediately makes the sign of the cross and lowers his head to his hands. Then he says, "Oh god, no one has given him the last rites." He gulps down air as an automatic reflex causes him to rise from his seat.

Detective Keating grabs his forearm, "I'm sorry, Father, that will have to wait until the crime scene technicians have finished their work."

As if hearing the words crime scene for the first time the young man's body falls rigid and he sits back down with a befuddled look in his eyes.

"Did you enter the room, Father?"

"What? Uh no." Then in a low whisper he says, "I've never seen a murdered body before."

Acknowledging his distress, Keating says, "Hold on just a little while longer, Father. What did you do next?"

"I ran to the nave to get the organist. On our way back to the sacristy, we bumped into Sister Mary Margaret coming from the direction of the sacristy."

Turning toward Sister Mary Margaret Keating asks, "Where were you coming from?"

"The garden on my way back to the nursery to close up before going home."

"Can anyone verify this?"

"To my knowledge, no one saw me in the garden."

Sam gives an account of her movements that evening, "I was in the nursery until the last child was picked up at six-fifteen. I looked for Sister to say good night, not finding her I gather my belongings and head up to the main level when the seminarian and the organist run past me."

"And I take it with your level of curiosity you follow them?" remarks Keating snidely.

"Of course, but only to be of help?" says Sam contorting her face into the most innocent angelic look that she can.

"How do you know they needed help?"

"A deduction based on the panicked look on their faces and the speed at which they were running," spouts Sam smugly causing Keating to roll his eyes.

The four, still potential suspects, are held by detective Keating just a little longer, then are told they can go home but not to leave town.

48

Sam informs Grace by texts, abandoning the earbud thing after Sam's muttering to herself evoked words like crazy, senile, and batty to describe her behavior. Hobbs is on his way home until news of Fr. Santos' death turns him around forcing him to meet his friends at Sam's house for additional information. He speeds across town longing to be at the crime scene unfortunately he knows better than to show up at another one of Keating's investigations.

One by one the five friends arrive carrying takeaway containers from at least five different restaurants, each person catering to his individual taste. "Things haven't been the same since you got a job, Sam," comments Hobbs carrying his double order of burgers and fries to the end of the island remembering her home-cooked meals.

When all the plates are filled, drinks retrieved, and everyone is seated comfortably around the island, the first few minutes are consumed with chewing, swallowing, and sounds of enjoyment.

"Personally, I feel this murder will give us the break we need," blurts out Grace. Her comment turning everyone's head in her direction their eating utensils poised mid-air.

"I agree Grace. Santos has a history we can delve into, perhaps there is a connection with Francisco that we don't know about."

"I am sure that the murders must be connected, two priests die in the same church less than a week apart, that's no coincidence. Why? And most importantly who is behind this?" adds Margot. No one responds to Margot just the sound of thoughtful chewing can be heard until dessert is pulled out of the fridge.

Hot coffee and dessert are taken over to the family room where the electronic Lucite screen pops up from a credenza bearing a clean window waiting to receive clues learned from the Santos murder.

"OK, how was he killed? Did they find the murder weapon?" asks Grace as all heads turn toward Sam.

"He was shot, three times in the chest, no gun found," explains Sam looking worn out and confused. She grabs a fork full of dessert while giving a play-by-play account of her discovery.

"How could this possibly be the same killer? One victim was stabbed and the other shot?" asks Maria-Teresa.

"I must admit," says Hobbs, "there must be two killers unless the motive for the deaths is different. Why would the same killer change his or her method of killing?"

"Maybe the killer is trying to throw us off the scent by using different weapons," suggests Sam. The air is filled with silence as they ponder Sam's comment.

Grace adds, "Why kill two priests who barely knew each other?"

Chewing stops and Margot asks, "Is there anything that Francisco and Santos have in common?"

Shoveling the last bit of his second piece of cheesecake in his mouth Hobbs shakes his head and says, "Damn, Keating is really under the gun. I feel kind of sorry for the bastard." Then as quickly as the sentiment rolls off his tongue his competitiveness marches in behind it. "I think we need to solve this case for Keating. Showing him up in his own backyard will make me rest better at night," states Hobbs with a sinister grin.

Margot pipes up with, "Whew, I am glad things are back to normal. You had me worried thinking you were going soft for Keating. I agree we have to solve this case because as a whole we are better detectives than Keating."

Grace rolls her eyes, "Now that you kids are finished, Sam, tell us again everything that happened this evening." When Sam finishes for the second time, Grace says, "List all the questionable things, people, or incidents connected to these murders. We have established that Santos did not know the first murder victim, although they posed a striking physical resemblance to each other from behind."

After reviewing all the relevant information, they narrow the list down to two, Sister Mary Margret and Lea Cardenas. Maria-Teresa says, "From where I'm sitting, the only common denominator between our two suspects is Fr. Santos. Everything still leads back to the church."

"I don't know about these two suspects. They seem too obvious, too neat," suggests Grace turning to Hobbs. Receiving no support she continues, "I agree Fr. Santos is definitely a lynch pin, but I think we are over-looking something that is staring us in the face," says Grace now pacing in front of the floor-to-ceiling windows.

Grace's hunch that everything is too neat and tidy causes more silence among the group, furrowed brows, and head-scratching. "How can you disagree, Grace? Sister has a crush on Santos, and Lea is his long-time lover," remarks Sam looking confused.

"Jealousy is a tried-and-true motive for murder. Of these two people, one of them killed Santos. We just have to find out which one," says Margot resolute in her reasoning.

"My money is on Bishop O'Leary," says Hobbs.

"Are you saying Bishop O'Leary is the killer?" asks Maria-Teresa a worried look on her face thinking one more person will shatter her faith.

"No, no. He's the one person who knows both priests and may be able to give us more insight," answers Hobbs again relaying his less than hospitable encounter with the bishop. "He is hiding something about Francisco's murder for sure and he might know something about the Santos murder too."

"Why don't we just pay the bishop a visit," says Maria-Teresa hesitantly still reeling from just having all her beliefs about the catholic church turned upside down.

Looking at Hobbs, Margot says, "The bishop wasn't that forthcoming the last time you dropped in on him. You think he'll be any different with us?"

"Sam is pretty good at hearing confessions. I'm sure she can get him to talk," chuckles Hobbs. Everyone has a hearty laugh reimagining the image of Sam doubled up on the floor of a tiny confessional.

"All joking aside, you may have something there, Hobbs. This string of deaths all starts with Francisco, who was sent by O'Leary. It stands to reason that O'Leary has to know what's behind all this," adds Grace.

"Yes! I think it's high time we pay the Bishop a friendly visit," says Sam.

49

The morning gathering of the four ladies is like herding cats due to miscommunication and oversleeping. Sam's Land Rover finally leaves her driveway everyone comfortably seated engaging in deep discussion concerning the possible outcome of their meeting. The archdiocese remains the same sterile beige stucco building inside as when Hobbs visited complete with the row of hard wooden chairs in the anti-office.

The rotund bishop enters his anti-office dressed in a black suit and clerical collar to find his receptionist absent but replaced by four determined faced women. His recognition of them from their past involvement in other community exploits gives him an instant headache.

The circles under his eyes and deeply drawn lines on his face scream lack of sleep. His slumped shoulders give all indication of a person who has given up, thrown in the towel, and admitted defeat. Exhaling a sigh of relief he asks, "What do you want?" over his shoulder as the ladies follow him into his office.

Quickly, Sam takes in the décor of his office noticing first the large number of books in the built-in bookcases on three walls. Through a half-open closet door, the bright colors of formal vestments complete with a staff contrast sharply against the black cassocks and suits hanging next to them. The light pouring through the windows accentuates the worry lines on the bishop's face. Grace's question snaps her back to the task at hand.

"Who was Fr. Francisco? And please don't feign ignorance," says Grace forcefully while the other three stare at him from their positions on three sides of him like herding dogs staring at a stray calf ready to block his exit if necessary.

He looks at each woman with a bleak expression and slinks around his desk to plop into his high-back desk chair. There is no fear in his demeanor, just secrets causing him weariness. All his secrets have done is produce death.

In a resigned voice, the bishop says, "Fine. He was a private investigator. The archdiocese hired him." The beleaguered bishop rests his face in his hands for a few seconds before continuing, "I've already told the police." His head lowers then raising his chin up briefly he says, "Nothing matters anymore, the death of two people on my watch seals my fate. My diocese is helping another diocese provide a sting operation."

"A what, why?" asks Maria-Teresa thinking her lifetime faith is dissolving before her eyes, and the others exchange confused looks.

"Apparently, there is a couple going from parish-to-parish blackmailing priests. The female gets them in compromising situations and demands weekly blackmail payments to keep quiet. The diocese wants to catch them."

"Other than that, was Francisco looking into anything else that could have caused his death?"

"We didn't think so," he looks away from them then adds, "I guess we were wrong."

"What's Francisco's real name?"

"Frank Hester, a detective out of northern California. We sent his body back there after the autopsy."

"What do you know about a journal that is kept in a safe deposit box?"

O'Leary's head snaps up from his hands his eyes wide with surprise. "How do you know about that?" Then just as suddenly his shoulders drop down to signal his resignation with trying to hide the whole mess he says, "Never mind I suppose it doesn't matter who knows now."

"So, it's true he was communicating with you through the journal?"

"Yes, Fr. Francisco was communicating with me through the journal. I don't even know where the journal is now." No one tells the Bishop they are in possession of the journal.

"Who is SMM from the journal?"

"Sister Mary Margaret," says O'Leary in a low voice.

"Why didn't you use a real priest to do the investigation?" asks Sam.

"Priests gossip like village women on wash day," says the Bishop hanging his head. Then lifting it again with a pleading look he says, "We need someone with no allegiance to the church, someone with no dog in the fight, someone with no axe to grind, someone—" O'Leary is about to go on with another analogy when Sam says, "OK we got it."

"Do you have any idea why he was killed?" asks Grace.

Shaking his head he says, "Not a clue."

"We also need to know how much you know about Lea Cardenas, Sister Mary Margaret and Fr. Santos; they could be the lynchpin to the murders." O'Leary divulges everything he knows about Santos and Sister Mary Margaret. He admits he knows nothing of Lea Cardenas.

"What does the sting investigation have to do with St. Francis de Sales?" asks Maria-Teresa.

"We got word that the couple is operating in the Mesa area."

"Why didn't you call in the Feds? Isn't blackmail their sort of thing," asks Margot.

Not making eye contact with anyone he says, "We couldn't risk the story getting out to the public. The plan to nab the couple seemed simple. Put a good-looking person in the church undercover and catch the perpetrators. But now all of this death, their blood is on my hands. I sanctioned this fiasco. My career is over."

"Have you found the couple?"

With red-rimmed eyes, he looks up at them and says in a tone that can only be described as a moan "No" then he lays his head on his desk and weeps. The ladies quietly excuse themselves.

50

Sam sits with her iPad and coffee at her kitchen island, trolling the morning news. Articles with headlines like **Priest Killer on the Prowl**. **Twice Hit Church Marked for Murder**. **Murder by Prayer** are popping up all over the internet. The latest killing fills the air waves as the newscasters and journalists speculate whether there is a serial killer on the loose.

Sam puts down her iPad and heads over to the church. Sam and friends feel the answer to solving these murders is still hiding somewhere in the St. Francis de Sales Catholic church. Police patrol cars greet her as she turns onto the once quiet street where the church is located.

Those curious parishioners who filled the pews after the first death, no longer come to church. Making her way to the nursery Sam is very surprised to see Sister Mary Margaret zombie-like in her demeanor but there at the church nonetheless.

"Are you alright? What are you doing here?"

"That's what Bishop O'Leary said this morning when he called. If there is a madman on the loose, I must protect the children. Besides about a half dozen parents pulled their kids out this morning. Afraid for their safety and all," answers Sister.

"Looks like it will be a light day, why don't you go home and get some rest?" suggest Sam.

"I can't rest. I keep seeing Fr. Santos' dead body lying there on the floor." Sister lowers her head to her hands and her shoulders move up and down silently as she cries. Sam puts her arm around Sister's shoulder and leads her to the nursery office to sit down.

Sam waits while Sister composes herself, "You may be the key to this investigation. You have been at the church the longest and you know Fr. Santos well. Do you have a hunch about anyone who could do such a thing?"

Dabbing at her eyes with a tissue Sister says in a hopeful voice, "I told the police I think Rosalea Cardenas killed Fr. Santos. I guess they'll investigate." With a shrug of her shoulders, she says, "I don't know, maybe I am wrong."

"What makes you think it was her?"

"Well, they are very close, Lea and Fr. Santos. You know I see the looks that pass between them, the whispers, the early mornings, and late evenings together. The way people carry on who are having an affair." Then to substantiate her knowledge of how people act when having an affair, she straightens her posture and adds, "I read books."

In Sam's mind, Sister relays her suspicions with a tinge of judgment in her voice, causing Sam to wonder if she is casting doubt away from herself or if jealousy has anything to do with her suspicions. Sister realizing how she must sound and says as a follow on, "Just because I'm a nun doesn't mean I don't know things."

As an afterthought with her nose slightly raised upward, she continues in a subdued but still defiant voice, "Besides, I told you I think I saw her in the church that morning."

A musing smile curls Sam's lips looking at Sister's mouth fixed in a defiant pout and her back ramrod straight in righteous indignation. Hiding her amusement Sam asks as earnestly as she can, "Is there anyone else or anything at all you can think of that might help us find the killer?"

The Sister is deep in thought when one of the five kids they have left comes barging into the office. The truth-telling is interrupted. For the rest of the day, things seem almost normal, excluding the twelve absent little voices.

51

The usual investigative team assembles at Sam's about to delve into any clues, speculations or evidence that may have gleaned from their sources that day. These sessions keep Hobbs apprised of their investigation and affords him the opportunity to give, in his mind, his expert opinion.

The sound of Sam's doorbell rings causes everyone to look around mentally confirming all the members of the investigative team are present and accounted for. Clearly surprised by the sound they remain seated until the doorbell rings for a second time. All eyes turn to Sam whose facial expression shows as much surprise as her friends.

"Well, don't just sit there, go see who it is?" says Hobbs who is fixated on the dinner that is waiting to be served. Sam pulls herself up from the sofa padding off down the hall to the front door. She swings it open wide forgetting about the newly installed camera.

"James?" she says at James Wilding's thin frame, sunken chest, greasy ungroomed hair standing in her doorway. "What are you doing here? Book club meeting isn't for a couple of weeks," says Sam forcing a smile noticing he is anxiously shifting his weight to the balls of his feet as if his body is at the starting line of a foot race his hands working nervously at his sides.

"I was so worried when I heard the news about Fr. Santos. I was just wondering how you all are holding up?"

"Fine. We're just about to have dinner." There is nothing in Sam's DNA that will ever allow her to be less than a gracious host. "Would you like to join us?" Halfheartedly she extends the invitation hoping he is gracious enough to turn her down.

Without answering her question, he brushes past her, knocking her back on her heels, and heads for the family room. Regaining her footing she follows him wondering why he is so eager to join them. Walking behind him Sam reaches the family room in time to see her other guest all turn and stare at the interloper.

"Hey everybody. I just had to come as soon as I heard about Fr. Santos. I umm, is there anything I can do?" says James again shifting from foot to foot in the doorway.

"Who is this yahoo?" asks Hobbs in his usual loud unhospitable manner, mincing no words.

Sam walks around James into the room, "Detective Hobbs this is James Wilding, he joined our book club a short time ago." James's eyes widen with fear and a flash of panic clouds his face.

Hobbs gives the young man a cold unsmiling up and down perusal before nodding an acknowledgment of his presence. Using every muscle in his body to keep himself from running, James slowly enters the room and perches on the edge of the sofa.

"Are, are you here on official business Detective?" asks James trying to sound mildly curious and tamp the fear in his voice.

"Would I be eating dinner if I was on official business?" Hobbs says flatly as Sam gives him a plate of food. The four women turn their attention to James who squirms like a bug caught in the web of a watchful spider.

"Ha, ha," James lets out a nervous laugh, realizes how stupid he must sound. His erratic behavior puts him under the watchful eyes of detective Hobbs who is an expert at eating and watching, a skill honed during hours of surveillance work.

"Oh no, nothing for me, thanks," says James declining the offer of food from Sam. During the uncomfortable moments that follow James becomes aware of a little nervous twitch of his mouth and he shifts his body on the sofa, turning his head away from the group rather than place his hand on his mouth to stop the movement.

Hoping no one else notices his nervous movements he says, head slightly turned, "You must be devastated hearing of this second death."

The ladies all say yes or shake their heads in the affirmative while chewing staring at their guest, exchanging questioning glances among themselves. Maria-Teresa is the only one showing sadness for the death of Fr. Santos. The rest of the ladies are more shocked than sad and now they ponder the reason for this unexpected visitor.

"James, tell us about yourself, are you married or single?" asks Maria-Teresa.

For some reason, this question catches him off guard. "No. I mean yes."

Grace raises her eyebrow. Hobbs' eyes narrow. Margot says, "You don't know if you are married?"

"Ha, ha, uhm," James gives another nervous chuckle.

"Where is your wife? Does she work or does she stay home? Do you have any kids?" asks Sam.

James fidgets in his seat and quickly says, "My life is dull. I um, I'm just your average grease monkey at Eastgate."

"Is that the airpark?" asks Sam.

Instead of delving any further into his life, he looks off to one side and asks, "Who found the dead priest? Do they know who the killer is?" his mouth still twitching at the corners. Maria-Teresa's sadness about the priest's death doesn't go unnoticed and he asks her, "What do you think happened?"

Chewing stops, everyone turns to Maria-Teresa who looks very much like the weakest link in the herd as she looks down at her lap refusing to answer. Receiving no response, James plucks up his courage, "Do the police have any suspects? Do they know how he got shot?"

Everyone stops mid-action, mouths open, narrow eyes they look at James. "Shot? Who said the priest was shot?" asks Hobbs beating Grace to the question.

"That's not true?" asks James whose face immediately turns red realizing his faux pas. He is also unable to control the perspiration glistening on his nose and forehead. Perhaps wanting to add credence to his previous statement he says, "I am sure I heard that on the news."

"The police have not released any details about the death to the news media. You seem to know a lot about this killing. Why is that, where are you getting your information?" asks Hobbs his senses tingling his brain firing on all cylinders. James realizes he may have overplayed his hand and he quickly recants his statement.

"Sorry, I may have gotten the details mixed up with another news story," as abruptly as he came in James jumps up and says, "well, I really need to get going. I'll see you all soon for the book club meeting." He walks toward the front door and Sam follows him to make sure he is gone.

When Sam returns to the room, she finds Hobbs thoughtfully stroking his mustache, "Just a hunch but I think we can add another name to our lists of suspects," he says with finality.

"I certainly think he is strange. I thought so the very first time he showed up here, but a suspect?" says Margot looking for support among her friends.

"Why is he acting so jittery like a person with something to hide," says Grace still not fully on board with Hobbs's train of thinking. "I don't know, Hobbs, as far as we know he has absolutely no connection to the church or the priests," says Grace in an unsure voice.

"Maybe it's the murders? A killer on the loose can cause nervous erratic behavior," says Maria-Teresa always approaching everything with compassion.

"But why should he be nervous, he doesn't really know either one of the dead people. He only met Fr. Santos once, why react so strongly to his death," asks Sam directing her comment to Maria-Teresa.

Hobbs talks over Maria-Teresa and says, "I think he's much too eager to find how what we know. Do we know anything about this yahoo?"

"Clearly not enough. He works nights at some airpark as a mechanic. We don't even know where he lives. Let's put him on the top of our suspects' list," says Grace finally giving in to Hobbs' hunch and the gnawing in her gut.

"We need to check him out. Something about that guy makes the hair stand up on my neck," says Grace indirectly giving the ladies their next assignment.

52

After dinner, Sam and Grace start their search into the life and times of James Wilding. The internet brings up a few James Wildings, none of them fit the book club James, either in physical appearance, age, or location.

"This is getting us nowhere. We've spent hours searching and we got nothing."

"He works nights but where?"

"Uhm, wait I am sure he said an airpark. Quick google airparks in the area if I hear the name, I'll know it," vows Grace.

"Eastgate Airpark is the only one in this area."

"That's it! Grab your things, let's pay our friend a visit. He always shows up on our doorstep unannounced, it's time we repay the favor," says Grace.

The small box shape building is about a twenty-minute drive from Sam's house. They pull into a deserted parking lot at the front of the building where through the chain linked fence separating the airfield from the parking lot a lone Lear jet sits on the tarmac. Through the front window of the one level building, Sam sees a well-lit office space where a young woman sits behind a counter laughing with a young man in coveralls. When the ladies enter the front door, the two young people turn to stare at them with confused looks on their faces.

"Hello, we're looking for a friend of ours. James Wilding, he's a mechanic here."

The young man chuckles causing the young woman to snicker. "You must have the wrong place," she says turning around immediately to resume her flirting.

Sam is immediately incensed that this slip of a girl is dismissing them and bangs on the counter, "Does James Wilding work here or not?" demands Sam.

Annoyed the young woman turns around her frosty green eyes lock on Sam. She pops up with such force that her chair slides back banging the wall behind her as she leans over the counter her face just inches from Sam's and says, "I told you, you must have the wrong place. I never heard of him."

"Are you sure James Wilding doesn't work here? He's a tall lanky white boy, in his late twenties," asks Grace more politely.

"Are you deaf, dumb, or just old. Of course, I am sure. If you are not interested in chartering a plane, I have work to do," pointing to the door. The young man claps his hands loudly for his companion's performance throwing back his head letting out, 'burn' mixed with a loud guffaw.

Grace having the foresight to see a possibly bad confrontation on the horizon says, "Sorry, we bothered you. Perhaps we have the wrong location," as she pulls Sam by the arm exiting the office.

Sam is giving the young woman the evil eye over her shoulder and continues to stare while mimicking the young woman in a falsetto voice she says, "If you don't want to charter a plane—"

"Oh, Sam, come on. Just stop it."

"She's being rude. She didn't have to get such an attitude."

Grace spins around placing both hands on Sam's shoulders shaking her lightly, "Listen to what she said, he doesn't work there, and she never heard of him. HE LIED."

Sam stops talking, letting Grace's words sink in and they both smile. Arms interlock they practically skip to the car chanting "He lied, he lied, he lied." Now, they just need to find out why.

53

News of Fr. Santos' death hits the parishioners of the St. Francis de Sales Catholic church hard. Volunteers drape black cloth over all the statues, the altar and the doors. A sadness prevails throughout the church and rectory.

The book club ladies are more intrigued than ever by the murders. Two people with nothing in common die in the same church just a short time apart. Frank Hester's background does not intersect with Joao Santos' life in any way. The more the ladies piece things together the more it seems like the first murder may be a case of mistaken identity. The intended target could be Fr. Santos all along?

"We need to do a deep dive into Santos' everyday activities. The obvious person to help us is Sister Mary Margaret, SMM. That is the same thing Frank Hester, aka Fr. Francisco, thought."

Grace takes on the task of questioning Sister and they set out immediately for the church. Sister Mary Margaret will give anything to close the nursery, but she realizes working parents have no other place to take their children. She braves her own grief and opens the nursery every morning on time.

The sound of laughter and squeals from the few children still enrolled is the only reminder that life goes on. When a tragedy hits, there are generally two types of mourners. Those who want to talk about the tragedy and those who don't. Lucky for Grace and Sam, Sister is in a talkative mood.

"So many things will have to be rearranged or halted," says Sister as she nervously moves things around in the nursery. "The Bishop says he will send over someone permanent next week."

"What are some of the things that need handling? What did Fr. Santos do all day?"

"Well, there's the nursery addition project but you know all about that." She puts her hand up to tick off the other things she knows about. "The spiritual counseling of the parishioners, some in their homes and some here at the church. Of course, there are the church finances." Then she stops as if remembering something important.

"You know he was always very busy going and coming," she says frowning, "but I don't know what made him that busy."

"You mentioned counseling, who did he counsel and when?"

"I'll have to look in his daily diary. It should be in his office." Sam stays behind while Grace and Sister go to the sacristy. "I don't know if the police have it. He keeps it hidden in the cabinet with the wine."

"How do you know where he keeps it?"

"Well, let's see now, I had to retrieve it for him once when he was out of the office on church business. He needed to check the time of a counseling appointment."

"Was he in the habit of leaving the book behind?"

"I don't think so, it was just that once. He was to meet Elaine Fisher at her house for counseling. I assume she is a shut in," answering Grace's questions as she feels around in the wine cabinet for the diary.

Sister brings the diary out from behind three rows of wine; Grace opens it and searches for names and addresses. Grace takes photos of all the pages starting one month before Fr. Francisco, aka Frank Hester's death, and all the pages up to Santos' death.

"Sister, did you show this to the police?"

"No, it slipped my mind until just now when it came up during our conversation. I am surprised that it is still here after their search of this office."

"Well, I think you need to replace it. If the police do find out about its existence, please don't tell them you showed it to me."

54

"Thank you again, Sister, for your help."

"Just catch whoever did this," says Sister gathering those few students for outside play.

"Well, I guess by that pleased look on your face, you found out something," exclaims Sam eager to hear about the clue.

On the way up the stairs to the main level, "Finally, I feel like we are not going around in circles," says Grace as she explains what Sister found in the sacristy wine cabinet to Sam who is practically jumping up and down begging for more information.

Once in the car Grace shows Sam the pages of the diary, "Flip that page back, look," says Sam pointing to the name Elaine Fisher. "That name is listed three times a week every week before and after Frank Hester's death."

"Come on, we need to speak with Elaine Fisher," says Grace pointing her car in the direction of the address written in Fr. Santos' diary. The atmosphere in the car is charged with excitement, the women giggle like schoolgirls preparing for a first date at the possibility of finding out anything that will move their investigation forward.

Following the navigation system's instruction, the ladies find themselves at an apartment complex not far from the church.

"I like the Ocher trim in Moss green," says Sam referring to the exterior paint of the three separate stucco buildings. Grace studies the group of buildings and surmises each building has three floors with two apartments on each floor.

After parking the car, they make their way on foot up a floral-lined path to the entrance. On one side of the entrance to the apartment complex sits a row of eighteen silver mailboxes mounted on a pedestal. After scrolling the names written on the mailboxes, they find there is only one tenant with the last name Fisher.

The label on the mailbox says E. and J. Fisher. "Do you think Elaine has a roommate?" asks Sam.

"Well, she has someone living with her. Since they have the same last name, they are either related or she's married," answers Grace.

A few men wearing large brimmed sun hats and long sleeve shirts tend to the landscape as the ladies pass them on their way to apartment number seven. They knock. Waiting a few minutes with no response from inside the apartment they knock again. As is the case in cramped housing there is one neighbor who knows everything that goes on with all the residents in their building.

This know-it-all just happens to live next door to Elaine Fisher and peers out of her front door when she hears the ladies knock on Elaine's door. The neighbor opens her door wide just as the ladies are about to leave, she leans out and says, "Nobody's home."

The ladies turn toward the helpful voice and Sam says, "Hello! Is this where Elaine Fisher lives?" The neighbor shakes her head up and down jiggling her hair curlers slightly. "You know when she'll be back?"

This time the neighbor shakes her head side to side before saying, "I haven't seen her since yesterday."

"Does she get many visitors?"

"Just the good-looking man that comes when her husband is gone." The word husband confirms Grace's suggestion at the mailbox.

"What does the visitor look like?" asks Grace in a stern authoritarian voice.

"Are you with the police, I want to be helpful to the police?" her tiny eyes blink rapidly.

"We are helping them, and you can help us," says Sam in a syrupy sweet voice playing the good cop role.

The neighbor describes Fr. Santos to a tee right down to the green and yellow baseball cap displaying the Brazil soccer team emblem. According to the neighbor, he dresses in street clothes. That tidbit coupled with Santos' reputation with the ladies, tells them that his counseling may be more than just spiritual.

Just to make sure they are not drawing the wrong conclusion and perhaps the priest visits for legitimate reasons Grace asks, "Does Elaine have any physical disability," the neighbor gives a hearty laugh, "Elaine is definitely no shut in."

55

Later that evening at the nightly debriefing meeting, the four ladies sit in the family room trying to make heads or tails out of the latest turn of events when the doorbell rings. Not expecting anyone else Margot says, "Gosh Sam, do you have a sign on your house that says Do Drop In?"

"Is Hobbs or anyone else coming?" asks Grace.

"No and no. It's probably just the church folk door-to-door canvassing again. I'll get rid of them," says Sam always forgetting to look at the newly installed exterior cameras.

She opens the door, her face fixed in stone to convey her level of irritation at this interruption when she hears, "Surprise" from the lean young man on the other side of the door.

"James? Look, now is not a good time for a visit," as she half-turns away from him to shut the door.

"Now is a very good time," remarks James putting his hand against the door to prevent it from closing. In what is fast becoming his usual style, he brushes past Sam and walks confidently toward the family room. Slamming the front door behind her she pads after him until there is another persistent ring of the doorbell causing her to stop.

"What the hell is this Grand Central Station?" says Sam as she swivels on her heels to retrace her steps to the door. Swinging the door open wide, her hand planted firmly on her hip she looks up at two uniform police officers who also enter her home without an invitation.

"Do come in," says Sam in a sarcastic voice to the backs of the officers who are headed further down the hallway. Their voices are loud and officious sounding when they turn to her to say, "We'd like to ask you a few questions. Is anyone else here?"

"What is this about? I am entertaining a few friends."

"Please ma'am, this won't take long."

Now, Sam takes the lead as the officers follow her to the family room. The first thing Sam notices upon reaching the family room with the police is James's absence. She shoots a puzzled look at Grace who nods her head toward the bathroom.

"What can we do for you officers?" asks Sam.

"How well do you know Elaine Fisher?" Sam shoots a curious look at Grace before saying, "I don't know her. I have never even seen her."

"Why did you visit her?"

"We didn't exactly visit, no one answered the door. We spoke with her neighbor," says Grace knowing how important it is to use the correct words to describe a situation when speaking with the law.

"Why all the questions," asks Sam.

"Elaine Fisher is dead. Do you know anything about her murder?"

"Dead? How? When?" says Sam in disbelief.

"How did you know to check on Elaine?" asks Grace.

"We got an anonymous tip. I thought you ladies might know something about that?"

"Murder? Are you sure it's murder?" asks Sam still unable to grasp the officer's words.

"It is unlikely she strangled herself," answers the police officer in a tone that reeks of professional snobbery. Sam and Grace look at each other stunned. Margot and Maria-Teresa are not as affected by the news since neither of them have been told who she is or why Grace and Sam visited her.

The police end their short visit with the following words of advice, "We've heard about you ladies—stay out of this investigation." Then they make their way to the front door.

James is down the hall listening intently to the conversation with the police. He cannot hear every word spoken but hears enough to cause perspiration to bead on his forehead and wet his palms.

As soon as he hears the police leave, James wipes his face and hands on a towel and makes his way back to the family room, his initial confident and belligerent attitude changes to meek, "Was that the police?" Sam is the only one who responds with a silent nod of her head. "What did they want?" presses James.

"Another member of the St. Francis de Sales church has been murdered. They just wanted to know if we know her." Without another word, James turns around and heads for the front door leaving everyone stunned.

"That boy is very strange, never let him in this house again," says Maria-Teresa.

"He never asks the identity of the dead person. Why not?" interjects Margot.

"Do you feel like death is chasing us?" asks Maria-Teresa.

56

Before anyone can respond to Maria-Teresa's question about death, Sam's doorbell chimes for the third time. This time she opens the door to Hobbs' asinine grin that makes her wonder if he is trying to be adorable or supercilious. He wastes no time asking his favorite question. "What's for dinner?"

"And here I thought you came for the friendly family atmosphere," says Sam stepping aside to let him pass.

"What's got your face and mood in the toilet," asks Hobbs as they make their way to the family room.

Sam sighs, "Nothing, just a night for uninvited guests."

Reaching the family room shedding his gun and holster he asks, "Who was that tearing out of your driveway like he was on fire?"

"That was James Wilding, you know the 'yahoo' who dropped by uninvited the last time you were here."

"Something about that guy tingles my 'Spidey senses'. Stay clear of him," warns Hobbs in a parental tone. Hobbs knows his surrogate family members are prone to involvement in dangerous often life-threatening situations.

He heads straight for the food then makes himself comfortable on the sofa with his plate. The ladies fill him in on the latest murder victim who also happens to be connected to the church. With these many murders in this short period of time, Hobbs is unable to hide the panic-stricken look on his face.

"Look, you know I don't have the flexibility at work that I used to have. Please be careful." He chews thoughtfully then says, "That archdiocese is definitely hiding something. All these murders come home to roost under the umbrella of the St. Francis de Sales Catholic church. That bishop guy is at the head of the whole thing I bet you." Then he promptly returns his attention to clearing his piece of chicken from its bone.

Grace says, "Yeah and that nosy neighbor of Elaine's may be able to shed light on her death."

Maria-Teresa comes alive at the possibility of interviewing the neighbor, "You may be on to something, let's all visit Elaine's nosy neighbor."

Hearing Maria-Teresa's declaration Hobbs says, "Wait a minute. I don't want you all to go headlong into more danger."

As the words of warning roll off his tongue, he knows nothing he says will stop this crew. But he adds the following statement anyway, "Look, keep in constant contact with him from now on. I mean it!"

57

Elaine Fisher's apartment is in the second of the three buildings. "The buildings are well maintained, she must have a substantial income of some kind," says Margot admiring the landscaping and the newly painted building exteriors. They walk past the yellow crime scene tape crisscrossing the Moss green door to Elaine's apartment and Grace knocks on the nosy neighbor's door.

They hear movement inside the apartment for a few minutes before a pair of wide set eyes peer curiously through the sliver of glass on the side of her front door. Recognizing two of the ladies from their previous visit, she opens her door with an eager smile. Pink curlers dangle every time she moves her head while sprigs of loose bleached blonde hair pop out from them resembling little corkscrews.

She steps out of the apartment wearing a maroon and gold tracksuit with matching slippers the colors of the Arizona State University and pulls the door close behind her.

"I guess you heard," nodding her head toward the yellow tape she says without emotion arms folded across her ample chest. "I'm Annie, thought you'd be back with all that's going on."

"Hello, I'm Grace," stepping aside pointing to each of her companions as she introduces Sam, Maria-Teresa, and Margot, no handshakes are exchanged just nods all around.

"Yes, we heard about Elaine. We'd like to ask you some questions, do you mind terribly if we talk inside?"

Annie looks panicky at her closed door then back at the women, "I could use a little something to eat why don't we take a ride to the café," answers Annie surmising the information she has might merit a free meal. The women blink at her, wondering if she's forgotten she's wearing slippers and hair curlers.

"Perhaps another time we have a previous engagement and we're a little short on time," pipes up Margot a little embarrassed by Annie's appearance.

Sam gives Margot a sidelong glance and quickly adds, "Really, we only have a few questions. We won't be more than fifteen minutes."

Annie's attempt to wrangle a free meal fails and without a word, she opens the door to her apartment leaving the women to assume they are to follow her. She stands patiently inside, waiting for the ladies to join her. The soft hum of an air conditioner provides a backdrop for the deafening silence in the apartment while all eyes adjust to the sight of an unusually neat living room.

The open floor plan confirms that the rest of the apartment appears equally obsessively tidy with all visible walls unadorned.

Standing in awkward silence Maria-Teresa asks, "May we sit down?" she moves toward a chair but with no OK to sit, she stops. Annie still standing near the door studies the room like she's trying to unravel a puzzle as a pained look clouds her face.

Margot bored with this waste of valuable time launches in, "When was the last time you saw Elaine?"

"Two days before her death," answers Annie her face still in turmoil looking from sofa to armchair.

Ignoring Annie's discomfort Grace plunges on, "Did she live with anyone?"

"She lived with a man that I assume is her husband. They moved in about six months ago. He came back to the apartment late last night but didn't enter."

"Was he at home when the police found the body?"

"No, the police had to get the apartment manager to let them in. I don't know if either of them is employed. Never kept work hours, they never had visitors, well except one."

"Did you hear any unusual noises or fighting coming from their apartment?"

"Recently, they fought all the time. When I'm on my balcony and they have their slider open, I can hear quite a lot." All eyes move to the glass door leading to her balcony, but no one moves in fear of disturbing the Hoover marks on the carpet. "I can hear their music, TV, fights, and sometimes other intimate sounds."

"What were the fights about?"

"Every word wasn't clear, but he would say something about this is not the plan. How he's not a fool and that she better watch herself."

"What kind of plan?" asks Maria-Teresa.

Annie looks confused doesn't answer but adds, "I did hear something about another man."

"Was the other man's name mentioned?"

"No, not that I heard. I just assumed it was that guy I told you about the other day, the good-looking one in the baseball cap."

"The man she lived with, what's his name? What does he look like?"

"Well, let's see, he's a lanky young man not very friendly. I think I heard her call him James."

All the women turn to each other looking first alarmed then frightened at the name and description of Elaine's husband.

"What's the matter, did I say something wrong?" asks Annie.

"Not at all."

58

"You're not going to believe this," says Grace in a veiled attempt to hide her excitement talking over Hobbs' chance to say hello.

"What's got you so hyped," asks Hobbs punching the speaker button on his phone hoping whatever it is will not bring his surrogate family closer to danger. Telling them not to follow a lead is like telling a two-year-old not to have a temper tantrum.

"We're all here at Sam's, I'll put you on speaker. Where are you?" the question forces Hobbs to survey his small windowless office and the mound of cold case files taking up most of his desktop. He glances at the Think Positive poster depicting a kitten dangling from a branch looking down at a snarling dog one of two unofficial things adorning his office walls. Hanging just below the poster is a photo of his dream sailboat his eyes lingering for a few seconds longer on the boat, "I'm on the damn Riviera," he says sarcastically.

"Well, listen," says Grace ignoring his surly mood. "The neighbor confirms Elaine Fisher is married."

Hobbs' surly attitude results from his feeling of being trapped with no official murder cases to solve and without Turner to run interference between him and his captain the possibility of him getting fired looms over him like the sword of Damocles.

"Well, good for her that makes her husband a prime suspect. Who is he?" asks Hobbs flipping through a case file, showing only a mild interest in the conversation with Grace.

"Who's tall lanky jittery with fair hair?" yells Sam into the phone over Grace's shoulder using the anticipatory voice of a game show host. When she receives no response from Hobbs, she says, "It's James Wilding! He fits Elaine's husband's description."

"OK, so that general description fits that yahoo James, but his last name is Wilding not Fisher," says Hobbs shaking his head wondering if Grace and the ladies are slipping.

"Don't you understand!" says Grace in exasperation. "James lied about his job, what's to stop him from lying about his name. The murders are connecting," says Grace emphatically. "Oh Hobbs, get your head out of your butt, Elaine received regular visits from Fr. Santos, and she is no shut in."

Hobbs is not totally in agreement with what little he has heard preferring instead to read inadequate case notes from the folder open on his desk.

"Hobbs are you there, what do you think?"

"Umm, yeah."

The process of mentally preparing his rebuttal takes him more than a few minutes to formulate due to his inattentiveness during the conversation. A cell phone buzzes in Sam's home and all eyes look at Maria-Teresa who checks her phone, "Just got a text from Lea."

"Sorry Hobbs, give me a minute."

Grace turns to Maria-Teresa and asks, "What does she want?"

"Isn't she still a suspect?" asks Sam in the voice of a confused person tuning in mid-way through a movie.

"Well, she may very well be a suspect in the first murder. After all, jealousy is a strong motive. Could she have found out that Fr. Francisco was investigating her lover Santos. So, she kills him. Then she has a quarrel with Santos and shoots him. She kills Elaine, the new girlfriend in Santos' life."

"Case solved," says Sam popping a mini cookie in her mouth from the plate of treats on the table, chewing with satisfaction for both her case conclusion and the taste of her cookie.

"Let's not get ahead of ourselves. All the pieces could fit, but it doesn't explain the change in murder weapons. What does Lea want?" asks Grace.

"She wants me and Margot to come to the convent chapel in the morning. She doesn't say why."

"Look, you two need to be careful. Sam lays out a reasonable scenario giving truth to the theory that Lea could be a three-time murderer."

"Don't worry, we can handle this situation. She won't try anything in the convent," says Margot confidently flexing her arm muscles. Her arm movement garners eye rolls and a titter from the other ladies but does not instill the feeling of safety for anyone else in the room.

"Maybe you're right. We'll keep in touch if it'll make you feel better," concedes Maria-Teresa.

"Just send a text every hour. Send one asterisk if you are in danger and Sam and I will rush over with the calvary," says Grace.

"I am sure you're over-reacting, Lea is harmless but OK we'll keep in touch," says Maria-Teresa.

"We will be here at Sam's until you and Margot come over to tell us what she wanted."

Hobbs is still on speaker phone, relieved that he doesn't need a rebuttal and says, "While you're giving out secret danger signals, how about you and Sam send me a text every hour. If I don't hear from you, I'll think something is wrong and head right over."

59

The next morning Margot and Maria-Teresa enter the quiet halls of the convent just after morning prayers. Unlike their two friends, this is the first time they've laid eyes on the highly polished floors, the high ceilings that provide an echo when they speak causing them to lower their voices to a whisper.

Hand in hand they wander down the main corridor peeking into all the rooms with glass in their doors. They understand from Sam that the chapel is along this corridor where portraits of Popes and Mother Superiors line the walls. The stillness, the cleanliness, and the unadornments all add to an eeriness of an unknown energy filling the hallway.

Margot spots the chapel first and yanks Maria-Teresa's arm to prevent her from walking past. They find Lea kneeling in prayer in one of the pews near the back of the church. She is dressed in her street clothes, which the ladies find odd considering she is a novice, and the last time they met she looked the part.

Maria-Teresa enters the chapel genuflects makes the sign of the cross and continues down the aisle where Margot quickly joins her. They stand quietly in the aisle at the end of the row where Lea's is concluding her prayers.

"Thank you for coming," says Lea rising from her kneeler to greet the ladies, hands still clasped together. The sanctitude of the surrounding forces Margot's eyes to dart restlessly from the altar to the chapel door, to the confessional, and back to Lea.

Lea smiles saying in a comforting voice, "It's OK to talk here if we keep our voices down. No one else is in the room." All three look around again just to confirm that the rest of the church is empty.

"Why are you dressed in street clothes? Are you assigned to work in the community?"

"I am leaving the United States and going back to Brazil. I will finish my training there."

"Do the police know you are leaving town?"

"Yes, I have been cleared as a suspect by them. Fr. Santos' death has hit me rather hard. I will always carry the grief with me. I must go home where I am needed."

"You could have told us this on the phone?"

"I wanted to thank you in person and give you these." She hands each of the ladies' rosewood rosary beads blessed by the Pope.

"I know you are not Catholic Margot, but I hope you will accept them from my heart with the deep gratitude and the blessings I pray you will have."

The speech is made with such love that the three of them tear up and engage in a group hug after which they walk to the back of the church in silence still overcome by Lea's gesture. Near the door, Lea walks to a corner and retrieves a small suitcase.

"Can we give you lift anywhere?"

"No, thank you. Mother Superior has arranged for my transportation." They walk to the corridor where Lea says goodbye with a warm smile.

Margot opens the convent door, and they step out into the oppressive heat a detraction from the beautiful clear blue sky. Once in the car with the air conditioner on high, Margot sends Sam a text saying: *Leaving convent. See you in twenty.* The reply comes back immediately: *a thumbs up emoji followed by C U then.*

Maria-Teresa asks, "Do you believe Lea's reason for leaving town?"

"I don't know. It makes sense that she will say she is innocent and grieving. Until we find a murderer, we have to admit she's still a suspect and the police might miss their chance to arrest her."

"Yeah, I guess you're right," says Maria-Teresa thoughtfully. Adding, "She just seems like such a nice person, that's all."

Margot gives her a pitying look meant for someone with diminished capacity, "I'm sure a lot of serial killers seem like nice people too," chuckles Margot.

The drive back to Sam's neighborhood takes about forty minutes. As their car pulls up to the street running perpendicular to street that Sam lives on Margot suddenly stops hard, throwing Maria-Teresa forward in her seat.

"What's the matter? Why are you stopping here?" asks Maria-Teresa rubbing her neck. "I might have whiplash."

"Look over there in Sam's driveway," answers Margot pointing at the house. "Isn't that James Wilding's car?"

Maria-Teresa leans forward, squints, and dragging out each word says, "I don't know." Eyes still narrowed leaning forward face close to the windshield staring at the car she says, "Not sure if I ever saw his car."

"Well, I did. I know that's it," says Margot pulling her car close to the curb still on the perpendicular street and sends a text message to Sam. Holding her cell she stares waiting for a response that she doesn't get. She sends Grace a text likewise no response.

"Something's wrong," Margot says in a panicked voice. Maria-Teresa swallows hard looking wide-eyed at her companion.

"I'll call Hobbs. Better be safe than sorry."

60

Back at the police station Hobbs anxiously checks the time. It is fifteen minutes past Sam's check-in time. He waits five minutes as worry lines crease his forehead, his fingers drum absentmindedly on the open folder on his desk. Snatching up his phone he texts Sam, then he texts Grace no response from either of them.

Just then Hobbs receives a text from Margot telling him that James Wilding's car is parked in Sam's driveway.

R U sure? Give me the tag number, texts Hobbs. For some unexplained reason, Hobbs has never run a trace on James' tag number.

Margot relays the tag number to Hobbs, who feeds the number into the police computer a flashing banner pops up. There is an ABP out on this vehicle, it is registered to Elaine Fisher. The hairs on the back of Hobbs' neck stand up.

He calls Margot, "That car belongs to Elaine Fisher." He jumps up from his desk adrenaline heighten while yelling into the phone, "Keep an eye on the property but do not, I repeat do not approach the house. I'll be right over. I am bringing back up."

61

Margot and Maria-Teresa anxiously watch the property from their car while inside the house the scent of fresh baked bread fills the kitchen and wafts under Sam's nose before passing through the partially opened patio door to the backyard. The warm sunlight streams through the bank of windows in the adjoining family room, casting a warm light over both rooms and its habitants.

Anticipating the arrival of Margot and Maria-Teresa the lunch entrée and dessert are arranged artfully on the table set for four. The floral centerpiece on the table rounds out the idyllic scene. If it weren't for the fact that a matte black gun is pointed just six inches from Sam's face, one might see this as preparation for an ordinary lunch with friends.

Sam is pensively perched on the end of the U-shaped sofa, a shadow lining half her face casted by the uninvited person holding the gun. Her eyes are wide with fear, her chest heaves up and down.

Grace is seated on the other end of the sofa concentrating on the gunman whose slight hand tremor, he tries to conceal by clamping his free hand over the hand with the gun. She continues watching his hands, listening to him rapidly mumble to himself, his eyes darting wildly between the two of them. Contradictory orders to them like "Stand over there," seconds later "no sit here move close together," only to change his mind and say, "no sit farther apart," while pointing his gun from Grace to Sam.

Grace thinks the gunman's behavior indicates he is not a cold-blooded killer, her assessment is based on her extensive experience as a black Ops agent. However, she must keep in mind that if James committed the string of church-related murders, caution must be exercised to save herself and Sam.

Some scientists think fear has an odor if that's true, the odor of fear overpowers the other scents in the family room. Grace looks over at Sam whose once rigid body is sagging at the shoulders, and she wonders how long Sam can hold out before fainting.

"Sam, remember your professional training," blurts out Grace hoping Sam's training as a psychological analyst will kick in. Sam exhales her mouth dry, she fights to even out her breathing preventing a verbal response instead giving just an affirmative nod of her head.

Grace's suggestion to Sam causes James, the gunman, to turn sharply toward Grace brandishing his gun. He gives Grace a long penetrating look, while his free hand flies up to wipe the perspiration from his forehead. Sam crosses and uncrosses her legs, the sudden movement draws his attention back to her. A panic confused look clouds his face, his eyes look toward the table setting behind them like it magically appeared on the horizon.

Grace scrutinizes her captor as he paces back and forth in front of them, his gun still pointed in their direction. She counts the number of steps he takes before he turns to pace in the other direction. She counts the number of steps it will take her to cross the somewhat small divide to reach him. Grace cannot however gauge his response if she rises and lunges forward.

Will he turn quickly toward her and pull the trigger? A professional would. Will he try to tussle with her and fire wildly hitting god knows what or who. Sam is sitting eyes fixed still paralyzed with fear. Grace is sure Sam will freeze and not have enough sense to take cover when the shooting starts.

There is always the possibility that James will be quick enough to stop her in her tracks as she rises from the sofa. She cannot take any chances with her best friend's life. Totally convinced that her plan to attack will work, Grace sits on the edge of the sofa and leans her upper body forward.

Her thighs tighten as she places her body weight on the balls of her feet, ready to push off from the sofa. She is ready to strike.

62

The shrill ring of Grace's cell phone startles everyone as James rushes over, snatching it from her grip before she can answer it. Following the ring the sound of a ding signaling the arrival of a text sounds loud in the quiet room. James' face goes white reading, "Are you alright?" below Margot's name. The phone shatters hard as he slams it against the glass fireplace startling the ladies. "Where's yours," he asks Sam.

She points to the kitchen island where her phone also signals an incoming text. James takes one step toward the island and abruptly stops looking back at the women sitting far apart on the sofa. Sam straightens her posture, still sitting on the edge of the sofa her wide eyes glued to James wondering if the texts will force him into irrational impulsive behavior, killing them both before help can arrive.

"So, what's your plan, James," asks Grace trying to divert his thoughts.

"Shut up!" yells James glancing at the fireplace behind him. He exhales a long breath and in a calmer voice he says, "Let me think."

"You are not a killer, James. How did you get yourself into this awful mess? How are you connected to these killings?" asks Sam feeling able to put her fear aside remembering to keep the subject talking.

James swings his gun toward Grace his lower lip trembling, water filling his eyes and asks earnestly, "Have you ever been in love?"

Instantly, an image of Rhys, her handler, ex-lover, her friend, appears in Grace's mind and her heart aches. Looking him square in the eyes she says, "Did the woman you love drag you into this mess with dead priests and now hostages?"

Sam chimes in softly with, "I understand how love can turn from kindness, the giver of life into hate, revenge, and death in a split second," to which James' face softens, his mouth opens then closes without a word. "Tell us what happened, we want to hear your story."

"Elaine is my wife," says James his eyes pleading for understanding. His voice cracks as the words catch in his throat, "well—was my wife." James momentarily looks down shakes his head in disbelief then he goes silent.

"Did you kill your wife?" asks Sam in her most sympathetic voice.

Tears well in James' red rim eyes his chest sinks back to his vertebrae making him appear hollow. Sam looks at this shell of a man and her compassion for him threatens to overwhelm her.

"I know you didn't mean to kill her," she says, his hand holding the gun drops almost to his side, but the action doesn't last long enough for Grace to overpower him.

This pity fest makes Grace anxious as she perches on the edge of the sofa watching and waiting for an opportunity to strike at James. To Grace, confirming James as Elaine's killer makes all the previous sweet talk about love irrelevant.

The air in the family room takes on a dryness parching the skin and the palate. Sam reaches for a glass of water on the coffee table. She never takes her eyes off her captor and in doing so, she knocks the glass from the table.

Startled by the noise James swings around gun pointed squarely at Sam. She jumps up, throws her hands in the air. At the same time on the other end of the sofa, Grace leaps from her seat and lunges for James. Unfortunately, he is much faster than Grace thinks, and she is stopped by the gun jammed into her breastbone.

"Move and I'll shoot." Sam can almost hear Grace's brain calculating her risks.

"Grace, NO don't," pleads Sam. Grace stops and rocks back a little on her heals.

"Sit back down, both of you and don't try anything like that again," his voice edgier than ever.

Grace complies with James' requests while Sam looks toward the kitchen for a cloth to clean up the spill.

Sam says, "I need to clean up the spill. I don't want to stain the floor."

"Leave it! You won't really care what happens to your precious floor much longer," says James. Sam sits there watching as the liquid from the overturned glass puddles on her hardwood floor.

Unable to sit by any longer, just watching the spill seep into the floor Sam says in a stern voice, "I can't. You have to let me clean this up."

Acting as if he has just been chastised by his mother James says, "Use that blanket thing behind you," referring to the throw that Sam keeps on the sofa for those moments when her hot flashes suddenly turn to arctic blasts.

The ladies resume seats on the U-shaped sofa, but this time Grace sits further apart from Sam. She hopes by sitting farther apart her position will make it more difficult for James to keep them both in his line of sight. He may be inexperienced, but he's no dummy.

"What are you doing over there?" asks James waving the gun around, gesturing for Grace to move closer to Sam.

"James, you know this is where I always sit on the sofa. You remember that from the first day you came to the book club. You remember that don't you, James?" says Grace in an unusual sing-song voice. She remains seated at the opposite end of the sofa.

James blinks his eyes several times, looks off into the distance before saying, "Yeah, that's right," as if obliged to conform to some prearranged seating norm. Grace knows he is both irrational, inexperienced, and at this point she needs to make her next move with caution.

63

"You have to let us go, James. Detective Hobbs and the others will be here soon," says Sam.

"Stop talking!" The veins in his forehead protrude just under the skin's surface. He paces with the gun in hand. "Just shut up. I need to think," he demands.

"You don't want to shoot us, someone will hear the noise," offers Grace attempting to find out how open he might be to suggestions. James contemplates her suggestion and for the moment appears to think she is correct.

Ever since the ladies separated themselves on the sofa, the muscles in James's neck tense to the point that his veins become visible. James quickly tires of darting his eyes from one side of the sofa to the other to watch both ladies simultaneously. Sam keeps him talking, distracting him hoping that Grace is hatching a plan.

"James, you are married to Elaine. I guess you really love her to risk going to prison," says Sam. When he hears the word prison, his head snaps toward Sam, eyes wide with surprise. "I'm not going to prison. I've done nothing wrong."

"Did you kill your wife Elaine?"

"I stopped her from making a fool of herself." The ladies hear James make a throaty chuckle and says, "She wanted to run away with that priest Santos."

At this point, Grace says, "You killed Santos? You shot him, didn't you?"

"I'm the good guy here," declares James poking himself in the chest for emphasis. "I saved him the embarrassment of being defrocked. Now, he dies a hero."

Sam fans herself with her hand as the heat rises from her chest to the top of her head. "James, can I just go to the bathroom and splash some water on my face. Please?"

James gives her a suspicious look and a strong, 'No'.

Sam says under her breath and rolling her eyes, "Men will never understand the urgency a woman feels when her internal temperature gauge reaches the boiling point."

After a few minutes of unsuccessfully trying to self-cool, Sam suddenly stands up, turns her back to James, and takes a step in the direction of the door.

Sam has never heard the noise from a gunshot at close range. In fact, until she hears a loud pop and feels a simultaneous whoosh as the bullet whizzes close to her head she has never heard a real gunshot. There is a ringing in her ears that reverberates up the side of her face settling in her head paralyzing her with fear and just a little damp down one leg.

Grace seizes the opportunity to again lunge at James, this time coming at him from the side. Her stride is long as she crosses the divide between her and her captor. Just as she gets within grabbing distance of his body, her line of sight unexpectantly switches from his head to his feet.

Grace feels the warmth of the wet throw that Sam used to clean up her precious hardwood floors. She hits the floor with a thud giving James just enough time to swirl around and once more point the gun at Grace as she scrambles to get up from the floor.

"Enough of this shit. Grace, get over there next to Sam," yells James exasperated with their antics to escape. "OK, you two down the hall," demands James waving the gun toward the hallway. "Don't try anything else or I'll kill you this time," says James sternly.

Obliging their captor's request, they walk slowly arms in the air toward the guest bedroom Grace still calculating her escape risks. The sooner the two women are secured, he can relax and formulate his next move.

"Get down the hall now. Go on hurry," he says as he ushers them down the hallway to their possible death.

<h1 style="text-align:center">64</h1>

Margot and Maria-Teresa sit uneasily in the car watching the front of Sam's house.

"I can't sit here any longer without knowing what's going on inside that house," says Margot opening the car door.

"Wait, don't go, Margot," says Maria-Teresa grabbing her arm as she climbs out of the car and makes her way across the street to Sam's house. Maria-Teresa wrings her hands as she watches Margot dash across the street.

Margot creeps up the winding walkway keeping her body crouched ready to pin herself against the garage door if anyone exits the house. Back in the car Maria-Teresa puts the knuckle of one finger between her teeth careful not to bite down too hard.

Sam's front door is within fifteen feet of Margot's reach. Her intent is to listen at the door for any sounds of voices or worse torture. The frosted glass panes in the middle and along both sides of the door allow limited visibility into the house. The very most she might be able to see are shadows if the inhabitants are close to the door.

As Margot gets closer, it looks like the door maybe ajar just a little. Her heart beats fast with anticipation, knowing there's a possibility that she may be able to sneak into the house. Her movements become more measured, her body more tense the closer she gets. The thought of possibly entering the premises brings a smile to her lips.

Stealth-like in her movements, she quickens her pace careful not to let the possibility of good fortune cause her to make a misstep. Before her smile fully forms, she hears that unmistakable pop. The sound of a gunshot.

Instinctively, she drops to the ground landing hard on her left knee sending an excruciating pain so intense that using all her resistance can't hold back, "Ooh, oh, damn" from escaping her lips. She flattens her body to relieve the pain in her knee and remains on her stomach eyes still peering up at the door.

Maria-Teresa watches from the car seeing Margot fall to the ground and stifles a scream. Her hand is on the car door handle poised to leave the car, not knowing why Margot suddenly drops to the ground. Margot doesn't know if anyone in the house is hurt but not hearing any follow-up shots, she does what any sane person would do.

Pulling herself to her knees she shrinks backward away from the front door. If it's possible to limp while crawling, Margot is making an excellent attempt at both while making her way down the driveway head down wincing in pain.

"Arf, arf, arf, arf," causes her to stop, shift her weight off her injured knee and look up into the face of a barking snickerdoodle, poodle doodle, or one of those poodle mixes who is cocking its head to one side, eye-to-eye looking curiously at her.

"Punchy, come away from the crazy lady," says its owner tugging hard on the dog's leash like her beloved pet might catch whatever craziness befalls the woman crawling on the ground.

"How about helping the crazy lady," sneers Margot rolling her eyes at the woman's legs, the only body part at her eye level. Ushering her pooch away from Margot, she walks away continually looking over her shoulder with concern.

Margot makes her way to the garage door where she sits momentarily, wondering how she can gracefully rise to her feet. From a cat-cow yoga pose after several attempts, she pulls one knee forward between her palmed hands balancing on the ball of her foot then dragging the other knee to the same position before pushing off the ground with her hands to a standing position.

Unfortunately, halfway to a standing position, a muscle spasm hits her lower back making it impossible for Margot to straighten from the waist up. Although in pain, she makes her way back to her parked vehicle yelling to Maria-Teresa, "I just heard a gunshot. Quick, call Hobbs again. Where the hell is, he?"

65

The oppressive Arizona heat often lends to a significant percentage increase in violent crime making the east valley police station a bustling hub of activity on this triple-digit day. With all that's going on in the station, the captain still finds time to give Hobbs a tongue lashing. The adage it's easier to ask forgiveness than permission, floats through Hobbs' mind as he stands listening uninterested in the words his Captain spouts.

"The murder at the church and its suspects are none of your business. Why would I give you permission to interfere?"

"But sir, I think innocent people might be in danger. I need just a couple of hours to make sure they're alright. I'll make up the time," pleads Hobbs. Ignoring Hobbs' plea, the captain continues his diatribe his Adam's apple fervently jumping up and down with every word. The vibration of Hobbs' cell phone necessitates a furtive peek at the message from Maria-Teresa confirming he is wasting valuable time.

Without a word, Hobbs turns and walks out of the captain's office leaving the plump little man with the sparse hair red-faced and slack-jawed. Hobbs checks his firepower before heading to his car. The station parking lot is full as he steers in and around people searching for a space.

Once on the highway, he puts on his flashing lights and siren maneuvering his vehicle quickly through the streets to help his friends. Racing through the streets at unsafe speeds, the knot grows in his stomach. Grace's skill as a secret operative gives Hobbs hope for the women's safety.

"What if they come to harm," he says to the voice in his head. His stomach lurches, his tongue feels thick and dry causing him to swallow hard. Continuing the conversation in his head he says, "I will never forgive myself if I fail to keep them safe."

Hobbs may have just lost his job but worse than that he is running head long into danger totally on his own without backup. A string of swear words laces his thoughts before unloading them on the motorists impeding his progress. He rounds the corner in Sam's housing complex cutting the siren not wanting to alert James and possibly spook him into doing something drastic. Hobbs parks behind Margot's car as both women jump out of their car and run to Hobbs with panic looks on their faces.

"What the hell took you so long and where is your back up?" asks Margot in her typical judgmental tone.

"That's a long story one I don't have time to explain now. Just tell me what you know."

"I heard a gunshot about twenty minutes ago. No one has left the house." On the side of Sam's house just past, the garage is a path leading toward the backyard, but the entry gate is kept locked.

"This is what I want you to do," says Hobbs then he explains his plan.

66

Inside the house, at gun point, Grace and Sam are in the guest bedroom at the back of the house. They are not tied up. James' first mistake. Although ordinarily not being tied up means an easy escape for the ladies, climbing out of the bedroom window is not a simple method of escape in most Arizona homes.

Sunscreens are designed to keep out the relentless Arizona sun but, in doing so, they keep anyone inside the house from easily climbing out. Sunscreens are mounted to each window from the outside with screws that require a special tool to unscrew them. The guest bedroom where the ladies are being held is fully furnished for sleeping and to the average eye, it contains little else for escaping.

Wordlessly, Grace scrutinizes the sparse items that can be used to take down a gunman, two nightstand lamps and the array of reading materials intended for use by any visiting insomniac. Grace turns to her best friend, looks her in the eyes and asks, "Are you ready to die?"

Sam is taken aback by both the question and somber tone in Grace's voice but responds quickly.

"No and hell no! Do you need to ask?"

"OK, then we don't have much time," says Grace as she moves around the spacious room opening the closet doors revealing a bare space waiting for guest clothing. On the floor of the closet tucked in one corner is a long box containing pieces of extra hardwood flooring.

Sam unable to fathom what Grace is up to or how to help sits down on the bed glad to be in a space with no gun pointed at her and says, "I could really murder a chocolate chip cookie right about now."

"Must you use that word? This is not the situation in which the word murder should ever be used," remarks Grace conscientiously continuing her survey of the room's contents.

"What are you looking for, Grace?"

"I am looking for something to save our lives," whispers Grace as she continues taking in her options. The vase of fresh-cut flowers, the crystal lamps, and the clock that sits on the nightstand catch Grace's attention.

Grace picks up a crystal lamp, unplugs it, and tosses it from hand to hand to determine its weight.

"Oh, no. Whatever you're thinking Grace that lamp is off-limits. I love that lamp. Don't touch that lamp," pleads Sam. Grace doesn't verbally agree or disagree with Sam's demands.

In the hallway, James paces back and forth deciding he must kill the two ladies from the mystery book club. Talking to that voice in his head he asks, "Can I kill unprovoked by jealousy or rage?"

He calmly walks toward the bedroom door gun drawn with only one thing on his mind, performing his tasks and quickly leaving neither of his captives alive.

67

Sam and Grace are calm enough to look at their present situation as an opportunity to put a simple plan in action. However, just how to accomplish this simple plan hasn't been finalized when they hear the bedroom door unlocking. James cautiously enters the room holding the gun that now contains a silencer.

Hearing the door being open, Grace positions herself in front of the door, James' eyes dart wildly around the room looking for Sam. As James nervously advances into the room his gun held out in front of him, his eyes still scanning for Sam, "Where is she?"

From behind the door, Sam advances quickly and forcefully strikes the hand holding the gun with a plank of extra hardwood flooring from the closet. The gun hits the floor and slides out of reach.

Grace quickly moves forward and lunges at James. Before he can push Grace aside to retrieve the gun now spinning on the floor, Grace grabs an Elizabeth George novel from the top of the dresser and rushes toward him shoving the spine of the book somewhere in his throat.

Temporarily stunned and in pain, James staggers back a few steps holding his throat. Grace advances again for a second pass at his throat with the book. James anticipates another strike and deflects the book. This second attempt puts Grace squarely in his personal space giving him the opportunity to get both hands around her neck.

Sam comes from behind him and jumps on his back pulling a pillowcase over his head. Surprised again by this newest impediment, James temporarily releases his tight grip on Grace. With one hand, he tries to pull the covering off his head while his other hand regains his firm grip on Grace's throat. This stunt brings everybody crashing to the floor.

Grace is now on the bottom of the heap with James sandwiched between her and Sam. With his face so close to Grace's face, it is easy for him to regain his firm two hand hold on her delicate throat even though his head covering is only partially removed.

Sam, still laying on top of the heap of moving bodies on the floor scrambles off to find something else to hit James with. Frantically looking around the bedroom for something, anything to subdue her captive, she retrieves the same piece of extra hardwood from the floor. Holding the piece of flooring over her head poised for the strike, she moves side to side, careful to step over moving arms and legs.

Fearful that she may accidently hit Grace with the board she tries to match the movements of the tussling bodies. The floor is a heap of clawing, reaching, grabbing, and kicking limbs. It is difficult to gage when she should strike with Grace's arms and legs flailing about.

"Hold still, Grace!" yells Sam before she decides to move counter to Grace's movements.

Grace, totally uncaring about Sam's order to hold still, is thrashing around her life depending on freeing herself. Grace feels around on the floor to find something to get him off her.

Her hand finds a cord, she snatches it and skillfully catches the lamp at in of the cord, then she twists her body enough to gather the lamp in her hands. Holding it up in the air over the partially hooded attacker, she brings it down on his head just as Sam lowers the plank of wood flooring.

Both items hit James in rapid succession; first the crystal lamp followed quickly by Sam's blow with the piece of wood that breaks the lamp over his head. Looking down at the broken shards of glass on the floor confirm it's the very crystal lamp Sam forbade Grace to use. Desperately trying to detangle herself from under the dead weight of James' unconscious body, Grace wiggles to one side. She lays on her back on the floor trying to steady her breathing.

Sam sits firmly on James who is lying face down with a one thousand thread count pillowcase still draped partially over his head. Sam picks up what is left of her lamp and her heart sinks, unable to say anything or move, she remains seated on James's back.

68

Hobbs instructs Margot to phone in 'a shots fired, possibly officer down' call to the police. A call of this kind will bring the backup Hobbs needs and within three minutes of Margot's call, additional officers arrive. Hobbs is already poised near the front door when his fellow officers arrive at the scene.

They crouch at Hobbs, six ready to enter the house on his command. Hobbs creeps to the front door that's partially ajar. Quickly entering the quiet house Hobbs directs his fellow officers where to go as they break off in various directions searching each room. From the guest bedroom in the back of the house, the ladies hear what sounds like hundreds of elephants stampeding accompanied by the sound of loud voices announcing 'clear' as they move through the house making their way toward Grace and Sam.

Hobbs reaches the bedroom and slowly lowers his gun when he gazes at the mass of bodies in a heap on the floor. A huge grin spreads over Hobbs's face when he sees that Grace once again has the situation under control. Grace, hair disarranged, throat red is still trying to fully extricate herself from under James' unconscious body now that Sam has slid off him onto the floor.

Sam is crying softly sitting on the floor hugging what's left of her crystal lamp.

"There, there, Sam. It's over now. Let me help you up," says Hobbs feeling sorry for her then looking down at the limp body under her, he thinks perhaps he should be feeling sorrier for James.

"Can I get a hand up. I am wrinkling my clothes," utters the hoarse voice of Grace lightening the mood now that the calvary is onsite.

One of the other officer's grabs Grace while some officer grabs James, who is just starting to wake up. Sam is holding the pieces of her lamp and muttering over and over, "I love this lamp."

Surviving what could have been her last day on earth Grace is glad she has Hobbs to come to her rescue. Grace's hands gently massage the outside of her very sore throat. She looks at Sam and manages to squeak out, "I'll buy you another damn lamp. The fact that it saved my life means nothing to you."

"Throw those pieces in the trash," says Grace leaning on her best friend as they head toward the kitchen arm in arm. When the two women reach the kitchen, Margot and Maria-Teresa greet them with open arms, hugs, kisses, and warm mugs of T and T, a drink concoction of tequila and tea.

Hobbs asks a few preliminary questions and tells the women that they must come to the police station in the morning to give formal statements. He leaves the house, turning around long enough to say to the ladies with a wink and a smile, "Try to stay out of trouble."

69

Hobbs is coldly known by his colleagues as the James Dean of the east valley police department. Fellow officers grumble among themselves because no police officer was in danger and express the same misgivings to their superiors once they are back at the station.

Hobbs grudgingly spends the rest of his day completing paperwork. In his Incident Report, he gives an account of his involvement in the situation at the home of Sam Jones. He recounts exactly why Margot Towers placed a frantic call to him explaining that she is unable to reach either Sam Jones or Grace Liu. Receiving the second communication from Maria-Teresa Rivera prompted him to leave work.

He adds a little fluff here and there careful to leave out the part that he spends nearly every evening at Sam's home. His report will no doubt lead to disciplinary consequences following his rouge actions. As he signs his statement, he gets a chill down his spine, much like a premonition.

70

News of the apprehension of a suspect that might be linked to the priest's murders spreads like wildfire throughout the valley. When the news reaches the west valley police station, Detective Keating is neither sad nor altogether happy about the news.

One part of him is relieved that he no longer must chase a ghost that was always one step ahead of him. He is a little disappointed that he is not the officer apprehending the suspect until he hears that Hobbs gets the collar. Keating's blood boils.

The next morning Keating shows up at the still bustling east valley police station red face and snorting mad with Hobbs. Keating goes straight to the captain to voice his displeasure with Hobbs' involvement in his west valley case.

"You need to do something to keep a tighter leash on that maniac. Surely you will take disciplinary action this time," demands Keating banging on the captain's desk.

"I understand your anger, but we all do have the same goal, to apprehend criminals. Besides the suspect was apprehended within east valley by an east valley police officer for an alleged crime committed within east valley jurisdiction," says the captain all smiles trying to tamp down the voice in his head, "once again, the James Dean of the precinct has gone off the reservation, saves the day, and comes out a flipping hero."

"Fine, but I demand to be in on the interrogation of the suspect," Keating says acquiescing to the captain's explanation.

"Of course, I don't see a problem with that."

Keating's next visit is to the center of the turmoil, Hobbs. Keating makes his way down the hall to stand in the doorway of Hobbs' windowless office. Hobbs who has been in a very reflective mood since returning to the police station looks up from his desk and beams a Cheshire cat grin at the sight of Keating.

"Do come in. Sit, make yourself at home. It's not much," sweeping his arm around referring to the sparse office décor. "We busy detectives don't require much because we are always out bringing criminals to justice."

"Cut the crap, Hobbs. If this guy has any connection to the church murders, I have your captain's permission to sit in on the interrogation?"

"My suspect," emphasizing the word my, "is being charged with two counts of attempted murder of individuals within the east valley jurisdiction. Not the church, however my expert," again emphasizing my, "deductive reasoning tells me he is involved in the church murders."

"What makes you think he is connected to the church murders. Did your Fed buddies tell you that?" says Keating making it a point to sound snarky, but at the same time fishing for information. James has been a person of interest on Keating's radar too. Curiosity makes Keating want to know how Hobbs nailed James.

"How did you nail Wilding?"

"The mystery book club ladies are the key to cracking this whole case, Keating. Would you like to watch them work?" asks Hobbs sheepishly smiling.

"Work, what are talking about? They're not police officers what are you trying to pull?"

"Oh, Keating, don't be so suspicious, follow me," says Hobbs leading him to an interrogation room where James is already seated.

71

The suspect James Wilding refuses to answer any questions posed to him by the police.

Hobbs is kept out of the initial attempts to interrogate the suspect as punishment for his rebel attitude. His Captain is even thinking of ways to give the credit for James' arrest to another officer. As much as the police officers hate to admit it perhaps, they need Hobbs' involvement in this interrogation because James refuses to speak with anyone else.

Reluctantly, Hobbs is given the lead in the interrogation since he knows more about James than anyone and he apprehended him. Hobbs goes into the interrogation room reflecting on the skinny little twitchy person sitting in Sam's family room and how uncomfortable Hobbs makes him feel. It's absurd that James is willing to speak with him.

But being the ever-consummate detective, Hobbs knows all these murders at the St. Francis de Sales Catholic church are somehow connected but he needs James to tell him how they fit together.

"Let's start at the beginning. Do you know Fr. Francisco?" asks Hobbs.

"No."

"Do you know Fr. Santos?"

"No."

"You know we've got you on two counts of attempted murder and the victims are here ready to identify you."

"Where is Sam and Grace?" asks James looking around the small interrogation room. "I'll only talk to them."

Not letting pride stand in his way, even though the request is highly irregular for a suspect to confess to his victims. Walking down the hall to his office, the ladies are waiting ready to make their official statements.

Hobbs puts on his cheeriest smile and asks, "I need your help. Will you speak with James? He says he'll only give information to you two."

"No? I don't care if I ever see him again," says Sam turning away from Hobbs thinking of the man who nearly shot her probably intending to end her life for good and ruined her best crystal lamp.

"Yeah, of course, anything we can do to help," says Grace jumping out of her chair ready to follow Hobbs.

Sam turns her attention to give her friend a penetrating stare, "My life and fears mean nothing to you, Grace," sneers Sam adding, "I thought I knew you."

"Of course, I care about your safety. Remember I got us out of that hostage situation. Oh, come on, Sam, we have a solemn duty as amateur sleuths to follow the investigation to the end."

Grace's secret life in the shadows teaches her to compartmentalize her feelings in exchange for the truth. Grace turns to her friend who is breathing rapidly her hand on her chest.

"You don't have to do this. I'll go," says Grace.

"No! It's high time I face my fear of interrogation rooms."

Sam slowly exhales and walks out of the office holding Grace's arm. The interrogation room is small with one table two chairs set up on one side of the table and one chair sits on the other side of the table. A voice activated microphone is suspended from the ceiling.

The ladies each sit in one of the two chairs, there are two uniform police officers standing in the corner of the room. Detective Keating is already standing in the room with a rather disinterested look on his face. Hobbs stands next to him with a rueful grin on his face.

The suspect is seated across the table from the ladies, facing the two-way mirror mounted on the wall. His ankles are shackled together. He moves his feet around under the table trying to find a comfortable position and decides to tuck his feet under his chair.

James clears his throat and looks down at his wrists handcuffed to a large metal ring mounted in the table then raises his gaze to the ladies.

"Thank you for coming." He lifts his head and says, "I am sorry," as he suddenly leans forward causing both women to instinctively sink back in their chairs.

72

The two mute officers standing guard move closer to James with their hands on their tasers as a precautionary measure. Their movement causes James to withdraw his body toward his chair his eyes darting from one guard to the other.

"You must know I didn't want things to be like this, to end like this," says James.

"Why do you want to talk to us, James?" asks Sam curtly.

He looks in Sam's direction and moves his hands toward her but is hampered a full stretch by his wrist restraints. Sam again shrinks away from the table.

James says to Sam with tears welling in his eyes, "You understand. About love and all that. You know I did everything because I love her."

"James, just tell us everything from the beginning," says Sam sucking in air for courage. The following is a verbatim account of how a private investigator, one priest and a woman of wayward behavior all meet their demise.

"I will give you the condensed version. Elaine and I have been married for five years." James' voice quivers and he looks down at the table shaking his head. "I still can't believe things went so wrong." Then raising his head, he looks pass the ladies his eyes unfocused and regretful for a few minutes before continuing.

"We start scamming priests out of economic necessity. I lost my job and Elaine's job as a cashier didn't yield much income."

"Umph, that's a pretty flimsy excuse," interjects Sam.

"Don't judge me. We are not bad people. We went to church to pray for help with our misfortune. Honest!" says James emphatically eyes wide searching from Sam to Grace.

Sam is about to comment again when Grace cuts her off and says, "We believe you, James. Go ahead." Grace knows if she lets Sam continue to antagonize James, he will clam up.

"Well, Elaine notices how the very first priest we blackmailed leers at her. She follows up on her instincts by approaching him later. She tells him she needs spiritual counseling or some such thing and that is the beginning of our lucrative endeavor."

"What do you mean?" asks Keating as if he is some grade school kid who can't read between the lines.

James looks up at Keating, blinks rapidly narrowing his eyes then frowns, noticing for the first time that Keating is in the room. He turns his attention back toward Sam even though he responds to Keating's question.

"Elaine puts the priests in compromising positions, and I take photos," says James looking down. In a softer voice he says, "Then we ask them for money to keep the photos hidden or risk public exposure."

He straightens his body up tall, his self-confidence visible in his body language. He continues, "Our plan works so well in the first parish that we try the same thing at other parishes. As we move across the state, we get wind that we are being followed by the law. We think it is the police."

"When did you meet Fr. Francisco?" asks Sam wanting to get back to the murders at hand.

"I never met him, he approached Elaine. I don't know how he found us."

"So, he was going to turn you two over to the police and you killed him," says Grace waiting for James to confirm her theory.

"Uhm no. He wants in on the scam. Imagine, he is trying to blackmail the blackmailers," snorts James who is shaking his head in disbelief. A sinister smile forms on his lips. "Elaine goes to St. Francis de Sales church the morning he is killed to reason with Francisco, but he wasn't having it."

"And you killed him?" says Keating rushing to what he thinks is an inevitable conclusion.

Again, another loud snort and eye roll comes from James. Once Hobbs sees James' reaction to Keating latest assumption, he knows Keating is off the mark again. Hobbs mimics James' reaction in a more exaggerated manner.

"Elaine stabs Francisco in the back. She said that she panicked when he fell to his knees from the stab to his back and turns his head to look at her. She realizes she cannot just walk away, he sees her face, so she slices his throat and runs."

Reiterating in a pleading voice he repeats, "She has to kill him, you see. He wants to take money from us," explains James opening his hands palms up as if what he is saying is the obvious solution.

Not buying James' explanation for killing someone and more than ready to move the confession along, Sam asks, "Who shot Fr. Santos and why?"

"That was me," says James pushing out his chest. "Elaine refused to stop seeing Santos. Normally, once we take the blackmail photos, she never maintains a relationship with the mark. Santos was different, she falls for this guy."

A sinister smile spreads across his lips and he says, "He can't have her, she's my wife," he pokes his chest. "So, I go to the church, and I shoot him."

"You shot him three times, isn't that over-kill, pardon the pun?" ask Grace unmoved by James' explanation of jealousy.

"Over kill? That was genius!" boasts James now sitting very upright in his chair, his chest heaved forward with an indignant look on his face. "I shot him once for the father, once for the son, and once for the holy spirit. Get it?" a reminiscent satisfying smile forms on his lips. No one responds to James' genius.

Instead, the ladies change the subject slightly, "You went to an awful lot of trouble to protect Elaine. I am confused who killed her?" asks Grace.

James' face changes to a hurtful look as he explains. "When I returned home from shooting Santos, I found Elaine packing. She didn't know what I had done. She said she and Santos were running away together. I was beside myself with rage."

Turning toward Sam with a pleading look in his eyes he says, "Sure, I killed her, but it just happened. Something came over me, I barely remember strangling her. You understand, don't you?" again trying to garner sympathy for his actions.

At this point in James' confession, Hobbs pipes up, "Now, we have you on two counts of murder and two counts of attempted murder." James looks up at Hobbs standing behind Grace's chair and opens his mouth to protest. Just as suddenly he closes his mouth and shakes his head in the affirmative.

"I've got one question," says Grace. "Why is your last name Wilding and not Fisher if she was legally married to you."

"My legal name is James Wilding Fisher. I use my middle name so people will not connect me and Elaine as the blackmailer couple."

"I think we have everything we need. Your statement will be typed and printed out for your perusal and signature," says Hobbs.

Hobbs nods to the uniform officers and they escort the prisoner back to his cell. As James is leaving the interview room, he can be heard muttering over and over, "Why does God make some women like that? I ask myself that a hundred times."

73

Keating walks over to Grace and Sam, "How do you ladies know James?"

"Detective Keating, nice to see you again," says Sam with a wry smile. Her greeting more than meets with Hobbs' approval. Standing behind Keating he winks at Sam from over Keating's shoulder.

"James joined our mystery book club a little while back," says Grace in a straight-forward manner refusing to play into Hobbs' game of one upmanship. She adds, "You know that Fr. Francisco was an undercover private eye."

"Yeah, I got that much from the Bishop." Keating rubs his chin and says, "I still don't get how you wound up being so central to James' confession."

"A good detective never reveals her sources. Let's just say we have an inside track," says Grace with a coy grin, hardly believing she just did something that moments ago she silently admonished Sam and Hobbs for doing.

Keating refuses to let his question go unanswered and rephrases it hoping to get an answer from one of the ladies.

"I know from the police report that you two are the attempted murder victims. How then does a man who tries to kill you both turn around and want to confess his sins to you."

"I think it's time we let these two gentlemen return to their work. Let's go, Sam," says Grace taking her friend by the arm and strolling out of the interrogation room toward the station lobby.

After the ladies leave, the silence becomes a little awkward between the two men and Keating says, "I would say thank you, you've been a big help, but I don't like you."

Chuckling out loud and rocking back on his heels Hobbs says, "That's OK I don't like you either. Besides, I didn't do this for you."

At the doorway, the men go in opposite directions and silently hope to never run into each other again.

74

After all, the hoopla concludes and the paperwork is filed, Hobbs still senses dread. True to the feel in his gut the Captain summons him.

"Look, I'll make this quick. You're a good cop but your style doesn't appear to be a good fit for this department," says the Captain.

Ordinarily, Hobbs may disagree with him, but for some time he knows that he just doesn't fit in. He also knows that with the arrest of James, he successfully solves three murders and in a just society he should get an accommodation. The operative phrase is 'a just society'.

His familiarity with police regs tells him a few days suspension is on the table for disobeying a direct order from the Captain. Hobbs' attention temporarily drifts from the Captain's speech to his past. His compassion for the underdog and his keen sense of justice for those wronged led him to police work.

Hobbs is a child of the foster system with no known blood relatives and thinks of the ladies in the mystery book club as his surrogate group of loving aunts. He is hard wired to protect family.

"We obey orders—," says the captain snapping Hobbs' attention back to the conversation in time to hear, "we work as a team around here. You need to decide if you still want to play on our team. The next few days off will give you some time to think about your next move. I advise you to choose wisely."

Like any true gossip mill, everyone in the department knows about the three-day suspension before Hobbs reaches his office. A few officers line the hallway outside the Captain's office snickering and whispering as Hobbs marches, head held high, back to his office.

His fellow colleagues feel vindicated that finally Hobbs' behavior receives punishment regardless of his perceived Federal connection. Hobbs clears his desk and heads for home with the captain's words ringing in his ears. You are not a team player.

Pulling up to the front of his beige and brown stucco apartment building, Hobbs debates whether he wants to be closed in a stuffy apartment or if he should hit a bar to think things through. Realizing Turner is not around to bounce his troubles off, he's overcome with despair. Watching the desert landscape from his car he wonders what he will do next, what he wants to do, and what he should do?

Dragging himself out of his vehicle, the heat of the day causes little trickles of sweat to roll down his back. He unlocks the door to his apartment where the coolness of his air conditioner makes the perspiration feel cold dripping down his back. Hobbs is a true workaholic bachelor with little regard for creature comforts.

He deposits his brief case just inside the door and his suit jacket on the small dining table for two. Sighing he heads toward the fridge. The rancid smell of day-old Chinese food smacks him in the face, possibly indicating it's older than he thinks. Moving the carton to the side, he grabs a beer and seriously considers lingering there basking in the cold air before ambling over to one of two recliner chairs and turning on the television.

Flopping down in a chair without removing the dirty clothes from it, his eyes sweep over the bare walls and a feeling of sadness engulfs him as he mouths, "This is a place you pass through not settle into." With that realization, he chugs half a can of beer in one gulp, still debating the idea of going to a bar for company and a better choice of scenery. His cell phone buzzes loud in his pocket displaying the name Sam Jones. Of all the ladies in the book club Sam is his favorite, probably because of her culinary skills.

"Hello, Sam," says Hobbs in a less than enthusiastic voice.

"Don't sound so happy to hear from me," she says cheerfully.

"Oh, it's not that I just have something on my mind. What's up?"

"Surely, you don't think we can let another solved case go by without a proper celebration, do you?"

"No. Of course not. I guess it's tonight."

"I'll see you at seven," says Sam hanging up.

Hobbs gets up briefly to get a couple more beers before returning to his dilemma, is he a team player or not. Ever since his trouble with his superiors in his Baltimore precinct, there has been something nagging him about playing by the rules. He has always played by the rules, the rules of sports, and the rules of law enforcement, in his mind everything about him screams play by the rules.

Are they his rules, their rules or have the rules changed? The sun has set without him realizing that it is well past 7 o'clock. Hobbs knows everyone is expecting him at Sam's to celebrate. If he doesn't show up, everyone will want to know why. Having to explain why he doesn't want to go to the celebration is something that Hobbs thinks is best saved for another day. He knows he must suck it up, put on a fake smile, and show up.

75

Turner leans over the passenger headrest, "Can you hurry it up," he says to his Uber driver, a request that is ignored. The driver pulls up to a gated apartment complex and piggybacks on the car in front of it for entrance. Gathering his duffle bag Turner jogs up to his apartment opens the door and drops his bag on the floor.

He takes one quick look around his designer decorated abode, snatching his car keys from the bowl in the entry, he heads down to his Chevrolet Corvette, affectionately known as the Batmobile. Turner pulls into a parking space at the east valley police station. Entering through the familiar glass doors into the lobby, he is greeted by the desk officer and a few of his friends.

He rushes to Hobbs's office and finds the door locked and the lights off. Turner heads to the captain to update him on his plan to return to work. The captain doesn't mention Hobbs' suspension or the ultimatum that he issued. Turner doesn't ask him how Hobbs faired in his absence, hoping no news is good news. Leaving the police station Turner checks his watch several times while exceeding the speed limit on the freeway.

Within twenty minutes, he finds himself ringing Sam's doorbell. She opens the door with caution just enough to peek out. Seeing Turner, "Oh my god," she says followed by joyful squeals as she flings the door open wide leaping into his arms.

"Sam! Sam! Sam! Woo-hoo," yells Turner as he swings her around and around. The others hear the loud voices coming from the direction of the door and fearing the worse they all run toward the door to see what is causing the commotion.

The group rounds the corner to the hallway when the vision of the tall, handsome, impeccably dressed Detective Turner comes into view. When the ladies see Turner, like Sam, they run to embrace him, individually and then in a group hug.

Everyone fires questions to him at once. "When did you get back? Are you alright? You look great! He looks a little thin to me." After a few minutes of pleasantries, the five of them make their way back into the family room taking their favorite seats on the U-shaped sofa.

"Now that the band is back together, everything is complete," says Maria-Teresa grinning from ear to ear.

"Is this a celebration or just another night of food and fun? Tell me everything. What did I miss?" says Turner twisting in his seat to look once more at everyone. "Did you solve the church murder? Where's Hobbs? He was not at the police station when I stopped by." As if summoned by the divine, Hobbs rings the bell a few times before opening the unlocked front door.

"Never a good idea to leave your door unlocked, Sam," yells Hobbs chastising her as he makes his way down the hall to the family room.

All heads turn toward the family room door at the sound of Hobbs' boisterous voice. Jumping up from the sofa like a jack rabbit Turner embraces his friend then they hold each other at arms-length followed by back slapping and hand shaking.

"Hey man, when did you get back. You look good."

"I got back a couple of hours ago. I stopped by the station, but your office was dark."

"Let's get this man a drink and some food. How 'bout it. What's your pleasure?" says Hobbs choosing to steer all conversation away from the police station and his job. Turner pulls Sam aside and says with a boyish grin, "I really missed your cooking. What's on the menu for tonight's meal."

"We're having tenderloin with all the trimmings," looking over at Hobbs. "Had I known you were coming—"

"I know you would've baked me a cake," laughs Turner. "Don't worry I don't mind eating Hobbs' favorite meal."

In between bites, Hobbs asks, "Has the group filled you in on what they have been up to in your absence?"

"Not yet. Sorry I missed everything," says Turner.

"I think we will give him the cliff notes version," says Grace, realizing if the story telling is left up to Sam, they may be there all night. Turner is brought up to speed on the cast of characters when James' name and roll is introduced.

Hobbs interjects with, "What I want to know is how did James get in your house. When I told you, he could be dangerous, I didn't think I needed to tell you NOT to let him in the house." He turns to Grace, "I expect more from you," shaking his head in disbelief that she was caught off guard.

"We are not stupid," says Sam who folds her arms across her chest assuming an indignant posture. The rest of the group is looking at her waiting for her to continue the story. As if to concede to the wishes of the greater good for more details, she exhales and proceeds with her story.

"I got the camera fixed over the door like you suggested Hobbs. We saw James ringing the front doorbell."

"We don't let him in or let him know we're home. He bangs on the door and even calls out Sam's name. Then he walks away. We wait five minutes, always checking the camera, but he doesn't come back to the front door."

"OK if you are that cautious how does he get in?" asks Margot now quite curious to hear how James worms his way into the house.

"We are both just sitting in the family room waiting to hear from Margot and Maria-Teresa when Sam hears a noise at the front door. We check the camera and still see nothing. We hear what sounds like noise at the front door a couple more times."

Sam takes over the story telling and says, "Grace jumps up to check out the noise. She goes to the front door while I wait in the family room." They continue to tag team the story telling for dramatic effect.

"Like I said we are waiting and getting jumpy. We think we hear noises coming from every side of the house. Grace is at the door when I think I hear something at the kitchen window. I scream."

"When Sam screams, I had just opened the front door to peer outside. Without thinking I run back into the family room without fully closing the door."

"So, James gets in because you left the front door open?" asks Hobbs once again admonishing Grace.

"No! Sam and I decide our nerves are out of control and unlock the patio door to sit by the pool. We are just about to step outside when James appears from behind that damned overgrown purple sage bush. With a gun, he forces us back inside the house."

For a minute, Sam and Grace go off on a tangent debating the function of the overgrown purple sage bush that sits to the side of the patio. Specifically, they debate whether it provides much desired shade for the patio or whether it has overgrown its decorative purpose.

A few members of the group clear their throats or fidget in their seats indicating they wish to hear the continuation of the hostage story. Sam is still in disbelief as she relays Grace's heroic defensive moves used to bring down James.

Turner and Hobbs are well acquainted with Grace's athleticism, her defensive training, and her secret life. But they feign awe and wonder as Sam retells Grace's feats. Margot and Maria-Teresa sit on the edge of the sofa enthralled in the telling of the ordeal that Sam and Grace endured leading to James' capture.

76

Like any well played battle that results in victory, celebrations can last well into the night. Everyone is so stoked and eager to give his or her rendition of a battle fought and won it is only proper to let those who have been absent during the big battle also give their victories.

Turner is next to tell what little he can about his classified experience at the Mountain. His story telling is wrapped up in two short sentences. "It was the greatest experience of my life and I can't wait to put what I've learned to use."

Tweaking Turner's cheek Sam asks him in a voice that resembles an adult reading a rhyming kid's book, "It's OK. You can put your secrets away. We'll know about them one day. You had a good time anyway?" says Sam smiling her nursery schoolteacher smile.

Frowning Turner looks to the rest of the group with confusion occupying every inch of his face he asks, "What's gotten into her? What's with the sing song rhyming cadence in her speech."

"Sam has been hanging out with a bunch of preschoolers and I think she has lost her grip on the adult world. It's nothing personal. Just be glad she is not cutting up your food for you," says Grace.

Funny how things work at that moment, Turner's cell phone rings and he moves away from the group to take the call. He returns to the group quickly.

Grace can tell by simply looking at the grin on his face and the twinkle in his eyes that he is getting a chance to use his new skill set sooner than expected.

The group works its way through dessert when Turner stands up and says, "Sam, let me help you stack the dish washer." Once alone in the kitchen with Sam, Turner leans down and says, "I've got some good news bad news and I don't want to ruin the party. What should I do?"

Sam turns to look into his eyes and walks him to a corner of the kitchen. "I pulled this mug from the cabinet a few minutes ago. I think I know what you are going to say."

He looks down and reads the whimsical saying on the mug that Sam is holding. The mug says, Parting is such Sweet Sorrow. He lowers his head and Sam knows she and the others will be losing a good friend.

"Hey, what are you two doing over there?" asks Hobbs. He sees one of the prophetic whimsical mugs in Sam's hand and yells, "Oh help me, Hannah!" Dropping his head backward while raising his hands up above his head as he talks to the ceiling exclaiming in exasperation, "Not this again."

Margot, Maria-Teresa and Grace exchange glances fearing the worse is not yet over. Sam and Turner both turn toward the rest of the group and by the somber look on their faces the group can tell bad news is coming.

"Well, don't keep us in suspense, what does the all-seeing mug say," mocks Hobbs. The ladies walk over to the kitchen to read the mug, but Hobbs remains seated. Upon reading the latest prediction, Margot says, "When the hell did you get a bard collection?"

"You can blame it on Grace," says Sam proudly. "The last time she was in London she bought a few mugs back for me. There are three mugs in the bard collection, all of them have the likeness of the main character from the play that the saying is taken from. On this mug, there is a small rendition of Juliet on her balcony. Under the rendition is the saying in question with William Shakespeare's name written underneath."

"London, when did you go to London?" asks Margot turning to Grace with confusion and a little suspicion. Margot feels there is more to Grace than meets the eye and one day she will find out what that is. Once again, Margot's question is ignored by Grace and the others.

Grace's best friend Sam has learned over the years not to ask about Grace's impromptu absences and business trips. The two men already have first-hand knowledge of Grace's secret life. And Maria-Teresa just accepts Grace for her mystery.

Maria-Teresa pipes up with, "I'm confused we just got everyone back together, who is leaving?" she searches the faces of her friends for answers. She is unable to glean any information from their faces leaving her to wonder which of her friends is about to drop bad news. Turner lowers his head slightly before inhaling deeply and exhaling.

"Don't tell me Homeland Security's star pupil has been sent to the head of the class," says Grace seeming to joke.

Grace recognizes star quality in any young recruit because she has recruited a few herself. A self-satisfying smile creases her lips when Turner announces that in one week he will be leaving for parts unknown. The ladies are joyous, until they realize that Hobbs is not joining in.

"Where are you going? When are you coming back?" asks Maria-Teresa.

"Don't know where I'm going, just know where I am to report. From there, they will give me my final destination. I am going to miss you all so much."

Grace knows first-hand how the government works when it comes to covert assignments. Everything is on a need-to-know basis.

They hear a gruff voice from behind them say, "I might as well tell you my news too. I'll be leaving the police department."

"What? Why? What are you going to do?" asks Maria-Teresa unable to believe both their surrogate nephews are leaving them at the same time.

"Oh, I don't know. I was never a good fit for this department. I've got some money saved I'll just see what the future brings," says Hobbs trying to convince himself that he is making the right choice. The once jubilant occasion is now more like a wake.

Turner makes a toast hoping to lighten the mood, "Here's to new beginnings," then swallowing hard to loosen the lump in his throat, he continues, "may we all see each other soon," they raise their glasses.

Sam offers her own toast, "To the future, may it bring happiness to us all."

77

The next day finds each member of the crime-solving team in very reflective moods. Hearing the news that his best bud Hobbs is leaving the force spurs Turner into action. Turner doesn't usually make house calls at seven in the morning, but he has little time before he departs.

Turner brings breakfast hoping it will appease Hobbs for barging in on him at this early hour. Hobbs however has been awake since five in the morning, thinking although some might call it brooding. Sitting at his small dining table, the knock on his apartment door shakes him from his thoughts.

He swings the door open wide ready to blast anyone proselytizing or selling subscriptions so early. A big Cheshire cat grin covers Hobbs' face when he sees Turner standing there holding a bag out in front of him.

"Hey man, I brought breakfast." Turner steps inside the apartment and looks Hobbs up and down. Then he says, "Dude, you look like shit but bring it in anyway," as he stretches his arms out waiting to give Hobbs a bear hug despite his appearance and smell of stale alcohol.

"You look like you need more than a hug and definitely some sleep," continues Turner as they exchange their customary hug and back patting before sitting down to eat.

"I guess the shit with the captain took a turn for the worse in my absence," guesses Turner.

"Man, that's putting it mildly. But I can't blame everything on him. He thinks I am not a team player and I think he might be right."

"In our profession, we see the worse of humanity. Often times, the guilty go free. It's bound to get to anyone who wants justice for the victims. We all go a little rogue from time to time," says Turner who knows the captain is right about Hobbs' inability to play by the rules but tries to remain supportive as Hobbs struggles with his feelings.

221

Hobbs says, "It's OK man, I know I messed up again. I think it's best I take a break to decide where I fit in this world."

They finish their egg McMuffins and reminisce over coffee about their brief intense time as partners. Then in all seriousness, Hobbs asks, "What does a washed-up cop do for a living? What occupation allows you to legally carry a gun?"

Turner shakes his head taking exception to Hobbs' last question. He says, "Remember, you're in an open carry state, being legally armed is not your problem. It's what you'll look like in that—"

Hobbs chuckles knowing exactly where Turner is going with his statement and says, "before you say it, a security guard uniform is not on the list." They both laugh at the image of Hobbs protruding belly in a security guard uniform.

Turner says, "Seriously, it has been a pleasure putting my life in your hands. I am sure you will reach the right decision about your future."

Hobbs says, "Remember, just because you're all hush-hush now, once a cop always a cop." Turner looks at his friend nodding in agreement then lowering his head unable to prevent a tear from dropping he leaves Hobbs' apartment.

78

The next morning Sam looks out at the sun glistening off the water in her swimming pool. She opens the doors separating the kitchen/family room from the patio allowing the smell of fragrant lavender from the yard to fill her nostrils. Softly humming, Sam steps onto the patio where she arranges brightly designed plates, colorful cutlery, and salt rimmed Margarita glasses on the table. This morning the mystery book club ladies are having a decompression gathering.

"Good morning, isn't it glorious," says Sam raising her arms toward the morning sun as she opens the door to her first guest.

"Um hey," answers Maria-Teresa brushing pass Sam leaving her perplexed by the one person who should be the happiest. The other women arrive one by one each one looking more preoccupied than the next as they enter the family room making low keyed greetings to each other. At the direction of Sam, they somberly carry bowls of salad, fresh fruits, and small delicate sandwiches artfully arranged on platters from the kitchen to the patio.

"OK, what the hell is the matter with everyone?" asks Sam after the last dish is placed on the table. "We just cracked another case before the police where's the joy?" Standing defiantly with her hands on her hips looking from person to person, "Spill it," she demands.

Margot looks up her mouth tightening her eyes tired, but she doesn't mention her need to meet her estranged family. Maria-Teresa meets no one's gaze instead she fidgets her head down wishing she was home mending her relationship with Danni. Only Sam has nothing urgent to attend to so the thought that others have neglected their private lives to play sleuth never occurs to her.

Grace knows time is not on her side if she wants to get to the bottom of her colleague's death, and she makes the following suggestion, "I propose we each

"

take some time away from each other. Put the book club on hold for a while. What do you all think?"

"What, why?" asks Sam her question ignored.

Tense shoulders relax as each person silently weights the suggestion. Margot is the first to voice her opinion, "I think it's a great idea. I can use the time to focus on reconnecting with my family."

"Thanks, Grace. Danni will be glad to have me around the house and office more," says Maria-Teresa following her friend's lead.

"Well, I'll miss not having you around," says Sam her face clouding with sadness.

"It's not forever, Sam, we'll be close by," assures Grace as they all instinctively move in for a group hug. The atmosphere in the room lightens as each woman accepts the gift of temporary freedom to explore issues related to themselves and engage in an awful lot of drinking, laughing, and splashing in the backyard pool at the quiet house in the Mesa suburb.

79

On the first day of separation from the book group, Margot Towers sits alone in her small apartment. Her grey-streaked blonde hair hangs loose around her face, her green eyes remain wary staring into the distance beyond her kitchen window. The mystery book club serves as a refuse from her self-absorbed focus.

Through the exploits of the amateur crime solving, she feels more self-confident discovering her own quick wit, adaptability, and mental agility. Margot is the first to admit that almost getting killed really sucks but without the life-threatening sleuthing experiences, she probably would never have the courage to face some harsh truths about her life.

Standing up from her kitchen chair, her tall willowy frame moves aimlessly to a seat in her living room her thoughts on her estranged family members. Separating herself from her family was easy, she had her husband John to concentrate on. Then, after fifteen years of marriage John walks out taking their friends absorbing them in his new life.

She gets to move to another state, start therapy, and join a book club full of people she used to think had nothing in common with her but now they feel more like family than the one she grew up with. Her long legs drawn to her chest, Margot remembers the last conversation with her therapist.

M. Why delve into the past when things are finally going in my favor?

T. You tell me. Do you feel satisfied?

Then comes the dreaded pause, the never-ending silence, the therapist sitting and watching you allowing you time to feel like an idiot for not knowing the answer. Satisfied with what?

T. You said your mother did not choose to love you. Why use the word choose?

M. Well, don't we all choose who we love?

T. And your father did he choose?

M. I told you he chose my two brothers.

A desolate coldness overtakes her as she allows the memory of her family dynamic to enter her thoughts.

T. Don't you need to know why no one chose you to love?

That morning leaving the therapist's office Margot experienced the familiar knot in her stomach and the ache in her chest that became a part of her childhood. An ever-present dullness drumming inside her.

Sitting at home this morning she can't help wondering why she still needs her family's love. Just the thought that after all these years of no communication, she stupidly chases their love making, her question, her sanity, and hate her neediness.

"I feel like I pulled the short straw in a game I never wanted to play," she mumbles to herself.

"If I can stand up to a murderer surely, I'm strong enough to confront my family members to find out why they emotionally abandoned me." Feeling empowered she is ready to rid herself of the pain of her past.

After punching her parent's telephone number into her cell phone, poised to hit the icon to connect the call, her heart beats fast and her breathing is suddenly erratic. Inhaling deeply, her finger shakes but she presses hard on the phone icon.

The sound of a phone ringing can be heard from the speaker of her phone. The ring reverberates off the quiet walls in Margot's living room. The ringing stops and an aged female voice says, "Hello."

"Mama? Hey, it's me Margot."

There is absolute silence on the other end of the phone. For a split-second, Margot thinks she imagined hearing her mother's voice.

"Mama, are you there?"

80

Margot is prepared for the phone call, but her mother is not. "Yes, I'm still here."

Her mother's voice sounds tired and older than she expected. There is no warmth in her mother's voice and her coldness conjures vivid memories causing Margot to instinctively grab her stomach rubbing it gently as she plows through her attempt to converse with her mother.

"I guess you and Daddy are well?"

"Your daddy is dead," says her mother in a tone commensurate with telling someone the sky is blue. Without pausing she continues, "I suppose you have a reason for disturbing me. What do you want, Margot?"

Some things never change and the cold dismissive attitude toward her daughter is classic Mama. Margot doesn't know whether to offer her condolences or get straight to the point of her call. She doesn't feel sad about her father's death nor does her mother offer any explanation for not trying to inform her of his death.

Now, the silence is on Margot's end of the phone as she contemplates her next words. Her mother says, "I don't have time for your foolishness, child, what do you want."

Her mother's demanding voice transports Margot back in time, and she begins to stutter, "I, I, I just, just wanted to know why you hate me so much."

Margot hears a deep exhalation from her mother before her mother says, "When you left, I breathed a sigh of relief."

The bright sunlight shines through Margot's windows but the entire room feels dark and cold. Her apartment walls appear to lose their solidity, wobbling and spinning causing her to put her head in her hands. Choking back her tears she asks in a pleading voice, "I am your child? Why?"

"Don't you get it," says her mother in a frustrated impatient gravel voice. "You are that constant reminder to me and my husband that you're not his."

227

"I had to make him love me. I couldn't lose him. You—well you landed alright. Any family tension is your fault!" railed her mother. "You broke our family, our trust, our love."

"Without you nothing was wrong. We were happy." Her mother stops talking for such a long time that Margot says, "Mama, Mama, are you there?" Margot hears nothing and knows her mother has just disconnected the call.

Disappointment and despair flood Margot's mind and body. She swallows hard to choke back her tears but the first tear trickles down her face, she falls back against the sofa and sobs uncontrollably. Finally, closure.

<h1 style="text-align:center">81</h1>

Not far from Margot in a home where the eating space is a separate room from the kitchen, a red-haired woman reads her electronic tablet, her half-eaten breakfast still on its plate beside her. Maria-Teresa saunters into the room choosing to sit opposite her not beside her at the table so she can relish the sight of Danni's tousled hair and creased PJs before asking:

"Anything interesting? I haven't read the news in ages."

Not looking up Danni completes her reading not wanting to discuss the elephant in the room, the mystery book club. As the silence grows Maria-Teresa says, "You're awfully quiet. Something wrong?"

Dropping her tablet with a thud Danni raises her head, "I don't know how to say this," she gathers her thoughts and says, "look, I know you enjoy your book club and your friends. I get that," pausing again this time turning her head and biting her bottom lip not sure if it's prudent to continue.

"But," asks Maria-Teresa.

"I don't know how much longer," her voice cracks, "I can go on feeling helpless while you plunge yourself into harm's way time and time again." Looking at Maria-Teresa she says, "There is no way for me to protect you and I constantly worry about you."

"What are you talking about? I am not porcelain. After this last murder investigation, I realize I am stronger than I thought. I really can contribute to the team, help them solve murders," announces Maria-Teresa with pride wishing to receive acknowledgement of her new-found strength.

Shaking her head Danni throws up her hands in surrender and she says, "Never mind. It's just my problem. I'll deal with it," rising suddenly from the table scooping up her coffee cup.

Worry lines crease Maria-Teresa's forehead, she combs her loose brown curls from her face with her fingers as she watches Danni leave the room.

Sitting alone Maria-Teresa wonders what it will take to repair the riff between them.

For the rest of the day, they move around the house avoiding each other or they tip toe around each other, one entering a space in the house and the other one leaving the same space.

After college graduation, Maria-Teresa joined the engineering/architectural firm where Danni worked. Several failed attempts to advance in the company, they realized they should open their own firm. That was four years ago. Their romance blossoms a few years later.

By the end of the day, both ladies have had time to reflect on their feelings. How they feel about murder investigations and how they feel about each other. Maria-Teresa enters their home library where Danni sits quietly reading and snuggles next to her.

She leans her head on Danni's shoulder and says, "I love you so much." Danni turns toward Maria-Teresa and says, "I know. I hate to be ratty about my feelings. I worry about you. I don't know if I can live without you." Danni looks away not wanting Maria-Teresa to see her tears.

"Danni, you're right, helping my friends should not interfere with us but this last time I had no choice but to help myself. I'd love nothing more than to be held in your arms for a long deserved secluded vacation."

"Are you suggesting we take a little alone time?"

"Yes, that's exactly what I am saying. We can go anywhere you want." With hopeful smiles, they fall into each other's arms not expecting or demanding anything from one another. Wrapped in each other's arms basking in the glow of their love they try to ignore the truth.

The truth is they both know Maria-Teresa will never abandon her book club friends in a time of crisis. They both know someday she'll return to the book club. She'll get back in the game and there is nothing Danni or anyone can do about it. But now is not the time to deal with that realization.

82

Grace Liu stands five feet seven inches in her bare feet. She's built like a fashion model with long silky black hair that shows no signs of grey anywhere which is puzzling to her friends of similar ages because there is no indication that she dyes her hair.

With the downtime she has been given, she cannot concentrate on anything but Rhys. Is the agency she risks her life for lying to her. Why? She can't shake the feeling that there is more to her former lover's death than she is being told by the agency and makes a vow to find out all she can about his reported death.

The question on her mind now is why doesn't the agency tell her how Rhys died? He was her old partner and handler after all. Surely, she can be read in on the particulars of his death. Unless—unless he is not dead.

She can't enlist the aid of her friends who know nothing of her semi-retirement status and secret activities. Sometimes, she feels lonely with no one to confide in now that her third husband Stanley Wu is dead, and her long-time lover and agency partner Rhys may also be dead.

Grace picks up the burner phone that she uses to contact Rhys and hits lucky seven, his speed dial number. She hears a click and then silence. They have disconnected his phone, perhaps he really is dead. Still not ready to accept his death she hops in her car and heads for the open highway for a long drive to clear her thoughts.

During her drive she reflects on their relationship and feels certain that Rhys would want her to know how and why he died. She also realizes he would prevent her from unintentionally risking harm to herself and to any mission he may be undertaking if he is alive.

A couple of hours later she drives back toward home when she recognizes two red parallel horizontal lines chalked on a utility pole, the same markings they used in the past to converse with each other. On the next pole, the same markings are repeated.

Grace's heartbeat quickens as she whispers to herself, is he alive and needs my help? Her hopes start to rise when she sees the same markings repeated on two additional poles. The increase in her pulse responds exponentially to the acceleration of the speed of her car as she races toward their old rendezvous spot.

Their old rendezvous spot is a small park about thirty minutes from Grace's home.

Once at the park, she runs toward the benches where they would sit back-to-back and covertly exchange valuable information. Grace takes up her position on one bench and anxiously waits for someone to join her on the bench that backs to hers.

She sits on the bench trying to look inconspicuous to the few people who walk through the park. After an hour of waiting, her hope turns to skepticism. Did she see something that was not there? Those markings were not on those poles earlier in the day. Is her grief carrying her down a road of make-believe? She closes her eyes exhales and clutches the edge of the bench for support.

Despair sinks into her bones as her shoulders sag toward her chest. A wave of dizziness grips her and she leans forward to rest her head on her legs. After regaining full control of herself, she walks slowly back toward her car with deliberate sometimes stumbling steps.

A part of her does not want to believe she made a mistake. In her hazy thoughts, she still looks around the park fully expecting to see Rhys appear from cover. Her eyes come to rest on a small military statue and a smile slowly raises the corners of her lips.

There are two red parallel horizontal lines on the base of statue. Horizontal rather than vertical lines indicate there is a message waiting. She races head long over to the statue and feels around its base. She frantically searches every inch of the statue above the pedestal. When her eyes drop toward the ground, she sees the foil from a chewing gum wrapper.

Grace almost misses the small piece of paper that is lying up against the statue like the wind has just blown it there. Grace looks around the park again before bending to retrieve the gum wrapper. She holds her breath and hopes that she is right about this dirty gum wrapper.

She unfolds the wrapper and sees writing on the inside. There is just a series of numbers printed on the paper. 1 12 9 22 5. Her heart leaps when she sees the five numbers. Rhys' code is elementary using the numbers to represent the letters of alphabet.

She turns three hundred and sixty degrees scouring the park's landscape, hoping to glimpse him. No such luck. Grace feels mixed emotions of sadness at not seeing him and ecstatic happiness because he is alive and wants her to know. Until he reaches out to her again, she will just have to wait and relish in the joy that he is alive.

Translated the note reads one word, ALIVE. Grace has part of the answer she is seeking. Now, she just needs to find out why the agency wants everyone to think Rhys is dead. She burns the message and leaves the park.

83

It's been several weeks since Sam's friends decided to take some time away from each other with only the occasional text between them. Sam occupies her time with baking and freezing her delights or volunteering at the local food bank. With her freezer full and her house clean, she sits at her kitchen island wistfully gazing off into space.

She has successfully shopped for new clothing in various sizes vowing as she does every year to lose weight. She buys smaller sizes to wear when she reaches her goal weight, but not wanting to feel the sting of failure if her ample figure accidentally expands, she procures larger sizes hanging them in the closet hoping never to use them.

Looking around her expansive abode, a veil of sadness replaces Sam's normally sunshiny disposition; her large home reminding her of her ex-husband because this was to be their dream retirement house. Unfortunately, his dream happens to include their twenty-something yoga instructor.

How long will she have to wait for her life to be full again? Lamenting her loneliness takes her down a road she doesn't want to go. This time, she is literally saved by the bell, her cell phone. Looking down at the number, she thinks he still has the same cell phone number and for some dumb reason, she still remembers the number.

Words to a popular song flash through her mind, should've changed that stupid lock—if I'd known you'd be back to bother me. The phone rings a second time; she still stares at his number reminding herself, I've grown strong. On the third ring, she hits the green icon accepting the call and his bass voice booms, "Hey Pumpkin, it's me."